Praise for *USA TODAY* b

"Black seamlessly ble
infusing enough tensi
Filled with heartbreaking
is both touchin
—*RT Book Reviews* on *A Stranger She Can Trust*

"*A Stranger She Can Trust* is just about as good as it gets when it comes to romantic suspense."
—*Buried Under Romance*

"The early connection between the hero and heroine was nice to see before all of the adrenaline-packed action. The hero's backstory was touching and added depth to the story."
—*RT Book Reviews* on *Heart of a Hero*

Praise for Lara Lacombe

"Aggressive action, terrifying suspense, delightful and dreamy romance in a well-written story."
—*Book & Spoons* on *Enticed By the Operative*

"An enjoyable romantic suspense, with plenty of danger and spice to keep a reader happy."
—*Fresh Fiction* on *Killer Season*

"With smart dialogue and a solid, intriguing mystery at its center, this story will draw readers in. Add two vulnerable characters with great, electric chemistry, and this story is one fantastic read."
—*RT Book Reviews* on *Killer Exposure*

* * *

The Coltons of Shadow Creek: Only family can keep you safe...

* * *

If you're on Twitter, tell us what you think of Harlequin Romantic Suspense! #harlequinromsuspense

Regan Black, a *USA TODAY* bestselling author, writes award-winning, action-packed novels featuring kick-butt heroines and the sexy heroes who fall in love with them. Raised in the Midwest and California, she and her family, along with their adopted greyhound, two arrogant cats and a quirky finch, reside in the South Carolina Lowcountry, where the rich blend of legend, romance and history fuels her imagination.

Lara Lacombe earned a PhD in microbiology and immunology and worked in several labs across the country before moving into the classroom. Her day job as a college science professor gives her time to pursue her other love—writing fast-paced romantic suspense with smart, nerdy heroines and dangerously attractive heroes. She loves to hear from readers! Find her on the web or contact her at laralacombewriter@gmail.com.

Visit the Author Profile pages at Harlequin.com for complete lists of titles.

KILLER COLTON
CHRISTMAS

USA TODAY Bestselling Author

Regan Black
and
Lara Lacombe

HARLEQUIN® ROMANTIC SUSPENSE

Special thanks and acknowledgment are given to Regan Black
and Lara Lacombe for their contributions to
The Coltons of Shadow Creek miniseries.

ISBN-13: 978-0-373-40237-3

Killer Colton Christmas

HARLEQUIN®
™ www.Harlequin.com

Printed in U.S.A.

CONTENTS

Dear Reader,

Happy holidays! It's Christmastime in Shadow Creek, Texas, but the town's jovial holiday spirit is threatened by Livia Colton, a manipulative killer everyone believed was dead.

Like you, I'm a huge fan of the many branches of the Colton family tree and it's an honor as an author to add this story to that world—at Christmastime, no less—with two special characters who have ties to the incredible Colton dynasty.

Emiliano Ortega grew up in Shadow Creek surrounded by a nurturing family, and though he leaves frequently for his FBI assignments, he always knows home is there, waiting for him to return.

For Marie Meyers, family is an elusive concept. Having grown up in the Dallas foster care system, life has taught her the only person she can count on is herself.

You might not find two people more different in their view of family, friendship, work and the holidays. But when Marie becomes a central target in Livia Colton's most recent game of revenge, Emiliano is tasked with keeping her safe until his team can resolve the threat.

Emiliano and Marie face an uphill battle of shedding their expectations in order to cooperate and reveal a criminal. Is it possible that in each other they will also find the genuine, lasting love they've both been quietly seeking? Fortunately, this is the season of miracles.

Live the adventure,

Regan Black

SPECIAL AGENT COWBOY

Regan Black

For Mark, Jordan and Robert. The three of you fill my holidays with more joy, love and laughter with every passing year.

Chapter 1

Livia Lives!

Marie Meyers cringed at the headline alert on her phone, the sugar-sweetened coffee in her mouth going bitter. It couldn't be true. A headline like that was an exercise in sensationalism. Click bait. Livia Colton, ruthless killer and crime boss of Shadow Creek, Texas, had died on her way back to jail when her car was washed into the river. True or false, this was almost the worst news Marie had ever heard.

As the chief digital officer for Colton, Incorporated, Marie defined her primary goal as creating a superb online experience for their customers and she worked to keep that positive experience a priority in long-term corporate growth strategy. Not only did that require her to collect data on their customers' habits, it meant being aware of what was trending in the media and analyzing the corresponding data to better anticipate their subsequent interactions with the company.

Marie's thumb hovered over the link on her cell phone, resisting the inevitable. She *had* to open the article, had to know what kind of message, rumors or facts were circulating out there, so she could be informed during the inevitable crisis meetings at the office today.

She set aside her coffee and held her breath as she

clicked the link, half expecting her phone to explode. Or implode. Didn't matter, as the result would be the same.

The banner for *Everything's Blogger in Texas* had been updated to reflect the top, scintillating story, and the article boldly declared Livia Colton, criminal mastermind *presumed* dead, was in fact back among the living. The blog promised to deliver every juicy detail of the hunt for the Queen of the Coltons in real time. There was a convenient link to subscribe for updates.

"Lovely," Marie muttered. A quick search proved *Everything's Blogger* did have the jump on other gossip sites and traditional news outlets. They posted quotes from victims and people connected to Livia's prior crimes and were weaving the story as they went along, connecting dots that might not even be related. The other sites were merely reporting the shocking news and waiting for confirmation, making them appear half a step behind.

Marie didn't expect the lag to last, and the more reporters covering this development, the tougher things would be at work. Her appetite gone, she skipped breakfast and headed into the office, the news following her on every station as she scanned the radio channels during the drive. Her grip tight on the steering wheel, she cursed the way one high-profile bad apple could ruin the whole bushel.

For Marie, Colton, Incorporated, was more than a career choice. The company had embraced her and she returned that welcome with a loyalty and affection as powerful as family ties. Now, thanks to one evil woman's machinations, her family of coworkers would be cast into a glaring spotlight as the authorities investigated Livia's connection to the company.

She'd seen it happen elsewhere. The most innocuous decisions and comments would be scrutinized for use as potential evidence, and as those details reached the press, the court of public opinion would weigh in first. Doubts crept into the customer mind-set quickly, and regardless of damage control, it could take years to restore confidence.

In the digital age, nearly everything lasted forever. Usually that worked in her favor as a CDO, sifting through data for patterns, identifying influencers and tailoring experiences for their customers. This process was known as data mining, but companies that mishandled the wealth of information had given a valuable process a bad name. She feared this kind of headline would work against her beloved company.

As she pulled into her parking space near the office, the radio went silent midbroadcast as if the station had lost the signal. In the next moment a new voice broke the quiet, speaking through an alteration device that hid the speaker's gender and identity. "The Cohort will prevail. We can and will expose everyone colluding with Livia Colton. We will see true justice is served."

"Not good," Marie murmured to herself as the normal radio hosts came back on air, apologizing for the strange interruption. The Cohort, a notorious hacktivist group, claimed to work collectively for pure transparency, holding the powers that be accountable. In college, her professors had built several lectures and case studies on the organization's methods, recruiting and most successful hacks. Unfortunately, they were often as destructive as Livia had been, despite their noble claims.

At thirty, Marie had experienced her share of bad days. Mentally, she shuffled today into her top ten list of worst ones, though there was serious competition in her history. She turned off the car and took a deep breath, resisting the urge to run flat out into the office and stay locked inside the building she loved until they stopped whatever the Cohort had planned. A thriving corporation connected by name and bloodlines to Livia would be an irresistible target.

Glancing around the parking area, she imagined someone hacking into the cameras and flashing her panicked race to work all over the internet with another headline full of negative insinuations about the company.

With that unpleasant image in mind, she forced herself to move with deliberate, calm purpose, belying the dread knotting her stomach. Purse over one arm, computer case over the opposite shoulder, she strolled into the gleaming twenty-five-story glass tower, hoping the lingering panic inside was hidden by her professional confidence and perfect posture.

The Cohort had a global reputation for following through on its threats. She knew Zane Colton, as head of security, would have precautions and heightened alerts in place, and the cybersecurity division would be shoring up firewalls and such to protect the company from a digital assault. As soon as she got upstairs, she would do everything possible to help ward off an attack.

The lobby door had barely whispered closed behind her when a wave of jitters surrounded her like a sudden storm. The air in the soaring atrium practically buzzed with nervous energy. She hustled to the elevators and upstairs to her office, just in time to pick up the phone ringing on her assistant's desk. "Marie Meyers. How may I help you?"

"Good—you're in."

"Zane?" she asked, startled by the obvious relief in his normally composed tone.

"You're needed in the conference room," he said.

No sense in wasting time with questions. "I'll be right there." The urgency was surely related to the Cohort broadcast. She wouldn't know how bad it was or how best to help until she got down there.

If she'd thought the building had a jittery vibe downstairs, it paled in comparison to the action in the conference room. A grim resignation pulsed through the air, as various people sat around the long oval table, murmuring stats and updates as they studied laptop monitors. At the head of the table, Fowler Colton, company president, stood with his brother T.C. and their stepbrother Zane. Today the company's top men wore similar expressions of anger, frustration and grave concern.

Had the Cohort made an attempt on the company already? It seemed impossibly fast, considering the news had just broken.

At a colorful oath, her head swiveled toward the presentation screen along with all the others in the room. Feeds from half a dozen computer monitors, presumably projections from those around the conference table, were displayed for everyone to see.

She walked closer to the screen, disbelief and alarm going to war with that knot of dread in her stomach. Under a black-and-white banner the names of the highest-ranking officers of Colton, Incorporated, were posted, including hers. Alongside each name were personal details, ranging from partial home addresses and phone numbers to bank accounts and social security information. While some of the information was shown for each name, other fields had been completed with Click for More links.

"What site is this?" she asked the room at large.

"Does it matter?" Fowler asked.

"It does," she replied, thinking of customers and their viewing habits. "We need to get it shut down—"

"Too late, Marie. The first successful breach of the firewall occurred just after five this morning and we've been scrambling to stop the digital bleeding ever since." Zane gave a nod to a young man at the table. "Show her."

That put the breach two solid hours *before Everything's Blogger in Texas* posted the story that Livia wasn't dead. Marie was trying to make sense of that when the screen flooded with a scroll of more names. She pressed her hand to her lips to smother the alarmed gasp. The Cohort hadn't just compromised the executives or those with the last name of Colton. It had systematically captured the personal records for *everyone* in the company.

"How can I help?" she asked, determined to fight back.

"You're looking at a dark website where the Cohort has started an auction," Zane told her. "We've contacted the FBI. They should be here any minute."

An auction for this kind of data would be irresistible to thieves, smugglers and human traffickers. The criminals who could afford the information wouldn't hesitate to use it. Although she had concerns for herself, she was only one person. Her heart sank for the employees and their families over the terrible consequences of identity theft of this magnitude.

How ironic that the Cohort, supposed champions of personal privacy, had just compromised the data of innocent people while she worked relentlessly to protect the information gained by her efforts.

"We have to move quickly and get an identity protection plan in place for everyone." Each of them faced more than just immediate inconveniences. With just a few hours' head start, bank accounts and retirement funds were already in jeopardy.

"We are," Zane said. "There's more, Marie."

"I've got it here," a tech offered.

"No," Zane said. "Send it to my office." He exchanged a stormy look with his family. His expression softened only slightly, his gaze holding hers while he crossed the room. "Come with me," he said, holding the door open for her.

What couldn't he say in front of the team? Her knees went watery under the combined weight of everyone staring at her. They couldn't possibly believe she had anything to do with this. A breach like this could end her career, even though it wasn't her fault. Her position as CDO had been a dream come true, allowing her to hit the pinnacle of her professional goals two years earlier than she'd planned. The Coltons had to know she would never jeopardize the opportunity.

To quell the worst-case scenarios stampeding through her mind, she turned her gaze to the stunning view of the city from the uppermost windows of the tower. Dallas sparkled below, rolling with glittering confidence toward the horizon. She remembered school field trips as a kid, standing on the sidewalk, tipping her head way back and staring up at this tower and others nearby. More than the glossy shine of excellent architecture and construction, she'd seen the security and stability she longed for as she watched executives, assistants and employees serving all levels of the businesses inside. Those field trips solidified her personal goals and she set out to achieve what many of those people probably took for granted—a place to belong. A place to make a difference.

"Marie, you should have a seat." Zane gestured to the visitor's chair in front of his desk.

She didn't realize how far afield her mind had wandered until she noticed him politely waiting for her to sit down first. Perching at the edge of the chair, she waited for whatever he didn't feel he could say in front of the others.

"As I said, the FBI is on the way," Zane began. "I'm sure once they arrive, we can come up with the best possible solution."

"Count on me to help out." She cleared her throat when he frowned. "Security is your area, of course, but whatever I can do to…" Her voice trailed off at his raised hand.

"I appreciate the offer." Shifting in his chair, he reached for his monitor and turned it so she could see the display, though it remained blank. "Unfortunately, I feel it's best for you and the company if we keep you far away from this particular situation."

"Pardon me?" *Please don't kick me to the curb so close to Christmas.*

"Our cybersecurity protocols folded almost instantly," he said, clearly disgusted. "Though we're chasing down the breach, the FBI will soon take over. We've switched our efforts to covering everyone who's been compromised with identity theft monitoring and protection."

"Good. You've seen the latest blogger headlines?" Her voice sounded weak and she straightened her shoulders. Social media and online trends were only a small aspect of her role. If Colton, Incorporated, wanted to manage the rumors and innuendo and keep customers content, they needed her analysis and assistance with the strategy to overcome this crisis.

Zane scowled. "Yes. It's ridiculous, though it's likely to get worse before it's over." He paused, taking a deep breath. "I'm sorry, Marie." He tapped something on his keyboard and more data from the piracy site flooded the monitor. Names and personal records scrolled through in alphabetical order, much as it had on the screens in the conference room.

When it reached the *M*s, the scrolling slowed, rocking a little as the information came to a stop. The process reminded her of a jackpot on a slot machine. Her name on the left. Her social security number dead center, her bank account and balance on the right. In bold red lettering, centered under those pertinent details, her job title was listed along with her salary and a call to action with a link.

Data mining is dangerous! Stop the snooping, CDO!

Okay, that was rough. She didn't appreciate her information being spotlighted by the Cohort simply because her job involved data mining to make customer interaction more engaging and valuable. Yes, the process was controversial, but unlike the hacktivists, she never publicly shared or broadcast the details she gathered. She performed her job with pride using the highest standard of security.

Leaning forward, she tried to make sense of the implications. It boggled her mind. "Where does that link lead?"

He clicked it, revealing a rant on the dangers of data mining ending with an input box. "I'm hoping the FBI can tell us what this is. My primary concern is for your safety."

Surely she would be safe if she stayed here until the FBI shut down that page and the links. "The breach and mitigating the effect on our employees should be our primary concern."

"Your loyalty is refreshing," Zane said with a half smile. "And valued. I want you to be the CDO here for years to come."

That was the first comforting thing she'd heard. "I'm not trying to be difficult, but what exactly are you saying?"

"This reads like a *personal* threat against you. Your information isn't in the auction—it's already been broadcast. I fear the Cohort has targeted you for some specific action."

Meaning what? She couldn't wrap her head around his assessment. Groups like the Cohort didn't go after people in person. They struck from the safe side of their probing computers, exposing and embarrassing their targets to promote the agenda du jour.

"I don't know anything about Livia Colton," she said, recalling the Cohort radio broadcast. Only what she'd read in the press or heard from her coworkers. "My only tie to the Colton family is my employment." Unless the Cohort knew something she didn't. She clasped her hands in her lap to keep from rubbing that tiny burn behind her sternum. *Not again, not now.* Calm, blissful years had flowed by without that annoying flicker of hope that she might eventually learn her father's name. How frustrating it was to discover no amount of crushing disappointment would extinguish it permanently.

"Regardless, the Cohort changed tactics. By definition, your job fundamentally offends the Cohort. Until we sort it out, I feel it's best if you take a leave of absence."

Those last three words reverberated in her head. She wondered where she could go and how she might fill her time. Zane explained the cybersecurity team's instructions for managing the identity breach issues. Password changes and notifications to her bank, credit cards, landlord and the IRS topped the list. Just when she wished she'd brought in a notepad, he slid a short stack of paperwork across the desk to her. "This is the packet going out to all employees by noon today."

Fast work, she thought, flipping through the comprehensive guide. "With all due respect, I'd prefer to stay and help."

Her coworkers were bound to be worried and the cybersecurity department would be flooded with calls and questions. Not to mention what they needed to do as a company to reassure customers that their data was safe. When she added up the tasks and the personnel, she knew they needed her here.

Zane leaned back in his chair and rubbed his forehead, debating something. "Handle the notifications," he said, "then come back to the conference room."

"Thank—"

He interrupted her gratitude. "I'll let you stay on one condition. You'll cooperate with the FBI's assessment of your safety. Whatever they decide, no arguments."

"Yes, sir." She hurried out of the office before he changed his mind.

As she walked to her office at the other end of the hall, she flipped through the guide, squirming at the long list of things she would now need to keep in mind. At least she didn't have a spouse or children to worry about. In her situation, not even extended family was a concern, since she'd been a ward of the state of Texas since her birth.

Marie's lips twisted and her throat went dry as those old questions tried to rear up from her past. Wouldn't it be ironic if the Cohort had discovered who her father was or even where her mother had gone after she'd abandoned her newborn with nothing more than a name?

Distracted, her head down as she passed the elevator, the doors parted, and she found herself tangled in the group entering the hallway.

She nearly bumped into the man in the lead and he steadied her with a light touch at her elbow. The dark suits and serious expressions identified them as FBI, even without the badges they wore in plain view.

"Excuse us," the first man said, his touch sliding away.

"No, pardon me." She offered a tight smile and stepped aside. In her heels, she wasn't quite eye level with him, though he wasn't the tallest of the group. With dark brown hair, straight eyebrows over deep-set brown eyes and a stern mouth framed by a trim beard, he radiated authority and he gave her a long study that put heat in her cheeks as he passed by.

What did he see? she wondered, striding away. Did he think he knew her? She couldn't shake the strange sensation that he had come to some immediate conclusion about her with only a light touch and one long look.

Special Agent Emiliano Ortega recognized Marie Meyers as he steadied her when she brushed by them. Her picture and résumé were in the initial briefing documents he'd skimmed when his boss called him to Dallas early this morning.

The FBI had assembled the fast-response task force Emiliano served on to investigate cyberattacks all over the country. They could even reach destinations overseas at a moment's notice to protect US interests. Reporting to Dallas meant a particularly short commute in this case, getting them on scene quickly and reducing the window of time in which the hacktivists could erase their tracks.

He hadn't had much time to delve deep into the file but he knew the key points on the top executives at Colton, Incorporated. Thirty, never married, Miss Meyers had earned her bachelor's and master's degrees in computer science and minored in psychology. No debts beyond a minuscule credit-card balance.

Everything about her appearance, from her glossy dark brown hair curling softly around her shoulders to the pricey designer high heels, shouted that this woman valued order and discipline.

He glanced back down the hallway, but she was gone. Why wasn't the CDO headed to the conference room? A cyberattack of this magnitude usually brought all hands on deck.

When his team reached the conference room with the obligatory massive table, monitors and floor-to-ceiling windows, the introductions were swift. Everyone seemed eager to hand over investigative control to the FBI. A typical reaction with attacks as aggressive as this one seemed to be.

He kept glancing to the door, waiting for Miss Meyers to join them as he and the team listened to the rapid-fire updates from the technicians and executives on hand.

The Cohort had claimed responsibility immediately: not the first time Emiliano and his team had encountered that strategy. Another stroke of luck, as the verification was swift and put them on the right track immediately.

As he and the team systematically peeled back the first layers of the breach, Emiliano soon realized the Cohort had employed a brand-new tactic. The trail of links from Marie Meyers's information led to a private message board called

Campus Martius, where Cohort Principes were encouraged to share ideas on how best to make an example of her.

"We have a problem," Emiliano said as he kept digging. He shared his display on the presentation screen and conversation around the room halted in stunned shock.

He spotted Zane Colton standing with his family near the wall of windows. "Where is Miss Meyers?"

Zane started to answer and stopped short. "Right here."

The notifications took longer than Marie expected, so she wasn't surprised to discover the FBI team had turned the conference room to crisis central by the time she returned.

Seeing her name and face plastered across the big presentation screen—*that* unnerved her all over again and she hesitated at the doorway.

Zane motioned her closer. "Marie Meyers, our CDO," he stated. "This is the FBI's National Cyber Investigative Joint Task Force." He gestured to the presentation screen. "They just drilled through the rhetoric to this direct death threat against you."

Despite the shock rattling through her system, she forced herself to stride forward.

The man with the dark eyes who'd studied her so intently in the hallway extended a hand in greeting. "Special Agent Emiliano Ortega."

She grasped his hand, momentarily distracted by the calluses on his palm. "A pleasure to meet you." She kept her eyes on him, rather than the presentation screen. His square jaw offered a much better view anyway.

His mouth tilted in a skeptical half smile before he introduced the three other members of their task force as Special Agent in Charge Selene Dashwood, Special Agent Finn Townsend and malware analyst Tristan Staller.

Despite the suits and no-nonsense attitudes, the task

force was a study in contrasts, from the sleek Dashwood, tall and lean with flawless ebony skin and no accessories beyond her wedding band, to the not-quite-rumpled Staller, who seemed reluctant to tear his gaze from his monitor. She knew his type well. In between were Townsend with his curling light brown hair and friendly smile and Ortega, who watched her closely.

"We're aware this isn't a good day," Ortega said.

Not her worst, either, though she kept the thought to herself. "How can I help?"

As Dashwood resumed her conversation with Fowler and T.C., Agent Ortega planted his hands on his lean waist. "Sometimes attacks like this one resemble battering rams. This attack, while large in scope, had some precision elements." He pointed to the screen. "As you know, they took everything in order to inflict the most chaos and damage to the company as a whole."

"Obviously," she agreed.

"Underneath the obvious, we believe the strategy was meant to blur their particular focus on *you*."

She bit back the rash of protests. It wouldn't help to point out she wasn't a Colton, had no connection to Livia or the horrible crimes she'd inflicted. Pressing a hand to her lips, she stifled an inappropriate and untimely laugh. This was absurd. Didn't the Cohort see the double standard of wrecking her career and threatening her life in their quest to safeguard privacy with criminal actions?

"The language is specific, Miss Meyers," Agent Townsend said. "The complaints target your abuse of privacy expectations and overreaching corporate authority. The Cohort is revved up and motivated against you."

She gaped at the FBI agent as she struggled for an appropriate reply. Was he actually accusing her of doing something wrong because she was good at her job? Her gaze drifted to Zane, who was scowling at the back of Townsend's head.

"Townsend." Ortega silenced him with a look. The other man returned his attention to the computer in front of him.

"Miss Meyers." Ortega pulled out a chair for her. "We need to walk you through these threats and review your options."

Marie sat down and the agent showed her what they'd unraveled. As if broadcasting her personal details and the vicious conversation in the message board weren't enough, the group had posted a new banner front and center where they were auctioning the stolen data from Colton, Incorporated.

Reward! Share your plan to end CDO Meyers and take a stand for consumer privacy!

The message board was exploding with real-time comments. She stared, horrified as the potential consequences drifted around her. Since when did groups like this offer rewards for real-life attacks? With every passing hour this day moved up the list, squeezing into her top five worst of all time. Not an easy feat, considering her rocky path through the foster-care system.

On the upside, if there was any credibility to the threats from the Cohort, she wouldn't have much of a future to dwell on it. The gallows humor didn't erase the icy rivulets of fear trickling down her spine.

Chapter 2

Emiliano studied the Colton, Incorporated, CDO, simultaneously impressed by her composure and wondering when the dam would break. No one could hold up indefinitely to the news of being hunted, online and in real life. Whatever had incited this attack, Townsend was right; the Cohort had zeroed in on Miss Meyers and they weren't letting up.

Why? During his work on this task force, he hadn't seen anything quite like the vitriol they were spewing at this particular woman. She seemed nice enough. Polite and competent. Pretty, too, though that was irrelevant. Nothing he'd heard so far gave him any insight as to how she'd landed on the bad side of one of the most dangerous hacktivist groups in existence.

Yes, the core of her career was at odds with the Cohort mandate on privacy, but why were they determined to incite direct violence?

She had courage in the face of the clear, physical danger, he'd give her that, and he had to assume integrity and commitment as well, based on how the executive staff treated her. And she was watching him expectantly from those wide, intelligent brown eyes shot with gold and framed with long lashes. He cleared his throat and got on with his job. "You can see the Cohort claimed responsibility immediately," he began.

Her gaze held his, serious and steady. "Because they think they can bring Livia Colton to justice? It's as if they believe hacking our personal records will prove the company is hiding her."

He'd expected the outburst, though she'd delivered it with admirable control. "It's a better reason than hackers usually offer," he said. "Public opinion will swing their way on this one."

Temper flashed in her eyes. "They've exploited innocent, hardworking employees. I'd think public opinion would go against them."

Across the table, Finn, one of Emiliano's best friends in the FBI, gave a snort. "Not with Livia Colton alive and on the loose. Do you have any idea—"

He held up a hand and cut him off again, wondering why Finn was so determined to terrorize Miss Meyers. They could cover the basic information without running the risk of sending her into a paralyzing tailspin. Her expertise might prove valuable on this case, assuming she wasn't in league with the Cohort somehow.

Her gaze shifted to Finn. "You believe the Cohort has turned the city against me, personally?"

Finn nodded, looking less than sheepish. Emiliano barely swallowed his aggravation. "Miss Meyers…" He waited until her gaze swung back to him. "Our team can unravel the digital details. We have methods to root out those responsible for the breach here. For your safety, it's best if you take a leave of absence. We'll assign a protective detail to keep an eye on you."

Her dark eyebrows arched high. She turned to the Colton executives gathered at the other end of the long table. "You're okay with this?"

"For the duration of the investigation, yes," Fowler Colton said. Beside him, Zane nodded emphatically. "This isn't a typical hack, Marie. Ignoring these threats could be a grave mistake."

"Shouldn't the FBI be keeping the Colton family safe?"

"We're taking precautions," Zane replied. "As you can see, the most immediate threats are aimed directly at you."

A fact that made this case more intriguing than any of the others he'd recently handled.

"You won't consider another option?" she implored. "I know I can help."

Almost in unison the men shook their heads. "We agree it's best to suspend your normal operations until the investigation is complete," T.C. said. "Don't want to give the hacktivists more ammunition."

"It's December, Marie." Fowler gave her a wan smile. "Get into the Christmas spirit. You haven't taken a real vacation this year. Take the rest of the month. We look forward to seeing you in January." He glanced around the room. "Surely she can resume her work by then."

Emiliano noticed no one on the task force made that kind of promise. Watching Marie, he caught the flash of panic in her eyes and the quiver in her lip before she dropped her gaze to the table. When she looked up, only a steely calm remained, her lips set in a tense smile.

In full investigative mode, he wondered what the woman was hiding. Most people would appreciate extra time at the holidays. He made a mental note to take a closer look at her file. Nothing indicated she'd be sympathetic to the Cohort, though he'd seen stranger things and known women who excelled in hiding their true natures.

Finn stood up and came around to stand at the door. "I'll drive you home."

"No, thank you." Although her lips curved upward, the expression couldn't be considered a smile. "I'll need my car to make the most of my unexpected time off." The resigned, almost sad glance she aimed at her bosses made Emiliano flinch inside. "Happy holidays, Zane, Fowler, T.C. Give my best to your f-families." She hurried away without waiting for a reply, leaving Emiliano and the rest of the room a bit stunned in her wake.

"We can't let her leave. Not alone," Finn appealed to SAC Dashwood. "She might be the access point the Cohort needed."

The brash remark drew everyone's attention. Astonished incredulity radiated from the faces of those who weren't FBI. Emiliano glared at him. They didn't publicly call out a suspect that way without evidence to back it up. Then again, Finn had been working for nearly an hour and he was one of the best at rooting out hacker signatures within computer code.

"Did you find something?" he asked.

"Call building security," Dashwood ordered before Finn could reply. "Have them hold her at the door."

"I'm on my way." Finn pulled his keys from his pockets and started for the door.

"No." Dashwood's stern gaze stopped Finn cold. "I need you here, Agent Townsend. You have the most experience with the Cohort and their primary hackers."

Temper moved over Finn's boyish face like a thundercloud, but he didn't argue as he returned to his seat. When Selene used that tone, none of them argued.

"Agent Ortega, you'll stick with Meyers until we can mute these threats. Her safety is your first priority as we work this case."

"Yes, ma'am." Emiliano closed the laptop he'd brought along and stowed it in his computer bag, no happier than Finn with the new orders.

Smart and gorgeous, all signs pointed to Marie Meyers being a difficult woman for him to keep an eye on. He'd done his best to clear drama and difficulty from his life. Guarding a suspect or potential victim was the least favorite part of his job description.

He hurried down the hall to Marie's office. She was already gone.

"Hang on, Ortega," Dashwood said, catching him at the elevator.

"So she *is* a suspect?" Emiliano kept his voice low.

"I didn't say that."

He waited for her to clarify.

"We both know this isn't typical Cohort strategy," she said. Only her narrowed gaze revealed her frustration. "I want to stop this before it becomes a trend. We'll work it from this side while you keep working it off-site. With or without the CDO's cooperation."

He understood what she wouldn't say outright in this building. They had to protect Miss Meyers based on the credible threats. In doing so, he would be close enough to catch her if she was cooperating with the hacktivists.

"When did you put her in the suspect category?" He knew some cyberattacks were assisted by insiders, but this felt like a big leap in judgment against Miss Meyers.

Selene spread her hands wide. "We're just getting started. I'm not ready to rule out anything."

"Let's move fast. I'm not looking forward to spending Christmas in my truck."

She rolled her eyes. "I'm sure it won't come to that."

"If it does, you can explain it to Scrabble." His beloved corgi would be grumpy if he wasn't home soon and she could hold a grudge. "I'll keep you posted," he said.

With a brisk nod, she strode back down the hallway to the conference room.

Alone in the elevator, Emiliano smiled as he thought of his dog patiently waiting for him back at his family ranch in Shadow Creek, several hours away. She had plenty of care and company out there; he didn't worry about that. It was the idea of being stuck in the city for the holidays that put a pinch between his shoulder blades. There was a fresh sincerity in small-town life he'd never found in the major cities he'd worked in. Only gone half a day, he already missed the rhythm and routine of the ranch that kept him grounded.

Dallas, in particular, set his teeth on edge. Despite the gloss and polish that impressed so many residents and tourists, he saw the unsavory elements lurking just under that pretty surface. And whose fault was that? he wondered with a sigh.

He stepped out of the elevator into the lobby and walked right into the unwelcome glare of Miss Meyers.

Marie could hardly contain her frustration. The FBI had ordered security to hold her here until an agent arrived to escort her. She had been taking care of herself, and doing a fine job of it, since turning eighteen.

She wished she could take back her promise not to argue this decision. Who would they send? Not the woman in charge, and probably not the rumpled-looking Mr. Staller. The idea of Agent Townsend hovering over her life turned her palms damp with nerves.

Agent Ortega stepped off the elevator and relief flooded her system. There was a kindness in his gaze, a compassion that she wanted to trust.

"Thanks for your patience," he said.

"They said I didn't have a choice." She gripped the handle of her purse with both hands, her computer bag over her shoulder. "How exactly will this work?"

He gave her a hesitant smile. "With your patience and cooperation you won't notice me at all." She almost laughed. Overlooking this handsome agent in any environment was unimaginable.

"The goal is your protection, not inconvenience," he said, holding the door for her. "We work quickly and should have your life back to normal by the holidays."

He couldn't know how little comfort that was—the holidays were always a study in loneliness for her—but she thanked him anyway.

"We'll take my truck to your car, and then we'll head to your place and make a plan."

Her heels clicked sharply on the pavement and she noticed he slowed his pace just enough that she didn't feel rushed. The heels put her at nearly eye level with him and she appreciated the sense of equality.

"A plan?" she echoed after a moment. "The FBI considers house arrest a plan?"

"You think you should be under house arrest?"

"No." Exasperated with the entire day, she puffed her long bangs up off her forehead.

He unlocked the truck and let her settle into the seat before he closed her door. After stashing his computer bag behind the driver's seat, he climbed in and started the engine. "Where are you parked?"

She gave him directions and then closed her eyes, silently counting to ten. There was a logical way out of this nightmare. When the truck didn't move, she opened her eyes and found him watching her intently, his lips tilted up at the corner.

"My mother used to do that when she got fed up with my brother and me." He pulled away from the parking space, his gaze on the road.

The man had a striking profile. "You have a brother?"

He nodded without volunteering any information. She got the impression he didn't make a habit of sharing personal details. A tactic she could respect. What people didn't know about, they couldn't judge.

"I could help this investigation, you know," she said as he pulled up behind her car.

The full weight of that dark, enigmatic gaze landed on her and she resisted the urge to fidget or plead. Would nothing convince his team or her bosses that she could be an asset? Didn't the FBI have safe houses or something outside the Cohort's reach where she could help?

"Right now the best way to help is to stay safe and give us room to work," he replied.

"This is outrageous." She pulled her car key from her purse and shoved out of his truck before her temper snapped and she said something she might regret.

Emiliano noticed there had been no searching or rooting around for her key. The woman was organized. He appreciated efficiency, focused on that trait rather than her lush feminine curves and lovely legs.

Both ranch life and FBI experience had taught him that calm was the best option when tempers turned hot. He braced for the slamming door. It would be easier to get a read on her once she relaxed.

Suddenly she turned back, her eyes flashing.

"I've never jeopardized or abused customer information the way the Cohort does."

He listened to her words and studied her body language. Hard to believe she'd willingly let in a hacktivist group.

"We do not share or sell personal information," she continued, in that staccato pattern that reminded him of her high heels on the pavement.

"Good."

"I knew programmers with hacktivist ideologies and skills. In school." Those dark eyes met his, held. "I didn't agree with them then and I don't support their criminal behavior now."

"All right," he said.

She sucked in a breath as if his acceptance offended her. "Do you know my address?"

"Yes." Her address, along with her cell phone number and the make, model and license plate of her car, was in her file. He plugged the address into his navigation app on the truck's dashboard. "I'll follow you over."

"Are you planning to stay in my apartment?"

He wasn't sure yet how they would work that out, only that he had orders to keep an eye on her. "Let's get over there and we'll talk."

Her lips twisted, though she didn't speak as she finally closed the truck door. The spunky Mini Cooper suited her, he decided. Painted creamy white with a dark green rocker stripe, it would be useless anywhere but the city.

And why was he analyzing her car? She put her purse and computer bag behind her seat and slid behind the wheel. He prepared to move his truck so she could back out, when she opened her door and peered at the windshield.

He powered down the passenger window. "What's wrong?"

"Nothing. A flyer or something." She stretched an arm out and he ordered her to stop.

"Let me see it first."

He grabbed his phone and hustled around the front of his truck to her car. Tucked low under the windshield wiper was a small square of white paper.

"Not a flyer," he said as much to himself as to her. He took pictures and used the flashlight app on his phone to peer under the hood. He dropped to the ground and checked the undercarriage.

She crouched beside him. "What are you doing?"

He deliberately kept his focus on the car rather than her legs. "Looking for any obvious signs of tampering or tracking devices." On his feet again, he called Dashwood and gave her an update.

"Tampering? You're a bomb expert, too, I suppose." She crossed her arms over her chest.

"Not an expert." He dusted off his palms and smacked

at the dirt on his trousers. Why couldn't he remember he was in a suit on the job, rather than in his work jeans at the ranch? "The FBI does keep us trained."

"Of course." She tucked a lock of hair, teased loose by the breeze, behind one ear. "I'm not handling this well," she admitted softly. "My work is everything to me and I don't appreciate strangers interfering with that."

There hadn't been any mention of a spouse or other family in her file and he'd assumed the rest of her background was in process. Now Emiliano wondered what that background would reveal. "May I?" He pointed to the note.

She shrugged, arms folded again. "Go ahead."

Using the end of a pen, he freed the note and unfolded it there on the windshield.

The image of a Guy Fawkes mask filled the top half of the letter-sized paper. Underneath, one sentence in all caps threatened her.

YOU WILL PAY FOR TRADING PERSONAL PRIVACY FOR PROFITS

Emiliano took a picture of the note and sent it to his boss by text message. Within two minutes she replied that an evidence team was on the way. The only hope for a lead was a camera on the parking area or fingerprints on the paper itself. The standard copy paper and black-and-white printing would be impossible to track down. Anyone could have printed this at home, an office or a copy store.

It took a little more than an hour for Emiliano to sign over the scene to the crime-scene unit. Miss Meyers wasn't happy about leaving her car to the investigators, but he convinced her it was temporary.

"That's one thing settled," he said as they drove away.

"One thing?" Another huff of frustration lifted her bangs.

"You can't stay in Dallas."

She gaped at him. "I certainly can't *leave*. Not without my car and not while the investigation is ongoing. Sooner or later you'll discover I can help."

"We've got it under control," he said. The woman had plenty of nerve to think they'd share information before they made a determination on her involvement.

She folded her arms over her chest. "I'm not leaving town."

She was wrong. "You're under my protection, so that choice is out of your hands."

"Third-worst day," she muttered. "Special Agent Ortega." She said his name with such respect it startled him. "I can manage on my own."

He believed her. "Since these circumstances aren't normal, I'm transporting you to a safe place until we sort this out."

He still couldn't quite believe what he'd heard himself suggest to Dashwood or that he was about to say it again. "The FBI has decided you'll stay at my family's ranch until we're sure it's safe for you to return to Dallas."

Chapter 3

Marie was sure she'd misunderstood Special Agent Ortega. Yet here she was again in his pickup truck, her suitcase stowed in the bed and the city she loved well behind them already. It was all she could do not to ask him how much longer they'd be on the road.

He'd stated in that infuriatingly calm tone that he was taking her to Shadow Creek, Texas. She'd done a quick search on her cell phone while she packed. Thank goodness, too, since he'd surprised her by confiscating her phone and laptop before they left Dallas. He'd made it clear that she would not be allowed any internet access during the investigation.

Located in the Texas Hill Country, the area's primary claim to fame was a quaint town center giving way to businesses surrounded by acres of cattle ranches. The idyllic pictures of rolling grassland, clear rivers, green hills and livestock dotting the landscape made her nervous. Checking the street-view pictures provided for Main Street didn't help. Not a high-rise in sight. The closest thing to a city-like feature was the Shadow Creek Memorial Hospital. She'd found it odd that a local hospital would feature so prominently on the search results until she read that it had been built by Livia Colton, hot story of the day.

As they passed through Austin and the landscape on either side of the highway gave way to the wide expanse of ranch land, she suspected they were getting close.

At the first sighting of a longhorn cattle herd grazing well back from the road, her palms went damp. She didn't do rural and couldn't imagine staying anywhere close to a heavy animal with horns like that. A city girl at heart, she'd only been camping once, though she suspected her experience wouldn't qualify in Special Agent Ortega's book. The excursion had only gone so far as pitching tents at the edge of the wooded greenway behind the youth center. Already the quiet beyond the low rumble of the truck's engine pressed in on her.

"Not much longer," he said.

She jumped on the first words he'd spoken in over an hour, needing the conversation. "How can you be a rancher and an FBI agent?" she asked, hating the nerves making her voice tight.

"Family effort," he replied.

He glanced her way and the look of contentment on his face launched a swarm of butterflies in her stomach. "You're moving me in with your parents?"

His eyebrows flexed into a scowl. "They're out of town right now," he said. "Plenty of room even if they were home. It's not like we'll be tripping over each other."

She gazed out at the wide-open landscape, wishing for the clear boundaries of a stable city structure. "I doubt anyone out here has that problem."

"Shadow Creek and the surrounding area will also make it harder for anyone wishing you harm to succeed."

She supposed he would know. Protection protocol wasn't her thing. "The note on my car can't really mean anything." If someone wanted to attack, wouldn't they have waited for her to show up? Although restating her earlier protest wasn't likely to make him turn around now, she felt she had to try. "The Cohort posted all my information for free already. Good grief, they knew my pay rate. Knowing what

I drive and where I park is the least threatening aspect of this nightmare."

Without a word he exited the highway at the sign for Shadow Creek. Under other circumstances she might let herself enjoy his handsome, stoic profile.

"I'd really rather deal with this in a familiar area," she added.

"So you've said."

"Can you blame me?" she asked. Were all FBI agents so unyielding? Townsend's face flashed through her mind. Initial charm aside, he clearly hadn't liked her and he might even suspect she was involved in the cyberattack. Investigators often looked for an inside source. Marie quickly counted her blessings again that Dashwood had assigned Ortega to watch over her.

"Not at all," he said. "What you're going through is very common. People don't like to be yanked out of the familiar routine. Not even FBI agents." He spared her a quick glance, then put his gaze back on the road stretching endlessly in front of them. "The FBI doesn't like for those same people to get hurt while we're investigating."

"At least you get to do your job." She couldn't fathom filling the hours she normally spent at work. "What am I going to do out here?" Too afraid of the answer, she couldn't voice the bigger question: How long would she be stuck out here?

"You might be surprised by how busy we are on a working ranch."

"If you're expecting *me* to herd cattle, you're in for a *big* disappointment," she said.

His low laughter was unexpected. "We do have a modest herd, thirty head of longhorn cattle, and plenty of help with that. There are also horses, goats, dogs, cats and an ever-changing variety of other animals. My parents are both veterinarians, and because we have space and staff, they tend to rescue more than their share of needy animals."

She kept her mouth shut. They might as well be from two different planets. One of her foster families had had a big orange tabby cat that wasn't a fan of children. There'd been a year of mutual hatred between her and a yappy little Chihuahua at another stop on her route through the foster-care system.

He lifted a finger off the steering wheel and aimed it toward a point in the distance she couldn't see. "We'll head down Main Street, give you a feel for the town."

Did that mean he'd allow her out of his sight long enough to come back into town? Was this a test? She understood she'd been threatened online and in real life. Understood no one wanted her help, which could only mean the FBI believed she might have assisted the Cohort's hack of her company's defenses. Things had spun so quickly out of her control today and she didn't grasp the new rules of the situation.

She wanted to ask him to be clear about his expectations for her, of her. Why couldn't she get the words out? Simple questions, really. *What are my chores? Where is my room? Is there a lights-out rule? Am I under house arrest?* Questions she'd learned to ask upon her arrival at a new foster home. Well, except for that last one.

They passed a beautiful white church spearing up from the landscape, backed by a lovely cemetery. She imagined the weddings, baptisms, funerals and weekly gatherings of families into a larger community that created generations of history. Her nose stung with tears she'd learned long ago to suppress. Tears were rather useless against loneliness.

As if inspired by that first church, Shadow Creek stretched out before them, buildings and businesses, and neighborhoods holding the vast Hill Country at bay. Bigger than she'd expected, it was merely a speck in comparison to Dallas or

Austin. Still, something inside her relaxed as they passed bed-and-breakfasts and a sign for a farm called Hill Country. That sounded like a friendly place.

With the tidy buildings and well-maintained facades exuding charm, Shadow Creek might as easily have been found in Hollywood serving as a backdrop for a Western movie. A movie set at Christmastime, she amended. Evergreen garlands climbed lampposts and draped over railings. It seemed every business had a different festive wreath at the door. She assumed tiny white lights sparkled delicately through it all at night.

Christmas. In her head she always emphasized the word with the same dismay Indiana Jones used when he said the word *snakes*.

She tried to give her spirits a boost as they passed businesses like the Shadow Creek Mercantile, the Cozy Diner and the Secret Garden floral shop near a thoroughly modern bank, a salon-spa and a printing shop. *A lovely spot for a weekend getaway*, she thought. Too bad she didn't bother with those.

Catching a glimpse of the tall, modern hospital was a harsh reminder of the Livia Colton announcement and the serious nature of Marie's trouble.

"Claudia Colton owns a shop you might like down here on Main Street." Agent Ortega pointed. "Honeysuckle Road. From the way the women around here talk, they love that she brought some New York City style to Shadow Creek."

"You're saying I'm free to walk around and go shopping here like a normal tourist?"

"You're not under house arrest, Miss Meyers." He glanced at her feet. "Although you won't want to walk from the ranch back into town in those heels."

"Call me Marie."

"Marie it is," he said, giving her another of those long

looks while they were stopped at a traffic light. "And Emiliano is fine."

She tested his name silently in her mind and decided the sensual cadence fit the sexy man perfectly.

"The FBI is simply trying to keep you safe," he continued. "We can do that more easily out here."

"Where strangers stand out?" She should be used to the feeling. There were so few times in her life when she hadn't been one of the new faces on the fringes, looking at groups with established routines and hierarchy, waiting for her to prove if she could fit in.

"Where neighbors aren't afraid to take a stand," he corrected. "It's a good-sized town, and the community isn't crammed up together like Dallas. Look around."

She had been. The businesses on Main Street sparkled as if the sun itself was happier shining here, reluctant to say farewell for the day. Sidewalks were clean and wide, and it seemed as if everyone smiled, a few people waving as Agent Ortega—*Emiliano*—drove by.

"Plus, with no ties to the area, no one will think to look for you here."

No ties anywhere, she thought, craving the safe anonymity of the city. Surely one of the gazillion hotels in Dallas would have been sufficient to wait out the hacktivists. Here, she suspected people knew where everyone else came from and would never forget about a foster kid's science project that caused a kitchen fire. Seeing a sign for another bed-and-breakfast, she felt her stomach twist. Although she'd learned long ago to deflect questions about her personal history, she'd rather not put that to a small-town hospitality test.

Dusk was falling, the sky growing heavy and deep, and as she'd suspected, those holiday greens started to sparkle. She was discomfited by the joyful, carefree vibe in town, and the space and distance of the ranch suddenly held far more appeal. "Tell me more about the ranch."

"It's quiet, not as big as some other ranches in the area." He stopped for another traffic light and pointed to Big Jim's Burger Shop. "Best burgers in town, in my opinion." He hitched his thumb back the way they'd come. "Aldo's vies for the same honor. We'll try both and you can weigh in."

Dinners, plural, with Emiliano? "Is the plan to show me around Shadow Creek?" Maybe he wanted to use her as bait to lure the hacktivists. It wasn't a pleasant idea, though she kept saying she wanted to help.

"Plan?" His straight eyebrows snapped together. "Just an option," he said, not looking at her. "The ranch is self-sufficient."

Contrite that he misunderstood her real concern, she tried to apologize. "Shadow Creek is lovely. I just wondered…" As his scowl deepened, she fell silent.

"You're wondering if I'll hang you out like a worm on a fish hook," he finished for her, a muscle in his square jaw twitching.

She wasn't quite as eager to cooperate when he said it like that. "It's a valid option."

"It's reckless," he countered, turning off Main Street. Within minutes the evening sparkle of Shadow Creek was a dwindling image behind them as he gained speed on a two-lane blacktop road.

Twilight crept across the landscape, the last rays of the setting sun painting the western horizon with bold streaks of fiery oranges and muted indigo. She felt small and alone in the world without the buffer of Shadow Creek between her and all that wide-open space.

He slowed to take a turn off the paved road onto a gravel driveway. They passed under an archway that declared their arrival at Ortega Ranch with a sign for veterinary services, as well.

She couldn't see much beyond the road in the fading light, just the rails of a fence and the shape of several buildings as he named them. "The drive splits here and circles around to the veterinary offices," he said.

She'd take his word, searching for anything familiar and latching on to the one-story stone house with a big chimney at one end caught in his headlights. A faint light glowed from a window deep inside the house.

"The cattle are farther out," he explained as he parked the truck.

Lights, apparently on motion sensors, flooded the immediate area in a bright glow. "Where will I be staying?" At last, she managed to voice one of the questions she should have asked earlier.

"At the main house with me." He left the cab to get their bags out of the truck bed.

She hopped out and her heels sank into the dirt. He'd been so eager to get on the road he hadn't given her time to change. This would not be the place for heels and skirts. Thank goodness she'd taken his advice and packed her sneakers and jeans, along with easy-care T-shirts and a couple of older sweatshirts.

What a mess, she thought, coming around to help him with her luggage. Moving in with an FBI agent, temporarily exiled from her work and distanced from the city life she loved.

"Plenty of room and all the modern conveniences. You'll hardly know you've left Dallas."

She jumped and turned at the sound of a soft woof. Uncertain of her options, she looked to Emiliano for guidance as a tall dog with a shaggy golden coat trotted out of the darkness from the direction of the barns.

Emiliano crouched down. "Hey, Gordo," he said, giving him a scratch between his ears.

"Gordo?"

"Short for Flash Gordon. My dad was in a mood that day. He found him on the side of the road and nursed him back to health after a broken pelvis. Gordo used to race up the drive as soon as he heard my dad's car. He's slowed down some." Emiliano stood up, smiling at her across the truck bed. "Come say hello."

"I don't know how."

He simply came to her, Gordo at his hip. "Sit." The dog complied, his ears cocked as he stared up at her. "Gordo, this is Marie. She's our friend. Shake."

Gordo lifted a paw and, at the agent's encouraging nod, she bent down and gave it a quick shake.

"Great job," Emiliano said.

She chose not to ask if he meant to praise her or the dog. Either way, she took an immediate liking to Gordo, and Emiliano's obvious pleasure at being home put her at ease.

"Let's get you settled in." He picked up the luggage, leaving her to manage only her purse as he walked along the wide covered patio that fronted the house. It was decorated with planters between each column and had padded benches set back against the firm stone wall of the house and separated by small tables, and she felt the warm welcome, even as a stranger.

Hearing the staccato barking inside, she stutter-stepped. "Another dog?"

"As I said earlier," he replied.

"Right." She gave Gordo a tentative smile. "I'm not used to being around animals," she said. "I'll figure it out." Blending in was the key to successful transitions. This was just one more temporary transition.

"As the son of two veterinarians, I can't imagine it any other way." The barking grew closer and a long white snout tipped with a black nose poked aside the curtains at the front window as they passed by. Bright brown eyes shone with happiness from a reddish-brown face, split by the stripe of white that narrowed as it flowed up between the large perked ears.

A broad smile transformed Emiliano's face. "That's my corgi, Scrabble."

"Another rescue?"

"Of sorts. She's one of our best herders." He stopped abruptly and she had to as well or run into his back. He turned, blocking the walkway. "Don't move."

At the window, Scrabble raised her voice again, her eyes on Emiliano, ears straight up and her small paws patting the sill. She seemed to bounce a little with every sound, as if desperate to tell him something.

"What's wrong?" she asked.

He didn't answer as he set the luggage down and drew his gun. He was in full federal-agent mode again as his gaze swept the area while he put his back to the house and the barking dog.

"Stay right there," he ordered.

A thousand terrible thoughts ran through her mind as he crept closer to the front door. Another note? A robbery? Something worse? No one knew until a few hours ago that she would be coming here, so it couldn't be related to her, could it?

Gordo wandered up beside her, leaned a little against her leg. She didn't care about dog hair on her skirt, taking comfort from the mutt's presence as she rested a hand on his head.

"Ace?" As quickly as he'd drawn his gun, he holstered his weapon, kneeling as he'd done to greet Gordo.

Another animal? She assumed this one was wounded based on Emiliano's tone.

Gordo whimpered and she absently stroked the dog's

ear, soothing them both while Scrabble continued her efforts to communicate with Emiliano. Why had she ever agreed to this? Coming out here gave too much weight to the hacktivist threats. She gazed out over the dark fields between the house and the deserted road and wondered what she could do to regain control of her life.

"Marie! Call nine-one-one."

"You have my phone." Was there an emergency response team for animals out here? She hurried toward him, only then seeing the man in the doorway. "Oh, no. He's not… Is he…is he dead?"

Chapter 4

"Ace!" Emiliano's heart kicked hard in his chest at the sight of Ace Gregor slumped against the front door. He pressed his fingers to the man's throat, searching for a pulse. Finding it steady, if slow, Emiliano drew his first deep breath of relief.

No sign of blood or wounds aside from scraped knuckles, which could mean anything for a man working on a ranch. Had he had a heart attack or a stroke? It wasn't outside the realm of possibilities. At sixty-three, Ace had been part of life at Ortega Ranch since before Emiliano was born. The man was as good as family and reliable as sunrise. He'd never done anything so uncharacteristic as passing out in a doorway.

Carefully, Emiliano felt around the man's head and neck for any obvious injuries. There was a large goose egg at the back of Ace's head, but no blood in the thin blond hair going gray at the temples.

Nothing out here on the porch would have caused that kind of injury and left Ace in this position, unless the man had fallen into the doorknob. An unlikely scenario. Emiliano looked around, seeing no signs of a struggle, which baffled him even more. Had the man knocked himself senseless and passed out before he could get into the house? Again, unlikely. Knowing the first-aid supplies were in the kitchen, Ace would have gone to the back door, not the front.

"Ace. Come on." Emiliano jerked out of his jacket and eased the older man flat on his back, pillowing his head. Stretched out, Ace seemed to breathe easier. Emiliano shook his shoulder gently, praying he'd come around.

Inside, Scrabble was going nuts, as if she was encouraging Ace to wake up. The antics didn't surprise him, as his dog and the ranch hand had a tight bond. Ace often used her to help with the cattle and he took the brunt of her care whenever Emiliano had to travel for work.

"You know him? He's alive?"

Emiliano turned, looking up into Marie's worried face. "Yes. He's our ranch manager."

"Do you still want me to call an ambulance?"

He let his gaze drift down her compact body, from her lovely face, over the shapely legs bared by her tailored skirt, to the heels that wouldn't last a day out here. His job was to keep her safe while they assessed the hack and her potential culpability, not catalog her finer attributes.

"Let's give him a minute. Help me get him inside." Dragging her out of Dallas and promising her safety, only to find a body in the doorway, probably didn't instill much confidence. It certainly left him rattled and wondering.

"Shouldn't you check for intruders or a break-in?"

"If someone was inside, Scrabble would've told me by now." He unlocked the door and pushed it open. Predictably, his stocky little dog squeezed through at the first opportunity and turned a happy circle at his feet before snuffling around Ace's face and neck.

She jerked back and sneezed, then startled him by growling at the older man. "Settle. Back it up, Scrabble."

The dog stepped aside and plopped onto her rump at his left foot. Her ears cocked for his next command, Emiliano saw her curious gaze drift toward Marie.

"In a minute," he said to his dog. He'd make introductions as soon as he got Ace inside. As gently as possible, he hauled Ace over the threshold and settled him on the nearest couch in the central room.

Marie followed with Gordo and the luggage, and closed the door.

"Kitchen's that way." Emiliano pointed. Scrabble put her nose under Ace's hand in a move that usually earned her an ear rub. Ace remained still. "Can you find a towel and wet it with cool water, please?"

Marie hurried off while Emiliano continued evaluating Ace. The older man didn't reek of alcohol and wasn't known to get sloppy drunk. The next guess was drugs, though that too would be out of character. Emiliano searched the man's pockets, found his cell phone and checked for any incriminating messages or callers, coming up empty.

Marie handed him the cool, damp towel and stepped back while Emiliano pressed the cloth to Ace's cheeks and forehead.

Scrabble studied the woman between her attempts to rouse Ace.

"We should call an ambulance," Emiliano muttered. "I just don't know what to tell them." Suspicions of heart attack or stroke wouldn't help a paramedic diagnose anything. With Ace breathing and a steady pulse, he decided to give the man another minute or two to come around.

They had a security system in place, but it was primarily aimed at protecting the vet practice. It hadn't been armed here when he'd opened the door, which told him Ace had been working nearby today. Wouldn't Scrabble have been out there with him?

Ace's hand twitched, his fingers sinking into Scrabble's ruff. The dog gave a soft woof and another nudge. The man's eyelids fluttered open. He looked around, winced and closed his eyes tight.

"Ace?"

"Emiliano?" he rasped. He coughed a little and tried to roll to his side.

"Easy, friend." Emiliano turned to Marie. "Water?"

She dashed to the kitchen, her heels snapping on the slate flooring between the thick area rugs.

"What happened?" Emiliano asked when she was out of earshot.

"How did I get in here?"

"I carried you," Emiliano said. "I'm calling a doctor."

"No. That's silly." Ace pushed himself to a seated position and clapped a hand to his neck. Scrabble hopped up, growled at the spot. "I'm good, sweet girl."

"Let me see." Emiliano pulled back Ace's work shirt, tugged aside the collar of the T-shirt underneath. "This looks like a bruise from a needle with a scratch to go with it. You need the hospital."

"No." Ace coughed. "I'm awake. I'll be fine."

"Here." Marie held out a bottle of water.

Ace squinted up at her. "Who are you?"

"Marie Meyers, CDO of Colton, Incorporated," Emiliano answered for her.

"You're pretty." Ace accepted the water, drank deep. "What's a CDO do?"

"Ignore him. Our Ace is an incurable flirt," Emiliano deadpanned. He pushed back to sit on the edge of an ottoman. "Give me a reason not to take you over to the hospital, old man."

"That's where I was," Ace said. He blotted his face with the cool towel and let it fall to his thigh as if that small movement exhausted him.

"You were at Memorial?"

"No, no. The vet hospital. Tires on the driveway." He closed his eyes. "It doesn't make sense. Everyone knows your parents are out of town."

Ace was right. Everyone in Shadow Creek knew the

veterinary offices were closed because his parents were taking a long-overdue extended vacation before the holidays. No one should have been driving around that part of the ranch. "Come on." Emiliano pulled his keys from his pocket. "I think the doctors should take a look at your head."

"My head's just fine," Ace protested. "Call in Dr. Ramirez if you want," Ace said stubbornly. "I'm not going to a damn hospital."

Considering the injection, Emiliano decided Ramirez was better than nothing, so he made the call. If Ace didn't have a clear recollection of the events that landed him in the doorway, they needed to be sure he wouldn't be dealing with any lingering side effects. "Why wasn't Scrabble with you?"

Ace smiled at the little dog resting her chin on his boot. "We'd gone out for a romp and I brought her in, gave her a treat."

"What time was that?" he asked.

"Around two, I think. That's normally when we go out." Under his sandy eyebrows, his pale blue eyes shifted to Gordo. "Then this one went with me to the back pasture to check on the horses." He took another pull on the water. "The tires on the driveway were too loud. Whoever it was came in too fast."

Emiliano checked the big clock over the archway between the great room and kitchen. It was a quarter past six, so Ace must have been out for the better part of four hours. It had been too dark for Emiliano to have seen any obvious skid marks in the gravel where the driveway split off to the offices. He'd have to take a closer look once Ace was steadier.

Marie couldn't help feeling like an interloper, no matter that she was here at the FBI's insistence. She wished there was something to do besides worry as the older man answered Emiliano's questions.

"The alarm sounded on your mother's office. I remember running that way. The back door was open." Ace rubbed his neck again. "A man stepped out, wearing some weird mustache mask thing." He waved a hand around his face. "I tried to confront him and got clocked. He must have drugged me, but why drag me over here?"

"We'll figure it out," Emiliano promised.

Marie wanted to wallow in his sheer confidence. The determination in his deep voice made her feel better despite everything that had happened today.

Emiliano reached for his phone as Ace described the mask. "Did the mask look like this?"

Marie caught a glimpse of the image of the Guy Fawkes mask used by more and more protesters in real life and online.

"Yeah. That's it," Ace confirmed. "What's this about?"

"Cohort," Emiliano murmured.

Although he was the investigator, she knew they couldn't dismiss the cyberattack in Dallas and the attack on Ace a few hours later as coincidence.

"They're a hacktivist group," Marie explained. "They attacked Colton, Incorporated, this morning. They breached the database and stole a great deal of private information on our employees." And posted a reward for her capture or death. Although she was here, it was still too bizarre for her to say it aloud.

"Huh." Ace's gaze moved slowly from Marie to Emiliano and back. "Why would they come out here looking for you?" he asked her.

"They wouldn't," Emiliano snapped. "The decision to bring Marie here for her protection was only made hours ago."

She bit her lip to hide the nervous trembling and followed his gaze as he stared at the needle mark on Ace's neck. Had this man been hurt because the Cohort was after her? The thought made her stomach pitch.

Emiliano stood up and drew his gun. "I need to check the drug inventory at Mom's office."

Marie almost told him to be careful, but this was his property, his job. She was certain he knew how to handle himself.

"You two wait here," he said. "I'll set the alarm system behind me." He looked at the dogs. "Scrabble, stay. Gordo, come." Scrabble sat up a little straighter between Ace's boots. Gordo lumbered to his feet and followed Emiliano. "We'll be back before Dr. Ramirez arrives."

Marie turned to Ace. "More water?"

"I'd rather have coffee," he said, in a hopeful tone.

She wasn't sure that was smart. "I'll brew some for you if the doctor says it's okay."

"Fine." Ace sighed and sat back. "You can tell me what a CDO does while we wait."

She would certainly do her best to keep him distracted.

As Emiliano jogged up the drive, he added up the various factors without any comfort in the preliminary solutions. His FBI career was no more a secret than his parents' vacation. Why would the Cohort come here? And if they could strike down Ace on Ortega property, was there any place where he could possibly hope to keep Marie safe?

At the fork where the gravel driveway split off toward the vet offices, he saw Ace was right. Someone had taken the turn too quickly. Near the office itself, he found skid marks where someone had pulled to a stop and left again in a hurry. He took a few pictures, though he'd have to take more in the better light of morning. At the office door, he took pictures of the broken lock. He would review the security system video after he checked the inventory. To drop a man as big and tough as Ace, the attacker likely went for xylazine, one of the tranquilizers his mother used in her equine practice. Like all reputable vets, Natalia Ortega kept careful records of the controlled substances. She used computer logs as well as a handwritten chart on a clipboard near the cabinet to track when each patient received what kind of dosage and why.

Sure enough, the locked cabinet had been busted off its hinges and two vials of xylazine were missing. Emiliano swore. It was a safe bet she was short a box of syringes, as well. A quick search confirmed that. He noted the signs of a brief struggle. Ace was tall, strong and wily. How had he seen the thief's masked face and still been overpowered?

On hands and knees, he found a syringe under the desk with a few milliliters of fluid in the barrel. His mother didn't keep controlled substances predrawn, which meant there had to have been two people here, one fighting Ace and another to prepare the drug. Emiliano pulled on exam gloves and dropped the syringe into a plastic bag, hoping to preserve any fingerprints.

At the security system panel, he checked the time of the alarm that had brought his ranch manager into range of the thieves. He and Marie had just gotten on the road out of Dallas when Ace was attacked here. Did that mean the incidents were connected or coincidence? He pulled out his phone to send a text message to his boss and changed his mind. Better to get more facts together. He could share this development on the team video conference scheduled for tomorrow.

Emiliano tucked his phone away. Knowing his mother's security codes, he moved the remainder of her controlled substances into a cabinet that locked properly. He was going to have to open a Food and Drug Administration report on her behalf, as well. With luck, being an FBI agent would make that process run a bit smoother.

He should probably call her, but he didn't want to interrupt their holiday cruise. It was the first big vacation they'd taken in years. The least he could do was handle things in their absence. Satisfied the meds were secure, he managed to get the door to stay closed with the dead bolt so he could reset the alarm. Tomorrow, he could make a decision about repairing or replacing the door.

He returned to the house just as Dr. Ramirez's sedan turned into the driveway. He and Gordo waited for the older man to climb out of the car with his bag. Together the two men and the scruffy dog walked inside, where Marie and Ace were chatting like old friends in the great room.

Emiliano opened his mouth to make introductions and stopped short. Scrabble hadn't met him at the door. She was sitting on Marie's lap in one of the leather armchairs, her canine grin expressing delight and pride in finding a new friend.

Huh. His dog was an excellent judge of character. It was uncharacteristic for her to become so friendly with anyone so fast, especially in light of Marie's inexperience with animals. Having her take that relaxed, affectionate stance toward a woman he hadn't completely removed from the suspect column made him reconsider Marie's position within the investigation.

"Who's the patient?" Ramirez asked. "You both look well enough to me."

"Ace is the patient," Marie said, gently stroking Scrabble's long back when the dog refused to relinquish her place.

Emiliano explained how and where they'd found Ace and the missing supplies from the vet office. Ace chimed in with what he remembered of the incident. "I'd appreciate you keeping this quiet," Emiliano said when the basics were complete.

"Assumed as much." Ramirez's thick salt-and-pepper eyebrows knit into a frown. He took blood and urine samples to verify the suspected xylazine and, after some additional evaluation, told them Ace had a mild concussion and would recover with a few days' rest.

"You'll be here, Emiliano?" the doctor asked, packing up his bag.

"Yes." This time of year the ranch ran on a skeleton crew so everyone had more time with family, although they would all pitch in and make sure Ace had enough help.

"Good." He snapped his bag closed and tucked his glasses into his shirt pocket. "I'm counting on you to be sure he doesn't overdo it or the recovery will take twice as long." He aimed a meaningful look at Ace. "I mean it."

"I heard you," Ace said.

"Pleasure to meet you, Miss Meyers," Dr. Ramirez said. "Enjoy your time in Shadow Creek."

Emiliano walked the doctor back to his car. "Ace had to be out for close to four hours," he said.

"I did the math," the doctor agreed. He unlocked the car and set his bag on the passenger seat. "That works in his favor in this case."

"How so?"

"Because being unconscious, his body was able to purge the drug without as much of a fight," Ramirez explained. "Once I have these labs back, I'll know if he needs more attention. In the meantime, water and rest will do him the most good. If he were in real trouble, it would be obvious in his breathing and heart rate."

It was small comfort, but he'd take it. "Do you think his assailants dragged him to the door?"

Ramirez chuckled. "Knowing Ace, he stumbled there on his own, trying to find help. He's too stubborn to let a head injury or sedatives have all the advantages."

While the last part was true, Emiliano was sure Ace would've gone for the back door over the front. It was habit. Then again, between the head injury and the drug, he couldn't have been thinking clearly. Maybe more details would come out as he recovered.

"I found a syringe in the office," Emiliano said. "I'll let you know what the evidence lab finds."

Emiliano watched the doctor drive away, the bagged syringe in his back pocket for the evidence team to process later, and his thoughts scattered.

At the sounds of small paws on the gravel, he turned to see Scrabble racing his way, Marie hesitating under the soft glow of the porch light. "Is Ace okay?"

"Just fine," she said. "He's hungry and I wanted to check with you before I invaded your kitchen."

Emiliano knelt down and patted his chest and Scrabble bounced into his arms, a trick he'd taught her when she was just a puppy.

"Impressive," Marie said as they joined her.

"Corgis are more athletic than people think at first glance," he said, his mind on more complicated issues. He was about to walk inside when she hesitated. "What?"

"Do you think your team will sort this out quickly?" she asked.

"Missing Dallas already?"

"Not exactly." Her mouth turned down as she frowned at him. "I told you Shadow Creek is lovely."

"You'll see more of it," he replied without thinking it through.

"But the Cohort," she pressed. "Do you think they hurt your friend because of me?"

"Time will tell. It's hard to believe these incidents are unrelated." He rubbed at the tension in his neck. "The Cohort isn't easy to crack, even when its motives are clear," he admitted. "Then again, the FBI is investigating and Christmas *is* the season of miracles."

She stared up at him for a long, silent moment.

Under her puckered brow, he read the doubt in her big

brown eyes. She didn't have to say the words aloud for him to recognize she was a woman who didn't have much faith in people, the FBI or miracles in any season.

Chapter 5

Once things had settled down last night, Marie had been shown to the guest bedroom. Decorated in a soft color palette that reminded her of the sunset, the space was fresh and scented with a bouquet of dried lavender. A warm, inviting space she couldn't seem to get comfortable in.

It had been a typical first night in a new house for her, rife with those old uncertainties she'd worked hard to bury or eliminate from her life since turning eighteen. She wasn't that girl anymore, blowing from place to place like a brittle leaf in a hard wind. This was temporary.

At Emiliano's insistence, Ace had spent the night on the couch, and she suspected Emiliano had slept out there as well to keep an eye on his ranch manager. The men shared a close camaraderie only time could bring. A camaraderie that had tripped her up emotionally when she'd thought she was past all of it.

Back in high school English class there had been a poetry unit she'd enjoyed. Though she no longer remembered the poet's name, she recalled the sentiment of his poems that described the way people interacted with each other. Some stuck and took root in a life and others drifted by, only involved for a time or a short purpose. The foster system had made her a drifter, and from the moment she'd left, she'd done everything possible to take root where she wanted to stay.

And yet, thanks to circumstance, here she was, drifting again. *Not the same thing.* She had friends at the office back in Dallas. Friends she couldn't contact while Emiliano kept her phone and other devices for the sake of safety and the investigation.

A pale dawn teased the edges of the curtains at the window and, hearing the men stirring elsewhere in the house, she rolled out of bed. She gathered her things and a change of clothes and headed for the bathroom Emiliano said was hers to use during her stay.

Showered and dressed, she went to the kitchen, where the rich aroma of coffee filled the air, anchored by the savory scent of bacon and spices. Emiliano stood at the stove, pouring pancake batter onto a griddle. No dark FBI suit today, he wore faded jeans that hugged his legs and a gray, long-sleeved T-shirt with the sleeves pushed back to his elbows. Both looks fit the man like two sides of a coin and left her a little breathless.

Ace, sitting at the table tucked into the bowed window, sent her a winning smile. "Well, good morning, gorgeous."

He was incorrigible. Helpless against the friendliness in his eyes, she smiled back. "How are you feeling?"

"Pretty near perfect," he said. "Hard to feel bad when Emiliano's dishing up breakfast and the loveliest lady around is about to join me." He patted the seat beside him.

"Take it easy, Casanova." Emiliano shot him a look as he stepped back from the stove and gave a pancake a perfect flip.

The man had surprising skills. "Need a hand?" she offered.

"I've got it," he replied without looking at her. "Pour yourself a cup of coffee."

She didn't know what to do with herself when no one needed her. She splashed a little cream into her cup, added hot coffee and joined Ace at the table.

"Where are the dogs?" The distraction would be welcome, while she figured out where she fit into this new scenario.

The older man grinned and tipped his head toward the back door. "Scrabble and Gordo are outside. Scrabble likes to count heads before we do. That one thinks she knows it all." Ace chuckled. "Gordo's just along for the stroll."

"Count heads?" Marie asked.

"She's a herder," Emiliano replied. "She believes it's her job to confirm everyone is in the right place. Stables, paddocks and chicken coop, she makes the rounds with us every day."

Emiliano brought over the pancakes and bacon, set the platters in the middle of the table one of them had already set with plates, cutlery, butter and syrup. He went back to the oven and returned with a piping-hot pan of diced potatoes.

Ace didn't hesitate. He filled a plate and surprised her by setting it in front of her. "Dig in."

She didn't argue. The hearty food was delicious. As Emiliano and Ace discussed the day, she listened with avid curiosity.

"I'll finish up around here, and Scrabble and I will head out to check the cattle," Emiliano said. "Ace can give you the full tour around here." He crumpled his napkin in one hand and picked up his coffee mug. From across the table he caught her gaze and held it. "Sound good?"

She brightened, picking up on the unspoken message. He wanted to be sure the ranch manager didn't overdo it. At last—a way to help. "Yes, thank you."

Pushing back from the table, he started to gather up the dishes.

"Let me do that," she said quickly. She took the dishes from him and her fingertips tingled when they bumped his. She swallowed. "Ace can help me out if I need it."

One of those dark eyebrows lanced upward. "All right."

He poured coffee into a thermos before heading to the door. "There's a conference call in a couple of hours to review the investigation," he said. "I'll be back in time for that."

He walked out before she could ask if there had been any developments.

"He's grouchy when his mind is on a case," Ace said, bringing dishes to the counter.

She only smiled, knowing better than to comment on Emiliano's mood. Shifting the topic to other things while she dealt with the dishes, she got Ace talking about life out in the Hill Country and on this ranch in particular. The man's love for his work and the Ortega family came through loud and clear, and she relaxed more than she thought possible as he told her how things had grown and changed through the years.

"The boys had their ornery moments for sure," he said of Emiliano and his younger brother, Dario, as they walked outside. "Brothers do that, y'know."

She didn't, but she nodded along. Her friends often fussed about siblings, yet she'd always envied the unbreakable bond of true family ties.

Ace guided her through the barn nearest the house, where the family's horses were kept in big, airy stalls. He told her about horses and goats, rescue dogs and cats. They found Gordo snoozing in a patch of sunlight, a small kitten snuggled beside him. "Aurelio and Natalia raised 'em right. They put a love for the land and all the animals on it into those boys."

"Neither of them stay to work the ranch?"

Ace looked almost offended. "They're capable of it, if that's what you mean."

It wasn't.

"It's a big world and young men have things to do." He ducked into a small office and opened an ancient refrig-

erator. He pulled out a couple of carrots and handed them
to her. "Besides, if those boys were here all the time, what
would I do?"

"Give ranch tours to city girls?"

He laughed loud enough to wake Gordo. "Allow me
to introduce our horses." He stuck out his elbow and she
looped her hand through it.

He guided her around the house to the fenced paddock
that bordered the driveway. Under the clear blue December sky, three horses were enjoying the morning sunshine.
Ace propped a boot on the lowest rail of the fence and
pointed to each of them in turn, giving Marie the names.
"Brandy is that solid brown mare. She's as sweet as they
come." He clucked his tongue and Brandy started their
way along with a colorful horse. "Where Brandy goes,
Picasso follows. He's a pinto and the boy never misses a
treat since Natalia rescued him years back. Now, that fair
color is called palomino. Our gal Rapunzel has a bit of
sass." When he whistled for the horse, she only flicked
her tail. "See what I mean?"

Marie laughed. As Brandy and Picasso reached the
fence, she started to ease back. The beautiful animals
were so much bigger up close. Until today, horsepower was
something she only related to cars or the Dallas mounted
police. *Definitely city girl to the bone*, she thought ruefully.

"Don't be shy," Ace said to Marie. "And don't be pushy,"
he told the horses. "There's enough for everyone."

The old ranch manager showed her how to touch the
horses and she reveled in the textures between their soft
noses, the sleek coats and the tickle of lips as they plucked
chunks of carrot from her open palm. Eventually Rapunzel got jealous enough, or curious enough, to join them. "I
haven't been this close to a horse since a field trip to the
zoo as a kid. They're wonderful," she said. "Thanks, Ace."

"Guess that means you don't ride."

"Never had the chance to learn," she replied. She didn't want to offend him with the truth that she'd never been interested. Her limited knowledge of ranches and rural environments came from entertainment venues like books or movies. Being out here in it gave her a new appreciation for why those characters loved it so much.

"You should ask Emiliano to teach you," Ace said as they started back to the house.

"Oh, I doubt I'll be here that long." Though she couldn't deny that she found the peaceful area almost as enticing as the man who'd brought her here.

"Time will tell." Ace gave her a wry smile, as if indulging a child's idealism while knowing the real world would clear things up soon enough.

There was something she wanted Emiliano to teach her. She needed to learn how to defend herself. In light of the attack on Ace, she decided to approach her FBI protector at the first opportunity.

Emiliano returned from his circuit of the ranch and caught sight of Ace and Marie with the horses out front. If by chance he'd missed them, Scrabble's alert would have corrected the lapse. His faithful companion had fallen in love with Marie, effectively the newest rescue on the ranch. The dog often showed more caution around new rescues and the attitude shift baffled him.

More unexpected was the undeniable attraction and connection drawing him toward Marie. Her delighted expression when he'd flipped that pancake had made him feel like a hero. And she'd immediately understood why he wanted Ace to show her around.

He'd had a busy morning, taking and sending clear pictures of the tire tracks near the vet offices to both his boss and Shadow Creek's new sheriff, Knox Colton. He'd ridden out to check the property lines and the herd for any signs of trouble or weakness. Scrabble was thrilled to be out and about, and she'd alternated between bounding alongside and riding up in the saddle with him.

Through it all, he mulled over Marie, the Cohort threats against her and the threat she might pose to the investigation. It was hard to look at her and think *enemy* when those dimples creased her cheeks and a smile lit up her big brown eyes.

He checked his watch, knowing he was cutting it close before the scheduled update conference call. Guiding his black-and-white gelding, Domino, into the corral behind the barn, he'd just removed the saddle and propped it on a rail when Ace walked up.

"Let me take care of this," Ace said.

Emiliano shook his head, removing the rest of the tack. Ace should be resting. "I've got it. Where's Marie?"

"Out front with another cup of coffee, I think."

"You think?"

Ace hooked his thumbs in his belt, rocked back on his heels. "I thought you had her babysitting me, not the other way around."

"Either way, you should both be *here*," he pointed out, inexplicably annoyed. "Scrabble, find Marie."

Ace snorted and reached for the saddle as the dog raced off.

"Ace," Emiliano warned.

"I've had as much rest as I can stand." He yanked the saddle off the rail and stalked off toward the tack room.

It wasn't until he was well away from the house that Emiliano had realized his mistake in leaving her with Ace, who, despite the declarations to the contrary, wasn't at the top of his game today. She might have done anything while he was gone, tampered with his computer, contacted the Cohort, tried to walk into town. Or found a ride back to Dallas.

And as she followed Scrabble to join him at the corral, a cup of coffee in hand, winter sunlight on her hair and that wide smile flanked by dimples, he knew all those possibilities were baseless. Mentally, he removed her name from the list of possible Cohort accomplices.

He'd done more background research last night after Marie had gone to bed and Ace had fallen asleep. He supposed being a foster kid explained her lack of ties to anything other than Colton, Incorporated, but it still bothered him. Who lived that way, without support or backup? No pets, as she'd said, a minimal social life and completely career-oriented.

When Scrabble sat, gazing up at him expectantly, he praised her and bent to give her a good ear massage. It gave him a moment to pull himself together. "How was your morning?"

"Great. Ace gave me the full tour. He showed me how to give the horses out front some treats."

"Good." Emiliano shuffled his feet and stared out over the acreage. She was almost too fresh and pretty to look at with her hair pulled up into a ponytail, her snug jeans too dark to have seen much use, and the half-zip sweatshirt with the faded football team logo over a long-sleeved shirt. She was in tennis shoes instead of high heels, so he had a better sense of how petite she really was, with those feminine curves balanced perfectly on her small frame.

At one time, she might have been exactly his type of woman. Thank goodness his work kept him traveling from one cyberattack to the next, effectively killing his chances to repeat the relationship mistakes of his past.

"I'm headed inside for the conference call," he said.

"Could I please join you?"

No. "Sure."

In the study that overlooked his mother's vegetable garden, he pulled another chair around to the working side of the desk so they could be seen on the call together. It wasn't exactly protocol, but it wasn't a breach, either. Scrabble stretched out on her belly between the chairs, her feet sprawled out like a furry compass star.

When Dashwood, Townsend and Staller were all online with Emiliano and Marie, Dashwood gave the preliminary general update that they didn't have a definite lead yet. Staller filled in the blanks on the malware that kept the firewalls vulnerable, adding his expectation of fixing the issue by the end of the day.

Beside him, Marie nodded thoughtfully. The others couldn't see the way her hands relaxed at the news that Colton, Incorporated, would soon be secure again.

Finn Townsend appeared as frustrated today as he had when Emiliano had left Dallas. "This code is definitely Cohort. I've found the standard references to their so-called leader, Sulla. Nothing so far that points us to a local Princeps."

One more deviation from standard Cohort behavior. The workhorses of the Cohort, the Principes often clustered near a cyberattack site to launch red herrings and other distracting challenges at investigators.

"There are typical tools and procedures within the signature, but the technique isn't on par," Finn added.

"Meaning what?" Emiliano wanted to hear something more substantial, something that would give them a hard target.

"Someone new." Finn scowled at his notes. "I'll keep digging."

"And you?" Dashwood asked Emiliano.

He reported about the attack on Ace and the xylazine theft. "Whoever it was killed the camera on approach, so no identifications. I'm still working out how they managed that. It's probably a local crime of opportunity," he finished. Pulling the bagged syringe from the desk drawer, he held it up for his team to see. "The sheriff will send this to the lab in Austin. Hopefully we'll get prints and a lead."

"Keep us in the loop on that. The timing doesn't feel like coincidence," Dashwood said, astute as ever. "In the meantime, be vigilant and let's all keep playing to our strengths."

Emiliano's strengths ran to computer forensics and re-search, and it seemed he would be spending the rest of the day on both.

"One more thing." Finn's gaze was brittle as he looked straight into the camera. "Going through the wreckage, I found trashed emails that someone at the company has been in recent contact with Hugh Barrington."

Emiliano didn't recognize the name, but it was clear from the horrified expression on Marie's face that she did.

"That's impossible." She turned to him. "He was a law-yer for the Colton family. When his rampant corruption was exposed, the company cut all ties with him."

"I'm looking at evidence to the contrary," Finn said with a shrug. "It'll be in the cloud for everyone to evaluate."

Dashwood wrapped up the meeting, leaving Emiliano wishing for the first time ever that he was in Dallas rather than on his ranch. Although he wanted to see Finn's new evidence firsthand, it was too risky. He couldn't take Marie back where the Cohort was hunting for her and he couldn't be that far away in case they managed to track her to Shadow Creek.

He'd barely ushered Marie out of the office when his phone hummed with an incoming text message. His boss was particularly irritated he'd allowed Marie to be on the call, and when Emiliano saw the accompanying screen-shot, he understood why.

The emails Finn had found were between Marie and Barrington. The content summary revealed a clandestine privacy breach the opponents of data mining were always warning against. His team considered her a suspect.

On a soft curse, he looked down at his dog. He just couldn't make himself believe the electronic evidence over his dog's judgment. Digital files could be fabricated while Scrabble didn't get distracted so easily.

No way would his team accept a canine opinion as fact, though.

"Something's off and we need to find out what it is," he said to the dog. After the break-in at the vet's office, he wasn't sure they had much time.

Scrabble rolled to her back and he rubbed her fluffy white belly while he considered his next step.

Chapter 6

Marie didn't know what to think. Agent Townsend's claim that someone from Colton, Incorporated, was communicating with Barrington couldn't be true. It had to be a smoke screen or diversion and she wished she had computer access to look into this herself.

She paced the length of the great room, up and back in front of the windows, and worried she might never get back to the company she loved if they didn't let her *help*. Ace wandered in through the kitchen door around noon and fixed ham-and-cheese sandwiches. Emiliano never emerged from the study to join them, so she covered his plate with plastic wrap and put it in the fridge.

"You look as antsy as I feel," Ace said. "Emiliano is almost too efficient."

"Almost?"

"He zipped right through the day's chores, but he hasn't gotten that door repaired yet."

"Which door?" None of the doors she'd seen on her tour of the ranch had been damaged.

"The one busted up over at the vet office. I'm headed that way to make the repairs. Could use an extra pair of hands."

She wasn't at all sure he needed her, but she needed to do something to fill the empty hours and distract herself.

Quizzing Ace about life on the ranch as they dealt with the repair, she learned there were plenty of things to keep a person busy, if they knew how to do those things. Life moved at a completely different pace on the ranch and in Shadow Creek.

Though they didn't move past the immediate doorway, she couldn't help noticing the signs of the fight in the office. It was disconcerting to think someone possibly with the Cohort had been in here stealing drugs that could incapacitate or even kill. The FBI was monitoring her compromised accounts and identity details and Emiliano was in charge of her personal safety, but this current level of protection wouldn't last indefinitely.

Her gaze drifted to the broken chair and cabinets. If she'd been attacked, she would have gone down in seconds. She needed to get serious about protecting herself. In Dallas, she'd sign up for a class. Here, she'd have to ask Emiliano for advice on that and transportation to and from a venue.

They were just finishing the job when the sound of tires on the driveway caught their attention. The Shadow Creek sheriff's car came into view, parking in the space closest to the door.

Her palms went damp in the quiet when the engine stopped and a tall man emerged from the driver's side, the gold star of his office glinting in the sunlight on his khaki uniform shirt.

"Ace. Ma'am." He gave a nod to each of them, though he didn't smile.

"Hey, Sheriff," Ace replied. He raised his chin toward the other man. "Knox Colton, newly elected, and we're all happier for it. This is Marie Meyers from Dallas."

"Appreciate that, Ace." He reached out to shake Marie's hand. "Welcome to Shadow Creek."

"Thanks." The name couldn't be coincidence, but she didn't feel right asking how he might be related to Livia.

Emiliano and Scrabble emerged from the passenger side.

He had a stride that put a delicious quiver low in her belly. The dog raced forward and sat obediently at Marie's feet, waiting for a proper greeting, and she obliged.

Emiliano stood back, gaping at them. "What are you doing?"

"Fixing the door," Ace said as if it should have been obvious.

Marie noticed his answer did nothing to ease the tension in either of the other men. "Did something happen?"

Emiliano planted his hands on his hips. "To start, it looks like you've contaminated a crime scene." His brown gaze shot daggers at Ace.

"We didn't go past this point," Ace said defensively. "I'm sure there's plenty of evidence to find inside."

Emiliano exchanged a glance with the sheriff before his eyes locked on her. "You didn't look at the computers?"

So *that* was the problem. Clearly the FBI had hauled her name to the top of the suspect list. "No." She tucked her hands into her pockets. "Ace asked me to help with the repairs. I assumed you knew."

"Of course he knew it had to be done. Too easy to bust through again," Ace said, tightening the screws on the dead bolt. "Not safe to leave it like this for another night when no one's staying close enough to hear trouble *before* the alarm."

"Ace," Sheriff Colton said, "can I have a word? Emiliano told me how he found you yesterday. Now I'd like to hear your take on it."

As Ace stepped aside with the sheriff, Emiliano stalked over to examine the repair. Her fingertips warmed as she imagined smoothing the tension from his jaw. "I take it Ace doesn't like to be idle for long."

"What was your first clue?" Emiliano asked, his voice rumbling through her senses. "You didn't go inside?"

"No," she replied, irritated at being asked twice. She

bent down and petted his happy corgi. Maybe when she went back home, she'd find a pet-friendly apartment and get a dog of her own. Of course, that meant cutting back her hours at the office. It would be worth it to bask in the unconditional love of a companion like Scrabble. "What did your team say that changed your mind about me?"

"What do you mean?" Temper snapped in his dark eyes.

"I'm not an idiot, Agent Ortega." She took a breath. "Something happened that has you treating me like a criminal." And still she wanted to comfort him, to find a way to ease the stress bracketing his mouth.

He sighed. "The email evidence Finn found points to you as the one in contact with Barrington."

Never. She wanted to shout it until he believed her. That company and the people she worked with were her family. Emiliano might have more than enough people in his life that he could toss away an extra friend or two, maybe even a spare cousin. Not her. Until Colton, Incorporated, she hadn't had anyone.

Feeling ill-equipped to have this discussion in her jeans and sneakers instead of her normal suit and heels, she rolled her shoulders back and lifted her chin. "In the process of my education, there were courses on cybersecurity."

"Right." He folded his arms over his chest.

She dragged her gaze away from the distracting flex of his biceps and locked on to his skepticism. "You've probably seen my transcripts."

"I have."

"Then you might want to take a second look. It seems you missed the part where I aced my course work and internships and worked my tail off to land the job I have." *Please, God, let that be the job I still have come January.* "I'm a bit of a perfectionist."

Under the rim of his hat, he cocked an eyebrow in challenge.

Leave it to her to find that sexy. Her foolish attraction added another layer to her temper. "Think about it, Agent Ortega. Why would I want to jeopardize any of that? And just in case I decided to turn on an employer I *love*, an employer that has treated me well, I sure as hell wouldn't have left behind something so blatantly incriminating."

She turned on her heel and started back to the house with Scrabble trotting along beside her.

Emiliano felt like a total jerk. "Marie, wait." He'd handled hardened criminals with more courtesy and finesse than he'd just shown her.

She spun back to face him so quickly her ponytail flew out in a wide arc. "What now?"

He didn't have an immediate answer and she'd apparently run out of patience. She continued on her way, her swaying hips distracting him for a long, delightful moment. Belatedly, he realized his dog was at her heels. Ouch. Though he suspected it was better for both of them for her to be under Scrabble's protection until they both cooled off.

Maybe he had jumped to the wrong conclusion. Marie wasn't his ex-wife and he had to stop looking at her through that same lens. Beth had been an expert manipulator and he'd ignored the signs in an effort to make his marriage work.

The evidence Finn had found was damaging, yet it didn't jibe with the curious, helpful woman under his protection. No, he didn't really know Marie. That took time. But in his gut he knew the accusations didn't fit.

Having been conned once, he wasn't eager to repeat the mistake. Although he'd not been fooled on a case, his career with the FBI having started *after* his divorce, he didn't want this to be the exception that proved the rule.

When the sheriff was finished with Ace and the vet office was locked up tight, the ranch manager dodged Emiliano's attempts to keep an eye on him at the main house for another night.

"No way. I saw how she left and I'm not getting in the middle of that," Ace told him. "I'll take care of the evening rounds. You'd best take care of those two ladies. Send up a flare if the pair of 'em goes on the attack," he said with a hearty laugh.

Knowing he needed a big gesture, he called in a favor at Big Jim's Burger Shop and ordered milk shakes and burger platters for delivery. He wasn't sure exactly what she liked, so he requested a variety of toppings on the side and an extra plain beef patty for Scrabble. Walking up to the road to wait for the delivery, he chided himself yet again.

His boss had texted him before the sheriff arrived, demanding proof of Marie's involvement with the Cohort or lack thereof. He was working as fast as he could, but this case wasn't unfolding the way other Cohort cases had.

Finn was right; someone new was in the game.

With the delivery in hand, Emiliano walked back to the house, only to drop everything on the table at the sound of a wild scream.

"Marie!" He reached for his sidearm, recalling too late it was locked in the study.

"I'm okay!" she called out immediately. "It was the television."

He skidded to a stop, his heart rate dropping closer to normal when he saw her posed in front of the television, Scrabble watching her from the chair. A strange scene played out in slow motion on the now-silent screen. "What's that?"

"Self-defense videos," she replied with an odd hitch in her shoulders. "They were on the shelf." She pointed. "I saw the mess at the vet office. I have to *do* something. Can you teach me? I can't expect you to protect me forever."

Why not? The visceral reaction shook him and he

quickly replaced those two words with a more appropriate response. "All right." He took a deep breath. "After dinner I'll teach you some moves."

"According to the demonstration on the DVD, the first move is screaming." She turned off the TV. "That was what you heard."

"Clearly loud noises do draw attention." He stepped back, still edgy from that moment when he'd believed she was being attacked.

In the kitchen, he pulled everything out of the bags. She chose the chocolate milk shake and bacon cheeseburger, adding sliced jalapeños from the extra sides and toppings he'd ordered. Scrabble, recognizing the scents, waited patiently by her food bowl, confident he'd ordered something for her too.

Marie didn't chatter aimlessly and Emiliano kept his mind on the case and sorting all the newest factors that didn't add up. The quiet felt easy between them, giving him one more thing to process.

Mentally setting the case aside, he considered her request. Basic self-defense was always helpful, building an inherent confidence that many assailants would instinctively avoid. Marie's situation was different, since she had been targeted specifically. He glanced up and caught her just as she looked away, a small smile teasing her lips. What had he done to earn that expression? The kitchen table suddenly felt too intimate, and he got up to give Scrabble her treat. He needed to pull himself together, but he found his gaze sliding toward her at every opportunity.

"Have you ever taken a self-defense class?" he asked when the three of them returned to the great room. Scrabble hopped up and curled into a corner of the couch, watching intently.

"One semester in college." She hooked her thumbs into

her back pockets. "I remember the emphasis on leverage and persistence."

"Good." Yet having seen the damage in his mom's office, she wanted to know more. Was she expecting to face something worse out here, under his protection? Her apparent lack of confidence in his skills tweaked his pride. "Attackers are usually looking for the easy mark. If you make it difficult, they'll often run away."

He was stalling, uneasy about putting his hands on her, but that was the only way to teach her what she needed to know.

"Except in my case, the Cohort is making it personal."

He couldn't argue with the truth. "We're working on that. All right, mirror me." He raised his hands to face level, palms down, fingers relaxed. "If the attacker comes in close—" he halved the distance between them "—use an eye jab." For safety's sake he aimed for her brow line, then caught her hands in his and demonstrated how the move would force an attacker back.

"Vulnerable spots. Got it." She let her arms drop to her sides.

They were too close. With her face tipped up she looked as if she were inviting a kiss rather than waiting for his next instruction. "Yes," he managed, his voice sounding rusty. "Blinding an attacker gives you room to run. Plus, scratches on the face are hard to hide and would leave DNA evidence under your fingernails. The whole point of self-defense is to find room to escape."

"Look at me." She spread her arms, laughing a little. "I'm not planning to turn a surprise attack into an MMA bout."

He raised his arms, lunging in slow motion as if he was going to pull her hair or grab her face. "Size doesn't matter in self-defense. It's about finding the angle. When an attacker gives you this opening, put your knee in the groin." He signaled her to try and she hesitated, rosy color staining her cheeks. "Pretend." He raised his arms again.

She giggled, her dimples flashing. "Sorry!" She clapped her hand over her mouth, tried to get serious and lost it. "It's just…" Another laugh slipped through those generous lips. "You look like a teddy bear trying to be mad."

He closed his eyes and searched for a mental reset button. All it took was an image of her being attacked rather than Ace. What if the FBI declared her safe too soon? She was right about needing these skills once she left his protective sphere. Determined, he decided to reverse their roles.

"Come at me, arms high."

She did, still grinning, and he raised his knee. Reflexively, she brought her hands down to protect herself and he went for her throat. Her hands came up and he raised his knee again. "Keep alternating soft targets of eyes, groin and throat until you have room to run away. If you're cornered, add in an elbow to get your opponent out of the way. Now you try."

She was a quick learner, and from the couch, Scrabble gave a soft woof.

"Thanks, sweetie," Marie said to the dog, breaking the lesson to go rub Scrabble's ears.

He stared at the two of them. "Choke hold."

Marie's eyebrows arched high as she gave him her attention. "Really?"

He caught her hands and put them on his throat, immediately regretting the contact. There was a warmth in her touch that left him craving her hands on other parts of his body. To save his sanity, he made her grip stronger. "Hold on. First, keep your head."

"All right." Her eyes locked on his mouth and she licked her lips.

A bolt of desire shot through his system. "Raise your

arms overhead and clasp your hands." He demonstrated and her gaze drifted up his arms to his hands and back down to his biceps. This was a bad idea. "Now sweep down and twist to one side." Gently, in slow motion, he showed her how to escape the hold.

"And run," she said for him when he was free of her.

"Your turn." He moved in front of her. "Ready?"

She gave an uncertain nod.

He wrapped his hands lightly around her throat, the blood in her veins fluttering under his hands. "This is practice," he reminded her as her eyes went wide and distant. Her hair was soft as silk against his knuckles. "Marie." He flexed his fingers, just enough to get her attention. "Keep your head."

He struggled to heed his own advice since everything inside him clamored to pull her into a much different embrace and discover if her lips were as soft as they looked.

"Uh-huh." Her arms came up, her hands clasped, and she executed the motion perfectly, breaking his hold and dancing out of his reach.

"Well done." He straightened his shirt, tucking it back into place.

"Thank you, Emiliano." She perched on the couch next to his dog. "That helps me feel better already."

Good news for one of them. Edgier than ever, he needed an escape. "I'll be in the study." He glanced at Scrabble, but she didn't budge from her place by Marie.

"Since you can't let me help, I'll be right here."

He left the room without another word. Her determination to be prepared and take care of herself made him want to lower his defenses and care for her. He wanted to explore the basic need she ignited within him. He couldn't afford that kind of mistake. His team was counting on him to do his part for the investigation and he would not let them down.

Chapter 7

Marie sat tall in the saddle on Brandy, the sweet mare Ace had introduced her to, relishing the height advantage over the corral, the distant hills, and the man with the dark eyes and reluctant smile teaching her to ride.

A gorgeous day had turned into a delightful afternoon, clean and fresh after an overnight rain shower. The air was cool on her face and hands, and a light breeze teased strands of hair from the clasp holding it up off her neck as the sun inched toward another brilliant sunset.

Emiliano had convinced her riding would help with her balance, essential for confidence and self-defense. Enjoying the experience was a pleasant surprise. She was on her first solo circuit of the corral, making small adjustments as he called them out. It tested her concentration since her gaze kept lingering on his easy grace and control in the saddle. Who knew that kind of view would be so tempting?

"You're a natural," he said, dismounting and slipping his hand into the bridle as the horse stopped in front of him with little guidance from her.

"Give the credit to Brandy. She knows way more than I do."

"Not for much longer."

Marie puffed her bangs up out of her eyes. His home was amazing and she appreciated his generosity and the tranquil pattern of the past week since the Cohort struck, but she hoped she wouldn't be here much longer. With

Christmas closing in, he had family and holiday traditions and she had…satisfying work to return to.

Though they'd kept the lesson relatively short, her legs wobbled on those first few steps after dismounting and following Emiliano and Brandy into the barn. "When does your family decorate for Christmas?" As a foster kid, she'd spent Christmas with various states of holiday decor, from over-the-top to nonexistent.

On the other side of the horse, his smile flickered. "Most years Mom starts on December first. With their cruise, she had other things on her mind. We'll get to it."

She couldn't decide if she wanted to see the house and ranch decked out or if it would only make her lack of holiday spirit more acute. The holidays always exacerbated that persistent sense of loneliness. She had friends, of course, but her friends had families and she'd felt like an interloper too often as a kid to repeat the cycle as an adult.

"How about you?"

Why had she brought it up? She shrugged. "Whenever." As in *never.* "It's not like hanging a door wreath takes a lot of planning." And she'd only started that because her neighbors in her building asked nicely.

She distracted him with questions about caring for Brandy, helping with the simpler tasks. Under his watchful eye and expertise, they cared for the horse and settled her into her stall. Once the saddle and tack were stored, and a treat offered, she followed Emiliano's instructions and started brushing Brandy. When Emiliano was confident in her technique, he moved to the other side of the mare.

"You have real history and heritage out here," she said, the brush bringing a gleam to the rich brown coat. "I only have questions." She peeked at him over the horse's back, but his eyes were on the animal. She could happily watch him move with that dedicated focus for hours on end.

"What kind of questions?"

Too many to dump on him, she thought. "For a split second, when Zane explained how the Cohort took aim at me, I thought maybe…" She had to catch her breath. "Maybe they knew something I didn't."

He stopped brushing and stared at her. "About your parents?"

"My birth record wasn't sealed. I know my mother's name and that she was a teenager when she gave me up."

"No mention of your father?"

She shook her head and tucked all those impossible, unanswerable questions back into that hole in her heart.

"You've never reached out to her?"

"No need." Marie shook her head, smoothing the brush over Brandy's flanks. The repetitive movements soothed her, loosened her tongue. "I've worked through all the stages of being abandoned. There's the fairy-tale dream of parents showing up and taking me home, lavishing love and gifts. Anger creeps in a little later, once the fairy tale dies under the weight of reality of life in the foster system. Eventually, when I hit my teens, I accepted she must have believed giving me up was the right choice. That's all any of us can do, is make the best choice in the moment."

"She could have arranged an adoption or tried to keep you," he pointed out.

"Those were possibilities, yes." Marie leaned into the gentleness of the horse. "It's too easy to judge with hindsight and no real facts. I was almost adopted once."

She hadn't meant to say it. Only she and the dusty records in the Dallas foster system knew about that. She'd never mentioned it to anyone before.

"When?" He moved the brush in long strokes down the mare's spine and Brandy huffed in pleasure.

Marie had to agree with the horse's sentiment. Emiliano had good hands and she'd only felt them during their daily self-defense lessons. Each time he demonstrated a hold or an escape, she battled the urge to move closer and cling to his athletic body.

She appreciated his quiet query, and maybe that was why it was easier to answer.

"I was four. I was the only child being fostered in that home. The woman had short blond hair," she remembered. "Her husband was tall and would put me on his shoulders when we went to the park." Her fingers curled now as they had then, gripping his hands for balance. "I didn't know they'd applied for legal adoption, not until years later. My room there was pink and lavender with a white four-poster bed. Just like a princess would have. They told me I could stay with them always and I believed them. Then one night they went out and never came home."

"What happened?"

"A woman came to the house and told me they weren't coming back. I didn't understand they were dead until much later. Hit by a drunk driver." The memory rattled through her, the fit she'd thrown when they pulled her out of that happy princess room. "I went back into the system. It was a valuable life lesson."

The true, brutal lesson hadn't sunk in until years later, when she'd been moved time and again, having been labeled "difficult." Looking back at her first eighteen years, she knew the seeds of her *difficult* independence had been planted that terrible night. The biggest wish of her four-year-old heart crushed in an instant by a nightmare.

Since she was grieving a loss she didn't comprehend, going through it alone, her emotional volatility shouldn't have surprised the child experts in the Dallas system. And yet. Reluctant to trust anyone, she'd done her part to embrace the label they stamped on her file.

"How so?" Emiliano asked.

"Pardon me?"

His eyebrows flexed, shading his perceptive, dark eyes. "What life lesson did you learn at four years old?"

A strange, prickling heat shimmered along her skin under that gaze. She wanted to touch the grain of the trim beard that accented his square chin. "In-independence," she managed, though her mouth had gone dry. She licked her lips and moved out of the stall. "I learned I was the only person I could count on."

"Four is too young to be jaded."

"So says the man who grew up out here with a family rather than in the Dallas foster-care system." His eyes turned hard, glittered with something she couldn't quite read. She forced herself to laugh lightly, verbal self-defense against the persistent bitterness that crept up on her every damn holiday season. "You're right—jaded came a little later." She shrugged. "But it happens to ninety-nine percent of us eventually."

Closing Brandy's stall, he joined Marie in the wide central aisle of the barn, scooping a hand through his hair and settling his hat back on his head. He whistled for Scrabble, who barked and zipped through the door to join them.

A flash of jealousy seared her system as they walked in silence back to the house. She'd seen the family photos, noticed the soft smile on his face when his parents sent a picture of some activity on the cruise. If something went wrong in his life, he had a fallback. He had several someones to lean on and talk to who shared his history. Did he have any idea how lucky he was?

Shame scorched her cheeks as she tried to shake off the unsettling emotions. He wasn't any more responsible for his birth than she was for hers. Life dealt the cards. "Haven't you ever wanted to move away from here?"

His lips twitched. "Are you asking why I still live with my mother at thirty-five?"

"You're thirty-five?"

He gave her an arch look from under the brim of his hat that quickened her pulse.

Agent Call-Me-Emiliano Ortega still wasn't inclined to share unless pressed. She pressed. What did she have to lose?

"Do you feel obligated to stay on the ranch?" she asked. That sounded like a reasonable question. Better than lashing out at him for having all the stability she'd craved and been denied.

"No," he replied. "I did move away for a time."

The answer did nothing to satisfy her curiosity. He'd been tasked with protecting her and with his investigative skills he'd managed to pull out all sorts of details about her so far. "For college or the circus?" Scrabble barked and raced ahead to the house, fully aware it was almost time for her dinner. "She says circus."

He opened the back door and laughed. The low sound rolled over her skin, the enticing sensation gone all too quickly. "It might have qualified as a circus," he said quietly.

"It?"

"My marriage." He pegged his hat, brushed the dust from his boots. "She pulled a few neat tricks in the divorce."

And now she felt like a heel for prying. "I'm sorry." Hanging up her jacket, she toed off her dusty sneakers.

"You really need boots," he said abruptly, his gaze on her socks.

She glanced back at him. "A few days ago we agreed I wouldn't be here long enough to break them in."

He scowled. "If you're going to ride, it should be in the right gear." He went to the refrigerator for a beer. "We'll go into town tomorrow and take care of it."

"Fine." Why argue? In truth, she'd appreciate a break from the ranch. Her imagination was running amok with

Emiliano as her primary source of conversation and Ace the occasional relief.

She was learning something new every day and fighting the sensation she'd thought she'd outgrown. As a kid, she used to look around and imagine herself fitting into other people's lives. Lives where lovers held hands, friends shared inside jokes, and the people in a home knew that the house they left in the morning would be the same house they returned to at night.

She'd longed to come home to a kitchen like this one, where an after-school snack came with genuine interest and she received warm hugs from a mother who wanted to keep her children close and safe forever. Lost in the fantasy, she felt a strong hand on her shoulder, heard her name spoken softly by someone who sounded as if they cared.

"Marie?"

She turned toward Emiliano's voice. He was standing so close, concern in his eyes and tenderness in his touch. Oh, how she yearned for the connection with him to be more than target and guardian. Trembling, she backed away, before she did something completely inappropriate. Like leap into his arms.

Knowing he'd catch her stirred up more longing. If only she could blame her desire for him on hormones and proximity. It was so much more. She found his steady confidence as appealing as his chiseled jaw, warm gaze and fit form.

And she'd repaid him by dredging up a painful memory. "I didn't mean to pry," she said in a rush. "About your wife."

"Ex-wife," he corrected her coolly.

"Right." The appetite she'd worked up during the riding lesson had evaporated. The idea of putting any food in her stomach while it twisted with wistfulness for things that had never been, could never be, made her queasy. "If you'll excuse me, I'll just, um…" She gave him a wide berth.

He wouldn't let her help with the investigation and had yet to return her electronics so she could keep up with anything outside this small pocket of the world. She rushed back to the guest room and the aching familiarity of being a temporary resident in a home she'd never be invited to call her own.

Emiliano watched her go, frustrated with both of them. She was holding back, but it wasn't at all what he'd expected her to be hiding. Her entire childhood—as a foster kid—was bottled up behind that dimpled smile and the big doe eyes. Although her scars were hidden, he had no doubt the cuts had gone deep.

Not knowing how to ease that wounded expression, he fed Scrabble, checked in by text message with Ace and piled thick slices of brown bread high with leftovers. Alone at the table, wishing she'd join him, he tried to separate the CDO from the woman, the woman from the investigation.

Failed.

The facts of her childhood as a foster kid were detailed in the background check his team assembled. She'd put herself through college and worked her way into that prime office space at Colton, Incorporated.

"Independent, not difficult," he murmured in Scrabble's direction. The dog stretched out on her belly near his chair. Her chin rested on her paws and her gaze remained vigilant for any wayward crumb he might drop.

"I won the jackpot with you," he said. Marie hadn't had anyone. "She won you over quick enough."

Scrabble cocked her head. The dog was one of the few females he trusted after Beth played him for a fool. He should have laid it out for Marie in the same matter-of-fact tone she'd used when relating that tragic failed adoption.

His failed marriage was old news. And yes, it had been essential to have a home, a place where he could retreat and rebuild from those mistakes.

He couldn't wrap his head around the idea of going through any disaster without his parents and brother at his back. Though he wouldn't cut short his parents' cruise or call Dario home from his freelance assignment, part of him wished they were all here to show Marie how strong a family could be.

Finished with his meal, he cleared his plate and made a detour to Scrabble's bowl, dropping in the bit of crust he'd saved for her.

Filling a glass with water, he headed for the study, where his and Marie's laptops waited for another night's effort. Maybe this time he'd get a lead rather than a hollow dead end. Instead of searching for online clues to the Cohort's leader, Sulla, he wound up digging into old records at the Texas Department of Family and Protective Services website. In theory, he could be searching for an old enemy of Marie's turned Cohort Princeps, except he doubted she had enemies. Whether or not she was a difficult foster kid, she didn't have a criminal record as an adult, and nothing in the court system suggested she had a sealed juvenile record. It made him ache, thinking of her as a little girl struggling to find her place.

Being part of the FBI meant he knew the low depravity to which people could sink. The foster system did good work, but every organization had its share of bad seeds. Had Marie been hurt along the way? The idea of her being that kind of statistic put an uncomfortable pinch between his shoulder blades.

She'd been in the system from birth, until they kicked her out at eighteen. She was born in the spring; he wondered where she'd lived during that summer before moving into college.

Independence. She wrapped it around her like armor.

He appreciated tenacity, and yet everyone needed someone. Like she needed him to resolve the Cohort threat so she could get back to her life.

Still, he dug deeper into her past, found her foster families and searched the names for any complaints. There was a picture of the couple who'd applied for adoption and been killed by a drunk driver. Had Marie ever seen it? He closed his eyes at the unfairness of life. After that, each subsequent relocation was blamed on a foster family's circumstances, her increasing reluctance to participate or connect with a family. Finding no criminal complaints wasn't much relief. He knew how often sexual assaults went unreported.

He worked for hours, researching the woman and eventually the hacktivists who'd painted a target on her back. There had to be a connection. The digital media outlets, both reputable and scandal-oriented, were still clamoring for Livia Colton, attempting to expose her criminal associates and insisting on transparency from the law-enforcement agencies hunting her.

In demanding Marie's resignation and restitution, as if she'd personally harmed the public trust, the Cohort had only chosen to get transparent about the things it could twist to its advantage.

Maybe it could, if it focused on exposing Livia rather than dragging down Marie. There was no public listing of Livia's birth date or social security number, no chat room dedicated to Livia's demise if she were spotted. Yes, data mining posed risks, but Livia Colton posed far more risks than Marie did. He sent Dashwood an email confirming his conclusion that Marie had no association with the Cohort or the hack on the company. He was getting to know her better with each passing day and she'd been right to call herself a perfectionist. The emails between her and Hugh Barrington were circumstantial. Anyone capable of the hack they were investigating could have injected those into the system to raise suspicion and sympathy, further riling the local Principes against her. Emiliano was confident that if Marie ever did go to the dark side of computing, she wouldn't make that kind of mistake.

While his boss would accept and trust his deductions about Marie, it would be best for everyone if he could find how those emails had landed in her sent-mail folder. He went to work, baffled when he discovered he'd been sent in circles. This hacker was good.

In keeping with what had become a distasteful habit, he returned to the message board devoted to brainstorming ideas to Silence the CDO. After the xylazine theft, he wasn't surprised to see that option show up in one of the many contrived scenarios that ended badly for Marie. Per his last contact with the sheriff, the horse tranquilizer hadn't been used in any other crimes nearby. Tonight's newest claim was a post that Marie had been sighted in Shadow Creek. Confirming the IP address was local, he stared at it uneasily. He forwarded the information to the team, hopeful they could uncover a physical address. It was too risky for him to take on that task while Marie was under his protection.

He glanced at the clock, surprised he'd worked until nearly midnight. Shutting down both laptops, he stowed them in the locked drawer and headed out, startled to realize Scrabble wasn't at his feet.

She must have deserted him for Marie again. This was getting ridiculous. Scrabble was *his* dog and he didn't appreciate her switching sides.

When his ex-wife had left him broke and reeling, he'd floundered for months, ashamed that he'd been foolish enough to believe Beth's convoluted lies about their finances, ignoring all the signs and warnings. His parents had welcomed him home, no questions asked, only an open invitation to share his troubles when he was ready.

He hadn't shared much of anything. What could he have said that would make any of them feel better? Instead, he'd diligently applied himself to taking his life in a new direction and eventually landed on his feet with the FBI. At the time, Scrabble had been a sort of welcome-home gift from his father, one of whose clients needed to place an unexpected litter of high-quality, energetic corgi pups. They'd clapped eyes on each other and been together ever since. That little dog had wormed her way into his heart, reminding him how good real affection, loyalty and love could feel.

Until now. He called her name quietly, worrying a bit when she didn't come running. It was time for her to go out before they went to bed and she knew the routine. Striding toward the bedrooms, he slowed when he saw the guest door cracked open, a soft glow spilling into the dim hallway.

Awkwardly, he paused at the door and knocked softly. "Marie?"

She didn't answer him, either. He put a hand on his gun, feeling ridiculous. If she'd been attacked, he would've heard the window break, the alarm sound, her scream or Scrabble barking.

Forcing himself to relax, he leaned around the door and stared. Marie was curled up on top of the covers, her hands under the pillow by her chin. Scrabble had tucked her little body right next to Marie's back and stared at him with a someone-had-to-be-here expression in her eyes.

Scrabble had never slept anywhere other than his room. Even when he had to be away on an assignment, his parents and Ace said she always slept on his bed.

He raised his chin and whispered a command. His dog glanced away from him. He was torn between amusement and frustration. She'd never shown a fickle side. "You need to go out," he whispered, tiptoeing to the bed and gathering her into his arms.

Marie stirred, but didn't wake. What would he have said if she had? Holding Scrabble with one arm, he flipped the bedspread over Marie so she wouldn't get chilled in the night and left her room, closing the door behind him.

When he and Scrabble returned from her outing, she stopped at Marie's closed door and sat down, staring up at him.

He kept walking. "Come on."

She woofed softly and held her ground.

"Seriously?"

She gave a little whine that, given time, could turn into a whistle that would wake up Marie.

"What if she'd rather be alone?"

She tipped her head to the side, then booped the door with her nose.

"Fine." He walked back and unlatched the door. If Scrabble wanted to be with Marie, she'd have to do the rest on her own. He wasn't going to give the woman under his protection any reason to doubt his motives or integrity.

With a happy wriggle, Scrabble nudged open the door and pranced inside, leaving Emiliano staring after her.

A few restless hours later, Emiliano was grateful for the first hints of sunrise. He dressed quickly and headed out to start on the chores, pleased when Scrabble finally came back to her senses and fell into her routine at his side.

Despite what he'd read online last night, Emiliano decided to keep with the original plan to take Marie into Shadow Creek today. He'd kept her out of sight as a protective measure, but since the person who'd left the prints on the syringe wasn't in any database, they'd hit another dead end. Though she'd assumed earlier that he would use her as bait to draw out the local Cohort Princeps, he didn't care for the fact that they might have to resort to such a move to advance this investigation.

His mother always claimed girl time and shopping perked her up when she was down. While Marie didn't have friends here, Emiliano was acquainted with a few women in town who would make her feel welcome. The longer she stayed on his ranch, the more pressure he felt to give her a few happy memories to carry with her when she returned to Dallas.

He blamed such an inexplicable urge on having her here in his home. Something about her open curiosity, muted by those flashes of sadness in her big brown eyes, made him want to give her the community she'd never had growing up. Though he'd deny it if openly accused, he knew he was overinvested in her reactions to his ranch, his home and the area he loved.

Heading back to the house with Scrabble, Gordo ambling along with them, he pulled out his phone and checked the store hours for Honeysuckle Road, the boutique owned by Knox's sister Claudia Colton. Claudia's friendly nature and eye for big-city fashion would do wonders for Marie.

Less than an hour later they were in his truck, headed to town. She was as quiet on the drive as she'd been over breakfast. He needed to find a way through the awkwardness of last night.

"I think you'll enjoy Claudia's shop," he said, trying to break the ice. "I'm not sure she carries the work boots you'll need."

"I thought the whole trip was for boots."

He felt the weight of her long look. "The stores are close enough we can do both if necessary." He shifted a little in the seat.

"Mmm-hmm. Did you make any progress on the case last night?"

"Some." He should tell her he'd dug into the foster records. "About my ex…" The words were out there and he felt as shocked by the topic change as she appeared to be.

"You don't—"

"You didn't touch a nerve, not like you're probably thinking. My bad marriage is water under the bridge." *Doomed from the beginning,* he reminded himself. He sought the matter-of-fact tone he used with victims on a case. "The marriage didn't just fail. Sticking with the highlights, she used my blind infatuation with her against me and stole my life savings and used that to fund an affair and another man's business." *Would the sting of admitting that ever go away?* "I didn't have any money to start over. Nowhere else to go but home. It wasn't easy to swallow my pride and I know I'm lucky, blessed, to have had the option."

"Okay."

Okay? He'd hoped by sharing, she'd share more as well, yet she kept quiet, her gaze on the rolling hills and cattle grazing in the fields stretching back from the road.

"When will you let me help with the investigation?" she asked as he turned onto Main Street.

"That isn't appropriate or safe, Marie."

"Then we should probably stop at a bookstore too. Make a day of it." She bit out each word.

"Why?"

She pushed a hand through her hair. She'd left it down today and it spilled over the shoulders of her faded sweatshirt in gentle waves. He shouldn't notice things like that.

"Emiliano, I'm going stir-crazy with only riding lessons and self-defense lessons. I'm not used to being idle. Coffee with Ace and time with Scrabble are nice, but I need more to do."

"I'll fix it." Clearly more time in town was the best solution. They both needed the distraction of other people. Being alone with her had become more of a challenge

than he'd originally anticipated. Every detail he learned
about Marie left him wanting to know more and to give
her more of himself. Each day in her company rekindled
his hope that he could finally shed the scars his ex-wife
had left behind.

Chapter 8

Marie wasn't sure she wanted him to fix anything beyond finding the hacktivists that kept her away from her work. Fortunately for Emiliano, Claudia Colton was an utter delight. They hit it off immediately and spending time with her was like a quick trip to Dallas. Even better, Claudia had managed to shuffle off Emiliano right after the introductions so they could talk fashion without him glaring daggers at every passerby on the street.

He didn't have to mention she was here under his protection; Claudia cheerfully explained that she'd seen Marie's face on the news and her name tagged in *Everything's Blogger in Texas* headlines. It helped Marie to learn Claudia and many other Coltons were often the target of that blog and generally managed to ignore the worst of the gossip.

"Has it been awful being sequestered at the Ortega ranch?" Claudia asked.

"Not exactly. It's a beautiful area, though I miss my work in Dallas," Marie admitted. "Agent Ortega confiscated my devices for my protection, so I've only heard what he wants me to hear lately."

"Probably for the best," Claudia said.

Marie's stomach clenched. "That bad?"

"More obnoxious than bad." She waved a hand as if wiping off a slate. "None of that brought you in today. Let's go have some fun."

Claudia's boutique focused on metro fashion, so she

took Marie down the street to get outfitted with boots better suited to barns and horses, while they discussed the pros and cons of Shadow Creek and ranch life.

"I've lived in Dallas all my life," Marie said when they returned to Claudia's store. "It's almost like walking on a different planet out here."

Claudia laughed. "The pace is slower, I'll give you that. And obviously, when I came back to town I saw a gaping hole in the fashion scene." She waved an arm to encompass her stock. "You should ask Emiliano to bring you out dancing one night. We know how to do that right around here."

An outing that resembled a date with Emiliano could draw out a Cohort attempt to silence her and possibly give the FBI a lead. Even if she got him to agree to that, she wasn't sure she could manage to keep a professional distance. The idea of dancing with Emiliano held too much appeal. "If we came back for dancing, what's the dress code?"

Claudia beamed. "Right this way."

"How do you handle living here under the shadow of Livia Colton's crimes?" Marie asked as she debated between three of Claudia's suggested outfits to wear during a night on the town.

Claudia's bright eyes dimmed. "Livia kidnapped my birth mother and stole me. Every family tree has its twisted branch. We've all learned to carve out our own lives despite her criminal enterprise. Most people around here understand Livia's nature isn't hereditary." She helped Marie into a cute denim jacket and met her gaze in the mirror. "I'm sorry your name's been dragged through the mud."

Marie rolled her shoulders as if her jacket had shrunk a size. "Agent Ortega is sure his team will get to the bottom of it." She just wished they would hurry.

"Emiliano and his family are fixtures here." Claudia winked. "That's a good thing." She rang up Marie's purchases and took a business card from the stack near the register. "Here's my number. Call anytime."

With a grateful smile, Marie tucked the card into her back pocket as Emiliano returned.

"Done?"

"Almost," Claudia answered, smiling at him. "My sister Jade and I planned on riding later this afternoon at her farm. We'd love to have you join us, Marie."

A sweet excitement rushed through Marie at the invitation and the idea of making friends who could distract her from Emiliano. "That would be nice, but I'm such a new rider," she protested.

"You'll be an excellent rider in time," Emiliano corrected.

"I'm afraid I'll only slow you down."

Claudia waved that off. "We're not barrel racing or tracking down lost cattle," Claudia teased. "It's all about the girl time," she added when Emiliano started to interrupt. "We all need it more than you handsome men realize."

Marie watched his mouth slip to the side, his brow puckering over his straight nose. Her childhood had taught her how to read people and she knew he was about to say no. "What if we stay on Ortega property?" She looked back to Claudia. "Would that be okay?"

"It's a great idea," she said.

Emiliano relented. "I'll make sure Brandy is saddled and ready."

Marie wanted to give Claudia a fist bump and decided to save it for when they were alone.

It was all she could do not to ask Emiliano a thousand questions about trail riding in general while they had lunch at El Torero's Mexican restaurant before heading back to the ranch.

She changed into her new boots and traded her sweatshirt for her new down vest, trying to stay quiet so Emiliano could work. Hearing tires on the driveway, she nearly beat Scrabble to the window, as eager as the dog was when she saw a horse trailer pass the house.

Jade was as open and friendly as Claudia, and Marie felt as if she'd found more than two temporary, passing acquaintances. She felt as if she'd made real friends who would want to stay in contact even after she left Shadow Creek. Until now, she hadn't realized how much she relied on her time-consuming career and the anonymity of a big city to protect herself from more heartache.

Thankfully, Claudia had been sincere about taking an easy ride and Marie relaxed in the saddle as the conversation darted between men, clothing, city life, men, animals and the perks of Shadow Creek.

For Marie, the main perk in the area was the man keeping an eye on her, though she claimed her favorite discovery was the land itself. "I never imagined spending time or feeling at home in this area. I knew it was out here, but Dallas…" Her voice trailed off as they watched the sun sink into the western horizon.

To Marie's surprise, Claudia and Jade asked her to meet them for coffee the next day. She felt about twelve years old again, having to clear it with Emiliano before she could commit, though they were both understanding.

Their reactions made her wonder what the Cohort and the gossip sites were spewing about her. It must be intense and she couldn't help wondering if this entire mess would be the end of her job before it was over. She couldn't serve Colton, Incorporated, if she lost the trust of Fowler, T.C., Zane and their customers.

The next day, Emiliano returned from his ride along the property line feeling surly and out of sorts. They weren't making any of the right kind of progress on this investigation and the solitude hadn't brought anything into focus. Holidays or not, he was wary. He'd have to call in a few ranch hands to help watch the likely access points in case someone came after Marie or more drugs.

His conference call with his team during Marie's ride with Jade and Claudia yesterday hadn't been productive. He'd hoped someone was making some headway, since he seemed to be stonewalled at every turn. Together they'd examined the brainstorming page. No one had posted anything about making an attempt on her in Shadow Creek. In light of that, Emiliano hadn't shared that he'd taken her into town.

Staller had managed to clear the lingering malware and overseen the enrollment of the Colton employees in identity theft monitoring services. Though the company was back to full operation, both his boss and the powers that be at Colton, Incorporated, agreed it was too dangerous for Marie to return to Dallas. If they'd expected him to break *that* news, they were going to be disappointed.

Taking care of Domino and the tack, he looked around for Marie. He was increasingly tempted to invite her to help with the investigation. Her work revolved around the analysis of data, and so far he hadn't cracked the elite levels of the Cohort. They couldn't shut down the ongoing call to violence against Marie from the lower tiers of the organization. The Cohort remained determined to make Marie's capture or death a cautionary tale that would put an end to the practice of data mining.

He used his hat to slap the dust from his jeans and whistled to bring Scrabble to heel when she got distracted over a new scent along the way. His mind made up, he walked into the kitchen, calling for Marie. It was his decision to let her assist him as long as they worked together. He could already picture the light in her eyes to get her hands on a computer again and the ability to help at last.

"Marie!" In the answering silence, he exchanged a look with his dog. "Go," he whispered to Scrabble. She took off in a red-and-white blur to search the house, happy to "herd" her new favorite person, and he poured himself a tall glass of water.

Scrabble came back too quickly, her expression a little dejected as she sat down at his foot.

He checked the clock on the stove and did a double take. Jade and Claudia should've dropped off Marie over an hour ago. On an oath, he scrolled through his phone for a message. Coming up empty, he dialed Claudia's number. No answer.

Idiot! Why had he agreed to let her go into town today without him? Oh, yeah. Because Marie had been pleading silently with those big doe eyes and Claudia had pulled him aside to remind him she and Jade were sisters of the new sheriff. She'd promised him they could handle any trouble as a group.

Emiliano reached for the phone on the wall and dialed Claudia's cell. No answer. He punched in Jade's number. No answer. He was forcing back the panic, since cell coverage could get spotty out here. He looked up the number for the boutique and called, only to hear that, although Claudia had popped in there nearly two hours ago with Marie and Jade, they'd only stayed a few minutes and were long gone. He called Jade's place, but they weren't there, either. His next call confirmed that no emergency calls had come into the sheriff's office. It wasn't enough to assure him that Marie was safe. He grabbed his hat and keys and slammed out the back door, Scrabble at his heels, eager for a ride in the truck.

Why in the world had he let Marie go with them? All the reasons he'd used to justify it didn't add up to one good excuse now. Where were they?

Blowing this protective assignment might well end his

career and he didn't give a damn. Too many images of Marie falling prey to the sick ideas posted on the Cohort's brainstorm page filled his head. If they succeeded, it would be his fault.

His fault.

He opened the door and lifted Scrabble into the truck. With his phone connected to the hands-free Bluetooth in case she called, he started the truck and tore out up the driveway.

He slowed down as another car turned off the road and into the driveway, rolling to a stop near the end of the front paddock. Music blared from the approaching car; he could hear it already. Through the windshield he saw Claudia's blond head bobbing to music, Marie next to her doing the same in the passenger seat.

Scrabble barked happily in the seat, delighted by the excitement, while he sat and fumed.

Claudia rolled down her window and stopped beside him. "Hey, Emiliano!"

"Where have you been?"

"Stuck in traffic," she said. "Must've been fifty head of Herefords blocking both lanes. We had to wait it out."

Marie hopped out of the passenger side, her face alight. "You should've seen it!"

"I've seen it before," he said to her. "You didn't call."

"No signal," Jade replied, climbing from the back seat to give Marie a hug.

"Where are you going?" Marie asked, petting Scrabble through his window as she stood between the vehicles.

He didn't answer. Claudia's smirk proved she knew he'd been worried about them.

"Nowhere."

"Claudia and Hawk are throwing a Christmas lunch and caroling party at Mac's tomorrow," Marie said, her excitement bubbling over. "It sounds like so much fun. Everyone's bringing cookies to exchange."

"We'll see," Emiliano said through gritted teeth. "Get in."

Her eyes went wide with fear and he felt like a jerk, knowing by the shudder of her shoulders where her mind had gone. He'd explain himself once they were alone.

Claudia pushed her sunglasses up into her hair and leaned closer through the open window. "Come over tomorrow, Emiliano. Whatever's going on, it seems to me you both need an infusion of holiday spirit. She's excited," she finished in a harsh whisper.

"We'll see."

Marie was in the truck; he just wanted to get her back into the house, where he could lock her behind the alarm system and let his heart rate settle.

"Your mom would have this place lit up by now," Claudia said cheerfully. "You two better get busy decorating before they get back. Christmas is only a couple weeks away." She looked past him to wave at Marie. "See you tomorrow!" Then she backed up the drive, her tires kicking up dust.

Emiliano sat there, staring at Marie, just soaking up the view of having her safe within arm's reach. Scrabble was snuffling her hair, making her giggle, and the happy sound just set him off.

He turned around, heedless of the ruts that set the truck to rocking.

"You're angry," she said when he parked at the house.

"Only with myself." And that wasn't the real problem. His sheer relief terrified him. He climbed out of the truck, suddenly weary of the emotional roller coaster.

She and Scrabble came around the truck bed. "Why?"

"Why?" Too late he realized he'd roared it.

She froze in place and Scrabble sat down between them, ears perked.

If he touched Marie, he'd shake her. Or kiss her. Either way, the smart move was to keep his hands to himself. "You are more than two hours late," he said, each syllable carefully separated from the others.

"Oh."

It wasn't nearly enough, yet the last fragment of his sane mind appreciated that she didn't offer useless excuses. He swore. "Marie." His fingertips dug into his palms, desperate to touch her, to pull her close just so all of him knew the worst hadn't happened.

"Did you have to tell your boss?"

"No!" He stalked off and turned right back to her. He'd tried to protect her from threats in real life and shelter her from the ugliness online. Without internet access, she didn't know all the sick and disturbed suggestions the Cohort was encouraging from the safe anonymity of computer keyboards. All it would take was one person to snap and the light in those big doe eyes would be extinguished. "I was scared for *you*."

What an understatement. The last time he'd been terrified of losing someone, it was already too late and not at all worth the effort. His ex-wife wasn't half the person Marie was, which made all these emotions churning through him a thousand times worse. She'd become more than an assignment and he didn't know how to get his feelings back on the right side of the fence.

"I'm sorry we worried you," she said softly, heading for the house.

"Hey." He caught her elbow as she passed. "I lost my head. I know none of this is your fault."

Her wan smile didn't reach her eyes.

He couldn't help himself, had to touch her. Draping his arm across her shoulders, he extended a peace offering.

"Claudia was right about my mom. How about I have Ace pick up a Christmas tree tonight? We can decorate before the luncheon tomorrow."

"No work on the case?"

He couldn't face it. "Not tonight."

This time, when her lips curved and her gaze met his, he felt like a superhero.

Chapter 9

Saturday morning dawned clear and cold and Marie hugged herself, still reveling in Emiliano's reaction to her coming home late. No one had ever cared so much about her whereabouts and she wasn't sure how to handle it. It was everything she'd ever dreamed of from such an obviously temporary source. She coached herself to enjoy the moment for as long as it lasted. It would give her something precious and happy to treasure when she was alone again.

She sipped her coffee, grinning at the kitchen counter covered in dozens of cookies for the luncheon. She'd made sugar cookies, snickerdoodles when she'd learned they were Emiliano's favorite, and chocolate chip with added mint for the season. While she'd been baking, Emiliano had hauled out boxes of decorations and helped Ace set up the fresh tree. She'd never had one of those before and she loved the way the crisp scent filled the house this morning.

After breakfast and the morning rounds with the animals, they wrestled lights onto the tree with plenty of help from Scrabble. In the past, Marie always felt like an impostor, dressing a home with someone else's stuff and pretending to belong. This time, as Emiliano shared stories about different ornaments and traditions, she experienced a rare sense of companionship, as if this could be her place too. She didn't quite trust the feeling, but she would treasure it forever. When the decorations were on and he hit the lights, she felt the glow inside herself, as well.

She wasn't nervous as she dressed for the luncheon, pulling her new holiday-red plaid shirt over a white thermal top. Claudia had told her a little about the ranch owned by her surrogate father, Joseph "Mac" Mackenzie, and she was eager to discover what ranch caroling was all about.

The classic white single-story house was neat as a pin and decked with lit garland around the porch rails. Trucks and cars were crammed in tight along the fence and people were milling on the big porch. Even in her wildest fantasies, Marie had never envisioned family by this definition. Between the introductions Claudia, Jade and Emiliano made that afternoon, she met so many people she'd never keep them all straight. Ignoring a varying chorus of half-hearted protests, Mac proudly showed her pictures of all the Colton kids that filled his home.

Full of food and riding on a high of engaging conversation, Marie nearly skipped along the path to the stable where three wagons had been lined with hay and decorated with holly and greens. Each team of horses hitched to the wagons had red ribbons in their manes and tails and bells on their harnesses.

Emiliano's hand lingered on hers as he helped her settle into the wagon. Sitting beside her, he shifted so his arm curled around her shoulders, and she caught him watching her. The heat in his gaze deliciously kicked her pulse up a notch.

"Happy?"

"It's incredible," she whispered. She was a little embarrassed by her enthusiasm, but no one seemed to mind. As the wagons rolled off under a cold, starlit sky, bells jingling, the group broke into a series of Christmas carols.

Emiliano's mellow singing voice warmed her almost as much as being pressed close to his side as the wagon jostled them together. His free hand covered hers and she laced her fingers through his, marveling at the strength and subtle promise of his touch. She had no idea Christmas could be this wonderful.

The wagons stopped near a clearing, where Mac had a bonfire blazing and thermoses of coffee and hot chocolate ready. Someone hooked up speakers and soon the night was filled with more music. On the other side of the fire, Hawk, Claudia's fiancé, tugged Claudia to her feet for a dance. Soon others were paired off, as well.

Emiliano held out a hand. "Shall we join in?"

"Rude not to," she said, placing her hand in his. He drew her close and desire swirled through her system as they danced. This was so new, so lovely, and she never wanted it to end.

Her lousy track record in relationships had convinced her she didn't have the emotional mettle to move from mutual attraction to serious commitment. Time with Emiliano made her yearn for the deep connection she'd been so sure was beyond her.

Overwhelmed, she rested her head on his shoulder. Oh, yes, this would be a memory with enough holiday joy to last the rest of her life. She finally had a *best* day that towered over her list of worsts.

Later that night, they returned to the ranch, flushed and happy from the caroling and camaraderie. Marie felt as if she'd finally had a real Christmas, even if it was ten days early. "That was a beautiful night," she said, wishing she could hold his hand as they walked to the house. "You have wonderful neighbors."

Emiliano opened the door and she knelt to greet Scrabble while he reset the security system.

"I'm glad you had fun," he said, taking her coat.

"Did you?"

"Yes." His smile sent a flutter through her. "I haven't done that in ages."

"Claudia plans to make it an annual thing." She tapped

her toe on the switch for the lights and the Christmas tree bloomed with dazzling light and color. A visual expression of everything she felt bubbling inside. Delighted, she stood back and simply admired it.

Feeling his gaze on her, she turned to find Emiliano standing under the mistletoe. *Invitation or happy accident?* she wondered idly. "Thank you," she said simply, crossing to him.

He might have been carved from marble, he was so still as she approached. Was he feeling what she was feeling?

She'd been fighting the quiver in her belly and the need prickling over her senses all night. His masculine scent when he was near, the rich tone of his voice as they sang, his laughter blending with the others and his arms around her while they danced.

She stopped in front of him, taking stock of every enticing detail in his face. Reaching up, she traced that hard, square jaw, delighted herself with the soft rasp of his beard against the pad of her finger.

Unmoving, he let her comb her fingers through the dark waves of his hair. "You're standing under the mistletoe." The lightest pressure of her fingertips brought that marble to life and at last he moved, just far enough for lips to meet.

Tender, warm and soft, it was over too soon as he eased back, breaking the kiss. Her body craved more, her pulse trembling as her palm trailed down from the nape of his neck, over his shoulder and away. She told herself to be satisfied with the sweet kiss. To be grateful she hadn't crossed into territory she couldn't come back from.

"Good night, Emiliano," she said.

He caught her hand, bringing her body close to his. "*You're* under the mistletoe now."

Her pulse leaped at the heat and longing in his eyes. His hand cupped her jaw, his thumb stroking across her cheekbone over her lower lip. It took an eternity for his mouth to claim hers.

Under the first layer of gentleness she found an urgency that matched hers. On a gasp, she clung to him for balance as his kisses spun her into dark territory full of secrets and promises lovelier than she'd ever imagined.

His hands spread across her back and lower, pressing her closer, molding her hips and gliding back up again. As if he couldn't touch her enough. The contact was glorious, swamping her senses in a rush that filled all the emptiness she had worked so hard to ignore.

Her head fell back and his mouth nibbled along her jaw, down her throat, ripples of pleasure drifting along her skin. She sifted her fingers through his thick, dark hair and arched into every sensation. The memories of the night air, dotted with starlight, evergreen, hay wagons and bonfires, mingled with his masculine scent, enveloping her.

His hands skimmed under her thermal shirt and she sighed, her muscles quivering in delight as those hard, calloused palms trailed up her ribs, his thumb tracing the curve of her breast.

He stepped back abruptly and she chilled, body and mind. If the Cohort had found her, it could wait. "Emiliano?" She was ready to beg him to forget how they'd met, why she was here, and see this through.

There was a sexy spark in his deep brown eyes, and a sizzle when his fingers laced with hers. She focused on the desire arcing between them as brightly as the Christmas tree in the window.

Backing up, he brought her along, plucking a throw from the couch. With a quiet command, he sent Scrabble to his bedroom.

"I had an idea," he murmured. "Earlier."

She remembered those glances he'd aimed at her while they'd decorated the tree. Thought the fantasies those glances had stirred were one-sided. Sweet anticipation prickled along her skin.

"What kind of idea?"

He spread the throw across the floor in front of the sparkling tree. He sank to his knees. His eyes locked with hers as he caught her hands, and he rubbed his thumbs across her palms. "Call it a fantasy."

"Oh." Who knew his strong and silent routine hid this delicious sensuality?

His hands stroked up, over her wrists, cruising back down to her fingertips again and again, melting her one languorous touch at a time. Without realizing she'd moved, she was on her knees, wrapped in his warm embrace, his mouth laying claim to hers once more.

As he stripped away her top and bra and set his mouth to her breast, she found her way past his shirt to the supple skin and chiseled torso beneath. He groaned when she touched him, the sound vibrating through his kisses as she learned the hard planes and mouthwatering angles of his body. The lights from the tree cascaded over his dusky skin. He teased her, pleasured her, discarding clothing and baring them both to the moment.

"You're so beautiful," he murmured against her skin. "This is like having you all to myself in a galaxy just for us."

She closed her eyes, as his words shimmered through her. Afraid of the myriad emotions she didn't recognize, she rocked her hips against his arousal, letting her body do the pleading as needs built and built.

She traced the curve of his biceps, up over his shoulders, levering up to kiss that sinful mouth. How did he have so much patience?

He hugged her close and then released her for a moment. She heard the tear of a condom wrapper before he drew her back into his arms, settling her over him. His hand smoothed her hair, twisting it around his fist as he kissed her. She leaned on those strong shoulders as she took him in, slowly, slowly, delighting in the passionate expressions moving over his handsome face.

"This was a good fantasy," she whispered, bringing his hands over her breasts.

He thumbed the hard peaks of her nipples as she rocked against him, found her rhythm. It was so right, this being filled and poured out and filled again. As if he had the strength and the patience and the answers to renew every dry well within her spirit, her heart.

She clenched around him, her pace faltering on a gasp as the climax crashed over her, her arms going weak.

He caught her, every weightless, sparkling piece of her, and brought her close so she didn't float away. His heart thundered at her ear a moment, and then he was over her, sinking into her again and again. Each thrust was more demanding and urgent than the last, until she was flying apart once more, and this time, with a shudder, he joined her.

There was a breathless laugh dancing on her lips as he stretched out beside her. She curled into him, pressing that bewildering happiness to his chest and throat with soft kisses.

Emiliano kept watch as she drifted off, her sumptuous curves tucked close to him. Did she realize the way she instinctively trusted herself to him? When she slept soundly, he carried her to his bed and slid under the covers to sleep beside her.

When the sun rose, he left her in his bed to tend to the ranch, his mind preoccupied with Marie and her case. He couldn't keep her all to himself forever. She had a career she loved and longed to return to. She had a thriving city she belonged in. Shadow Creek was an interlude, if not an outright inconvenience for her.

Yet she'd surprised him, adapting quickly to early mornings and the small-town pace.

One night of spectacular sex probably wouldn't change her mind or her career goals, though having her in his arms had changed him. He shoved the foolish thought aside in search of cold logic. She wouldn't have any kind of future if he couldn't shut down the threats against her. When it was safe, she'd return to Dallas and he would stay here where he belonged, waiting for the FBI to call.

He'd worked hard to create this career and give his life purpose and stability, especially after his divorce. His job was to protect her, not fall for a temporary, delightful version of her.

That was the kicker, he realized. He was falling for her. He'd sworn off the feeling after his divorce, never wanting to be that vulnerable again.

In the case of his ex-wife, love had blinded him. He'd told Marie as much the other day. He could just imagine his boss's reaction if it came out that he was dating Marie. He'd be the butt of every office joke, not that he spent much time in an office to hear his name used as a punch line.

He couldn't allow a hint of his feelings to show until her case was clear or the team would never accept his assessment about her involvement or anything else. He had to find a way to move this investigation along. For both of them.

Finishing the chores, he let the problem roll through his mind, bumping facts into new directions. When he returned to the house for coffee and breakfast, he had a tentative working plan.

With Scrabble at his heels, he walked in through the mudroom. Scrabble bounced on into the kitchen while Emiliano paused to remove his work boots and peg his barn coat, an echo of his mother's rules putting a smile on his face.

At the stove, Marie chattered at Scrabble while something in the skillet sent heavenly aromas through the air. Emiliano's stomach growled but his feet grew roots to the floor. She was a vision with her silky, dark hair gathered up high and snug jeans hugging her hips. Her fuzzy socks protected her feet from the cool tile floor and…and she wore one of his flannel shirts. Too big on her, she wore it open like a sweater, with the cuffs folded back to her elbows.

"Can I give her a *b-i-t-e*?" She pointed at a bit of bacon she'd set aside.

He nodded, struck mute by the moment.

Beaming, she carried the bacon to Scrabble's food bowl and made his dog the happiest corgi on the planet.

Something turned, opening inside him like the tumblers in a lock. He loved her. Not the blind and stupid version. This love had trust and hope woven in and… "You're cooking," he noted, dumbly.

She puffed her bangs away from her eye and sent him a quick glance. The happy glow in her rosy cheeks dimmed. "Not the first time," she reminded him.

Right. She'd made breakfast on several days for both him and Ace. But this was the first time she'd done so since he'd put a name to the emotions wheeling through him.

The twin lines of doubt puckered her brow as she gave the skillet her focus.

"It smells amazing," he said, pulling himself together. *Case first.*

"Good."

The short, cautious reply was confirmation that he was screwing up this morning-after thing. He crossed to the stove and, faced with the creamy column of her throat, barely managed to keep his hands and lips to himself. "Can I help with anything?"

She gave him a tight smile. "Set the table?"

He handled the task swiftly and poured coffee for himself, carefully topping off her mug near the stove. She'd assembled a hash of sorts with diced potatoes, thick chunks of bacon, onion, peppers and seasonings that set his mouth watering.

He watched her poach eggs as he sipped the coffee, wondering if this life—his life—would actually be enough for her. To hell with tomorrow and wrapping up the case first; he wanted another taste of her right now. Setting his coffee down, he reached over and nudged a loose strand of hair behind her ear, let his fingers trail down her neck. "Do I need to move the mistletoe in here?"

She stirred the blend in the skillet and finally met his gaze, a warmer smile curving her lips. "No."

He brought her close and kissed her, tasting the coffee on her tongue, inhaling the savory scents of breakfast clinging to her cheek, her clothing.

"You're in my shirt," he said, easing back far enough to trace his finger across her skin, just above the neckline of the T-shirt layered under it.

She quivered. "Is that a problem?"

He considered it an honor. "No."

The timer went off for the eggs and she jumped a little. When the plates were ready, he carried them to the table and sat across from her. He could watch her forever. Famished, he dug in. "Wow. The culinary world is missing out on a star," he said once he'd swallowed.

She laughed lightly, music to his ears. "A starving man is easily pleased."

"False humility," he accused with a teasing wink. "You should write down this recipe for my mom."

She gave him a noncommittal hum around a bite of food.

"I can't stop thinking about your case," he said. "You need to feel safe again. What if we could push the Cohort into a mistake?"

"We?" Her dark gaze lit with interest. "How?"

"The layers within that brainstorm page," he explained. "They want more xylazine and we have some. That should get me a meeting with one of the local Principes."

"Local?" Her fork clattered against her plate.

He reached across and stroked the back of her hand. "I discovered two IP addresses on that page that are local to Shadow Creek. Based on language and technique, Finn believes they might be high-ranked Principes."

"And if you get the meeting?"

"We make arrests. The FBI can encourage whoever shows up to roll over on Sulla and we have our case. Instead of the Cohort making an example of you, we make an example of *its members* and get on with living our lives."

She withdrew her hand. "Sounds like a plan." Pushing back from the table, she carried her dishes to the sink.

"Would you like to help me?"

She turned off the water and spun, excitement glowing in her eyes. "You mean it?"

"Two heads are better than one." He smothered his mixed feelings about her enthusiasm. She hadn't touched a computer in over ten days. In her shoes he'd be itching to get online too. The flip side was her realizing how much she missed her career. A problem for later.

Resigned, he swallowed the last of his coffee and took over the dishes. "Why don't you bring the laptops in here? I left them on the desk. Get your cell phone too. It will be easier to work side by side."

Alone with the cleanup, he knew loving her meant he would soon have to let her go back to the city life and career where she flourished. As their father often reminded Emiliano and his brother when they'd fussed about less pleasant chores, *no one said you had to like it.*

Two hours later, he wasn't any happier about pushing

the investigation than he was about the idea of Marie returning to Dallas.

Using FBI technology to mask his IP address and a screen name of Robin Hood, with Marie's perceptive assistance, he set to work baiting the hook. He'd finally found the right combination of rhetoric and vocabulary to earn an invitation to the ultra-secret next level of the Campus Martius, the Cohort message board. Discovering the hacktivists had been relentless in pursuit of Marie was disturbing, though now he could steer that discussion in a new direction.

"This is what you do at work?" he asked, skimming through the most recent conversation.

"It's basically being an excellent listener online." She scooted back in her chair, drawing a knee to her chest so he could see she wasn't touching the keyboard. "Then I tailor the interactive conversation they have with us. You're offended."

"Mesmerized." He shook his head. "This type of thing must be invaluable for customer service." He leaned over and set his lips to hers for a brief kiss.

She relaxed, sitting up again as they continued evaluating the people on the message board.

"It's understanding and juggling point of view. What our customers hear and how it affects their decisions. Companies have hired consultants to manage this data for decades. Computers just make it easier."

"For everyone," he grumbled. The current discussion on kidnapping Marie and forcing her to publicly backtrack and undo her work as a CDO was heating up. The loudest voices were citing a bogus article about her colluding with Barrington posted by *Everything's Blogger in Texas*. Someone else added a lousy cut-and-paste photo of her having coffee with Livia Colton.

"I might choke on the hypocrisy," she murmured, reading over his shoulder. "Hang on. Can you enlarge that logo?"

"Good eyes," he said. A chill brushed over the nape of his neck. Whoever fabricated the picture had used a candid shot of a café in Shadow Creek.

Her hand gripped his forearm. "Emiliano, that's from Friday. They replaced Claudia's face with Livia's."

"The day the loose cattle made you late coming home."

"Yes." She clapped a hand to her mouth as emotions washed over her face. Fear or hope? He wasn't sure.

He checked his case notes. That was the day after he'd confirmed Cohort activity tracing back to IP addresses in Shadow Creek. His team had tried to blame Marie, forcing him to defend his supervision skills. "We have to stop this," he said.

She nodded.

"If the Cohort has someone this close, let's get them out in the open. Help me sound appealing enough to risk a face-to-face."

"Tell them you know where I am."

"No." The idea made his gut clench. He couldn't take that kind of chance with her.

"You know it's the best option." She slipped her hand into his. "We can control the meet and take precautions."

"You're sure."

She nodded. "Let's end this." Her lips set in a determined line, she leaned forward. The clove-and-ginger scent of her shampoo teased him as they carefully negotiated his meeting with the local Princeps.

The next afternoon, Marie curled up in the big chair near the fireplace in the great room, pretending to read a book, her hand absently stroking Scrabble's ears.

Emiliano had gone out to speak with Ace, and although she'd been invited, Scrabble remained with her. Instead of the familiar annoyance or confusion about his dog's choice, there had been something closer to humor and happiness in his gaze as he kissed her on his way out the door.

That easy kiss left a residual of rightness and delight humming in her system.

She'd been watching the clock since the Princeps agreed to the meeting, unable to think of anything other than ending this deadly dance with the Cohort. When it was over, when she was safe, she would return home to Dallas and never enjoy this view of the Ortega ranch again.

It made her inexplicably sad and she cuddled Scrabble closer.

"You're such a love," she murmured. *Love.* The word echoed through her head. She was in love with Emiliano. How was it even possible, with her background? Clutching the book to her chest, she tried to deny it and couldn't.

She pushed out of the chair and paced in front of the Christmas tree. Should she tell him? What good would come of that? They were from two different worlds. No, this was her problem. He was handling too much for her already. Her heart would stay here, with him, once she was out of danger.

Hearing the chime for the kitchen door, she pasted a smile on her face, masking her tumultuous emotions as Emiliano walked in.

"I have the ranch hands riding the property lines as a precaution," he said.

"Thank you?" She wasn't sure what else to say. It was smart. From what they'd learned, she was now a trophy for the Cohort cause.

"I don't like leaving you alone even for a minute." He checked his phone again. They both knew he had to leave or risk losing the meeting. "Finn should've been here by now."

"I have excellent supervision." She smiled down at

Scrabble, dragging her thoughts away from a cliff of misery. Her heart was in enough trouble. Could her soul handle one more loss if he got hurt on her behalf? "And Ace is close enough if Scrabble needs any help herding me."

He scowled. "Keep your phone on."

"I promise." She waved the device, showed him it was charged up.

He kissed her with a resolve and urgency she understood. Ever since the mistletoe, and before that, really, a need had pulsed inside her veins that only he could satisfy. If she didn't get back to Dallas, back to work soon, she might start believing this idyllic time with Emiliano could blossom into something more permanent.

Marie stood at the window until his truck disappeared around the curve of the drive, hoping his meeting gave the FBI the arrests they needed. They both knew this was temporary and merely making the most of it.

She scolded herself for giving in to that first urge to kiss him. Now she knew what she would be walking away from when they brought the Cohort under control. Men like Emiliano valued family, stability and history. Everything she didn't have and could never offer a man who deserved that and so much more.

At her feet, Scrabble gazed up at her adoringly. "Maybe I should start my own family with a dog." Not that she knew anything about taking on that kind of responsibility. She could take a class or something. Her Colton, Incorporated, salary meant she could invest in a house with a yard so a pet would be happy. It wouldn't be Shadow Creek, but it would be more than her quiet, empty apartment.

"Let's go find Gordo," she said, heading toward the barn. "We'll all take some carrots to the horses."

Enjoying the pace of ranch life had surprised her. She'd been so sure it would be boring drudgery. Emiliano and his neighbors in Shadow Creek had proved her wrong. Beyond the daily adventures amid the routine care of a ranch this size, the sense of community pride and open acceptance of even her held immense appeal. Was there a place for her in Shadow Creek?

Scrabble barked at the sound of an approaching car. "That's probably my new babysitter," Marie said. With a sack full of carrots and a few sugar cubes in her pocket, she aimed for the paddock at the front of the house.

Although she hadn't seen him since the FBI had arrived at the Dallas office, she recognized Finn Townsend as he stepped out of the black sedan. He'd parked nearly on top of the porch and she swallowed a request for him to move the car back. Beside her, Scrabble voiced her disapproval.

"Hey!" His brown wavy hair was pushed back off his forehead, and in the navy polo shirt and khakis he seemed a little nervous, and lines of tension aged the boyish grin she remembered. "Is Emiliano here?"

"No." At her feet, Scrabble rumbled. Marie agreed with the dog. There was a weird energy rolling off Finn that had her wishing she'd stayed behind the security system in the house.

Scrabble edged forward, ears back and ruff rising. When he crouched down to greet her, she backed up closer to Marie.

"Easy, girl," he said, standing quickly. "Where are you two headed?"

"We're taking treats to the horses." Being comfortable around the horses didn't mean she was ready to go riding alone.

"I'll join you."

Marie handed him the bag of carrots. She could hardly stop him. She could, however, keep herself between Finn and the still-grumbling Scrabble. At the fence, she whistled the way Emiliano had taught her and Brandy strolled over, Picasso right behind her. Rapunzel feigned disinterest as usual. She crooned to the animals as she offered the treats, rubbing her hand over Brandy's long, velvet nose and scratching at Picasso's flicking ear.

"I wouldn't think they'd like Scrabble," Finn said.

"Emiliano says the horses know she's a good partner."

Finn chuckled as Picasso tried to stuff his head into the bag, searching for more carrots. "You must be eager to get back to Dallas with the holidays around the corner."

"Sure," she replied. Everyone on the investigation should know she didn't have anyone to celebrate holidays with.

"Great timing that Emiliano found a way to close in on the Princeps in the area."

She sensed an accusation under the words and slid him a look. "I think so."

"On the way in, our boss called. She wants me to take a look at the office where the perps grabbed that xylazine. It'd save us time if you could show me while we're waiting on Emiliano."

She wanted to say no. Surely an FBI agent could find his way, but she agreed anyway. "Come on, Scrabble." Maybe her help would finally convince him to stop looking at her as if she were a Cohort accomplice.

Chapter 10

On the drive into Shadow Creek, Emiliano listened to the hum of his tires on the smooth pavement, his thoughts flickering between the Cohort and Marie like a horse's tail swatting flies. Something wasn't adding up and his intuition clamored that he should've figured it out by now.

He blamed the distraction on leaving her alone, though he knew she was safe. Ace and a few of the other ranch hands were around, not to mention she'd earned Scrabble's devotion. For a self-proclaimed city girl, she showed a remarkable affinity for the animals on the ranch. Would she be willing to extend her visit?

And that kind of thinking wasn't putting him in the right mind-set to sell himself as her enemy at this meeting with the Cohort Princeps. Despite his precautions yesterday, he expected to be recognized and had to convince whomever showed up that he'd willingly turn against the FBI and jeopardize his spotless career. More, he needed them to believe he would deliver Marie to Sulla, according to the demand insinuated on the message board.

The Cohort had proved itself well-informed this time around, which was another anomaly. Typically, its members struck hard and disappeared. Why was this group so determined to make a personal example of Marie?

He parked on the street and walked into the tidy diner. Contrary to Marie's first impression of small-town life, Shadow Creek was big enough that he didn't know everyone and their history on sight. He did, however, know within moments that he was the first one there.

He walked over to the booth at the window designated for the meeting, prepared to wait. No surprise that new recruits were forced to cool their heels while being vetted by other Principes lurking behind surveillance cameras and devices.

As he sat down, playing the role of a man with all the time in the world, he saw a Guy Fawkes mask on the other bench seat. Emiliano didn't reach over. The man who'd stolen his mother's xylazine and drugged Ace had worn a similar mask, possibly this very one, though that would be a stupid way to leave behind evidence. Criminals were often caught by similar careless mistakes.

Thanks to his time on the message board, Emiliano knew a discarded mask meant a Princeps wouldn't show for a meeting. He ordered a cola and mentally replayed the setup, searching for the mistake that had spooked the Cohort.

No need to get antsy. Finn was with Marie and Staller was out on the street watching Emiliano's back. Once Staller realized the meeting was a bust, he'd come in and they could make a new plan. Emiliano's heel bounced impatiently as he glared at the mask. No Princeps and no contact from Staller. He glanced out the window, searching up and down the street for his teammate. Where was he?

The pieces aligned in a sudden rush, as the dead ends and sketchy evidence in Marie's case suddenly clicked into a clear picture.

The Cohort had turned Finn Townsend against them. He was the new player in this deadly game. Emiliano knew the rhetoric on those message boards could be convincing. Still, Finn? The shocking betrayal stung and Emiliano wanted to resist the facts. He considered Finn a good friend, yet the signs were all there.

Finn had pressed the theory that Marie had been colluding with Cohort. He'd found the incriminating emails. A programming language expert, he claimed there was a new player in Sulla's pocket. And Finn had insisted on protecting Marie today. No wonder the bastard had been late; he'd needed Emiliano to be clear to make kidnapping Marie easier.

Emiliano swore. He'd rolled out the red carpet for a fox to invade the henhouse.

He dropped money on the table to cover the soda and a tip and called Staller's number. No answer. He sent an urgent text to his boss, spelling out his revelation. No time to ask the other customers who'd left the mask in the booth. He'd been fooled and if he didn't hurry he would be too late to save Marie. He called her next, swearing when she didn't answer either her cell or the house phone.

With the hands-free option in the truck, he called Sheriff Colton and then the Austin FBI office, asking for backup at the ranch. He dialed Ace's number next; hopefully the trusted ranch manager was close enough to wreck whatever Finn had planned. Dread dripping down his spine, Emiliano stomped on the gas pedal. Saving her was going to require a miracle.

He skidded through the turn off the blacktop, the back tires fishtailing on the gravel driveway. Around the curve, he saw the sedan parked carelessly near the house.

Maybe he wasn't too late, but he couldn't wait for reinforcements to arrive. Changing his plan from one heartbeat to the next, Emiliano parked the truck to block in the sedan. No sign of Gordo, no greeting from Scrabble. It added up to significant trouble. He sent a text message, warning the ranch hands patrolling the property line to watch for Finn and to contact the sheriff if they saw him.

Checking his backup .22 in his ankle holster, he drew his service pistol before he left the truck. He paused near the front of the house, listening for any sound. Staying low, he crept closer and peered into the front windows, unable to see much around the Christmas tree.

The silence prodded him forward, and he tested the front door. Unlocked. Of course she would've let Finn in, not knowing the danger. The alarm sounded and he disarmed the system, hurrying through a search of the house. Acutely aware that every second's delay could be one second more than Marie had left, he forced himself to be thorough. It wasn't much relief to find the house empty and no signs of a struggle.

If Finn had convinced Marie to leave the house, Scrabble had gone along. The two had been nearly inseparable from the moment he'd introduced them. Outside the kitchen door, he found scuff marks in the grass and the shrubs that edged his mother's herb garden trampled. Not much of a trail. Where were they?

The ranch he'd considered secure, but he now saw as a minefield of potential tragedies. There was the back road out, several vehicles Finn could steal, not counting the horses he might have saddled to carry off Marie to a Cohort rendezvous point. *Think!*

He wanted to shout for Scrabble and couldn't risk giving away his position if Finn was within earshot. He whistled, the quick high-low call he used to bring Scrabble to heel when they were out with cattle or on a trail ride. No response.

Fury blazed through him. When he found Finn—and he would find him—the man would pay dearly for putting this desperate fear for Marie in his head. He cleared the barn near the house and moved on to the next building, giving another whistle. Maybe Scrabble had trailed Finn as he'd kidnapped Marie.

This time he heard Scrabble's answering bark, high and urgent, and her sturdy red-and-white body streaked toward him. She circled his feet and dashed several paces ahead, back the way she'd come. She barked again, then bolted toward the veterinary offices.

He cautiously jogged after his dog. Hearing the crack of a gunshot and a scream, they both broke into a run toward the recovery barn, a small space where his mother often kept her seriously ill equine patients.

He paused just outside the door to get his bearings. He could hear Finn, on a tirade about the abuse of corporations against citizen privacy. Emiliano glanced to Scrabble, signaled her to stay.

"Marie?"

"Emiliano!" she cried out.

"You okay?"

"Get the hell out of here, Ortega," Finn interrupted. "I just want the CDO."

Scrabble woofed and Emiliano stepped inside, gun raised. "Not gonna happen."

Finn leveled his gun at Marie. "The Cohort tasked me to bring her in." He sneered at Emiliano. "Dead or alive— they don't care."

"I care." At his side, Scrabble growled low in her throat. It seemed they both cared. Alive, he could find her. Dead, he'd be lost without her.

"Drop your weapon or I shoot."

Emiliano complied immediately. "What turned you?"

"Sulla understands the changing landscape and how to illuminate others' minds to the cause. We have to take a stand. Don't you get tired of being used? Making an example of Marie will force companies to think twice before employing data-mining strategies that violate personal privacy for the sake of corporate profit. We deserve to choose who knows what details." He waved the gun at Marie. "Can't you see she is a walking security breach waiting to happen? What she does turns our data and preferences against us."

Finn shifted, glaring at Emiliano. "I can't believe you still blindly follow Dashwood and the government. You're smarter than that."

Emiliano would've said the same about Finn once. "We took an oath to protect this country from threats like Sulla and the Cohort."

Finn stepped toward Emiliano. "The Cohort has a solution for greed, perpetrated by corporate puppets like Marie."

"Why steal the xylazine?" The timing had bothered him from the beginning of this case. "What does the Cohort want with horse tranquilizers?"

"There was a blanket request. It's a useful tool." He shrugged. "Thanks to you, I knew where to find some."

"You drugged a man." Emiliano inched forward. "Could've killed him."

"He lived." Finn's harsh laughter bounced through the empty barn. "Getting here before you and breaking into the office was almost too easy."

As Emiliano's friend and coworker, Finn had known when the ranch and vet office were practically unattended. The entire attack on Colton, Incorporated, on Marie specifically, had been orchestrated from inside the FBI. Emiliano was furious.

Scrabble growled again, her ruff high and ears back. He agreed with her.

"Call off your dog," Finn said, lowering his gun to take aim at her.

Emiliano shifted his weight to block the angle and protect his dog. "She never liked you. I should've trusted her judgment."

"It was mutual. She's a pest."

With a hand signal, he ordered Scrabble to go home.

Her movement drew Finn's attention. "Marie, run!" Emiliano shouted as Finn fired at the dog.

Scrabble darted out of harm's way and Finn twisted back to shoot Marie. She hadn't fled. To his dismay, she charged Finn.

No! They hadn't covered this in her self-defense lessons. Emiliano surged forward as Finn fired. The bullet went over her head, plowing into a beam above. She tried to knock the gun away. Finn anticipated the move, striking her across the cheek with the weapon.

She crumpled to the barn floor and Emiliano tackled Finn from behind. But Finn's longer reach was no match for Emiliano's wrath. He knocked the gun aside and landed an elbow strike that left Finn gasping for air.

They rolled and Finn pinned Emiliano, one hand crushing his windpipe while he sought the gun with the other. Emiliano couldn't quite reach his .22.

Black dots danced in front of his eyes and he brought his fists down on Finn's arm, breaking the hold and dragging air deep into his lungs. Finn screamed in pain, skittering like a spider across the floor. His hand found the gun just as Emiliano caught his ankle. Finn twisted, kicking against the hold, and pulled the trigger.

The next gunshot was a lightning bolt through his shoulder. Emiliano's left arm went numb instantly. Finn scrambled out of his reach. Marie shouted and Emiliano struggled to his feet, only to crash down into her arms.

Light poured in from both ends of the barn as the team from Austin finally arrived, blocking Finn's escape. He heard Scrabble barking, felt Marie's silky hair on his cheek. Ace bellowed and Gordo's deep howl joined a chorus of sirens approaching. Blackness pressed at the edges of his vision and Emiliano refused to give in to it. Within minutes Finn was shoved against the sheriff's car, hands cuffed behind his back, listening to another FBI agent read him his rights. With Finn in custody, they could contain the threat against Marie and drive the Cohort back into the shadows.

Ace and Marie helped him out of the barn. "I'm sorry," Ace said. "I was out—"

"Doing your job." Emiliano fought for control of his queasy stomach. "This was my mistake."

He looked to Marie, longing to kiss away the pain that surely throbbed in her cheek. "Forgive me?" If he'd figured it out sooner and listened to his instincts, they would have caught Finn before he'd ever had a chance to strike her.

Her lips curled up in a smile, though not enough to put that dimple in her cheek. At her feet, Scrabble whined, and she crouched down to pick up his dog. Scrabble licked her reddened cheek first, then wriggled toward Emiliano, but he couldn't hold her. He stroked her ears with his good hand, and they both lavished her with praise and the promise of cookies.

He gave a statement to the team from Austin while the paramedics dragged him onto a stretcher. They started an IV and pushed a painkiller through the line before they moved him to the waiting ambulance.

"Ride with me?" he asked Marie, his gaze locked on her face. Her shirt was stained with his blood and she was pale. She hadn't yet said she'd forgiven him, hadn't said much of anything to anyone besides Scrabble.

"They need my statement," she said.

"They can get it at the hospital." He couldn't let her out of his sight.

"I'll bring her over," Ace promised. "Once we settle the dogs."

"No." Every breath was another lance of pain through his shoulder. He shoved himself upright. "Please, Marie." Maybe it was the pain or the drugs, but he was afraid once he let her go he'd never see her again.

"I'm here." Her long ponytail swayed as the paramedic helped her into the back of the ambulance.

The fog of the morphine settled over him, and having her near soothed him as nothing else could. He reached over with his good hand, grateful for her gentle touch. Though her lips moved, he couldn't make out the words as the ambulance sped toward the hospital.

Chapter 11

Marie sat in the surgical waiting room, caught between the will of her heart and the wisdom of her mind. Her heart wanted Emiliano; to hell with the facts that her place was in Dallas at a job where she thrived.

Emiliano had friends and family, dogs and a life she could never compete with. Didn't want to compete with it. She wanted to find her place within his world. *Dangerous thoughts.* This was *his* place. He was built for Shadow Creek and the rancher's life; even his commitment and work with the FBI fit that solid framework.

She didn't have any experience with that kind of stability. Who would trust the girl without family or roots to stick? And what if someone else came after her? She couldn't bear for her troubles to put him at risk again. No, the sooner she took the right actions, the sooner she would feel better about letting Emiliano go.

Her heart beat a frantic protest against her ribs. *Wanting* a man was different from wanting what was *best* for him. Ace returned and handed her a cup of coffee from the vending machine. "Any word?"

"No." She glared at the phone on the volunteer's desk, willing it to ring with news on Emiliano.

"There was no exit wound." He scratched at the stubble on his jaw. "Shoulders are tricky."

She'd learned as much from a Google search that had done nothing but crank up her worry. Emiliano could lose the use of his arm. Because of her. She blinked back another wave of tears.

"What did Zane Colton have to say?" he asked after several endless minutes.

Zane had flown in from Dallas to check on her and give her an update of the situation on their side of the investigation.

"The FBI sent in a new team. They're combing through everything Finn touched, making sure the system is safe. They told me Finn was training a new team of Principes in physical assaults. It should be safe for me to go back to work. Zane has a team ready to keep an eye on me for a few weeks. A precaution."

"You're not staying in Shadow Creek?"

She sipped the hot coffee, scalding her tongue. "My career is in Dallas," she replied. She wouldn't call it a life, not after this time with Emiliano.

Ace fell silent. They both knew Emiliano belonged in Shadow Creek. He had been miserable trying to build a life with his ex-wife in another city. She wouldn't ask him to risk that again. Loving him was her problem, not his. And loving him, she wanted Emiliano's happiness more than her own.

As she left the waiting area to stretch her legs, it seemed easier to leave with every step. She should go now. Never look back. Leaving would hurt, but staying left her open and vulnerable to the inevitability of him walking out of her life when the city smothered him.

Stay in Shadow Creek, a voice in her head whispered. If only it was that easy. She wasn't ready to give up on her career, the only stability she had known.

Her mind drifted back over recent days, the feel of his body close as he taught her self-defense, his gaze on her as he taught her to ride and care for the horses. His smile for Scrabble, his focus on her case, and the way his trim beard felt against her skin. Running over and through all those sweet moments was the depth of his anxiety when she'd been late coming home. His words. She pressed the memory close. No one in her life had ever been so concerned about her. For her.

Stay in Shadow Creek.

Her heart clamored for her to find a solution that would allow her to stay for a while and give whatever was sprouting between them time to bloom. She had plenty of vacation time built up. Would they let her telecommute?

Silly to assume he even wanted her to stay. She'd brought dreadful trouble to his door and to his parents' business. She was too green about *everything* to be an asset on the ranch.

No, better to walk away and accept the only possible ending to this story would be the same as her previous relationships. In her mind, she started composing a note, and eventually, as the words flowed through her mind, she gave in. She couldn't leave him without any explanation, not after what they'd been through. Leaning against a wall, she drafted a farewell email to Emiliano on her phone.

Satisfied, she was ready to leave the hospital, the town. Ace would be here for him when he came out of surgery. His parents would be home soon, as well. Yet she couldn't make herself go without hearing his prognosis. Of course, Emiliano was fit and healthy and she didn't expect any life-threatening complications from the surgery, only threats to his lifestyle, should the doctors have trouble removing the bullet.

A wound he'd sustained trying to protect her. Her stomach cramped again.

Ace waved at her from across the waiting area and she noticed the surgical team heading his way. With Emiliano's parents and brother out of town, Ace was his point of contact. She hurried over, her hands shaking as she listened to the report. The doctors were able to remove the bullet without any further injury to Emiliano's shoulder structure and nerve damage was unlikely, though they had to wait for the swelling to subside and his initial recovery to know for sure.

Marie and Ace thanked the doctors, and when the ranch manager sat down, she joined him again. "That's such a relief," she said.

"I expect he'll be ornery about the limitations." He checked his watch. "I need to get back to the ranch and take care of things for the evening. Can you stick around while they get him settled into a room?"

"Me? No. I'm not sure it's appropriate."

"He shouldn't wake up alone." Ace pushed to his feet.

"Can't you call someone else?"

Ace shook his head. "Everyone is stretched thin over the holidays. Marie, he asked you to ride in the ambulance with him," he reminded her. "The animals can't take care of themselves. I'll be back in a jiffy. Want me to bring dinner?"

"Sure," she said, clearly outmaneuvered.

Emiliano had a hazy recollection of faces flitting in and out. Some asked him to talk or make a fist. Others chattered about heart rates and transfers. The reasons and information floated just out of reach, along with the dull sense that he'd been out a long time. He recalled Ace at the foot of his hospital bed. Dr. Ramirez had come by. And Marie.

"Marie," he rasped, blinking into the faint light. "Marie?" He reached for the side of the bed.

"'Fraid you're stuck with me" came the answer.

"Ace?"

"That's right. Just rest, man. We'll catch you up soon enough."

The next time he came awake it was easier. "Where's Finn?"

"In custody," Ace replied. "You saved the girl and the investigation. You're a hero."

Emiliano felt like he'd been flattened by an 18-wheeler. He rolled to his left and swore.

"Sounds like you're coming along fine," Ace said with a laugh. "Need a hand sitting up?"

"No." He fumbled with the controls for the bed, but managed it. "Where is Marie?"

"She stepped out," Ace replied. "You're pale. Want me to call a nurse?"

"No." He took stock of the flowers and balloons crammed into the room. "How long have I been here?"

"Overnight is all. I just got back from the morning rounds at the ranch. Doc says—"

"Where's Marie?"

Ace's gaze drifted to the ceiling. "She stepped out."

Emiliano had to wait while a nurse arrived to check his vitals and help him move around a bit. "Is she hurt?" he asked the moment they were alone again.

"Not a bit. Cheek is puffy, that's all. She said it hurts when she smiles."

He wanted to hear her say that for himself, wanted to *see* her. "When will she be back?" He was feeling steadier with every passing minute, though the ache in his shoulder was gaining steam.

"Soon enough." Ace wagged a finger at Emiliano's shoulder. "They say you shouldn't have any long-term trouble."

"Good." Emiliano aimed his bad-cop interrogator gaze at Ace. "What aren't you telling me?"

"I called your parents and Dario. Brought 'em up to speed."

"Great." Had Ace told them about Marie? He'd wanted

to be the one to share that with his mother, in particular. "Why not bring *me* up to speed?"

"I, ah, don't know any more particulars about the case."

"You know I'm talking about Marie." He checked the wall clock. Forty-five minutes had passed since Ace said she'd stepped out. He had a bad feeling that had nothing to do with the miserable ache in his shoulder or the last of the anesthetic clouding his mind.

Looking miserable, Ace handed Emiliano his cell phone. "She wanted me to give you this when you woke up."

Emiliano read the email, his heart sinking as he read that she'd returned to Dallas. As she wished him a happy holiday. *What the hell?* He deserved better than this sorry excuse for a breakup note.

"Sorry, man," Ace said.

"No." He read her note again and picked out each of her lame excuses for going back to Dallas. He'd listened when she told him about her childhood, or rather a distinct lack thereof. He'd kissed her, made love to her, and he recognized this letter was a cop-out. She was letting her old fears of abandonment decide for both of them.

He tossed the phone to the foot of the bed. "Where are my clothes?"

"She left you?" Ace shook his head. "I'm sorry, man."

He couldn't drive in this condition, but Ace could. Would. "My clothes, Ace. You're driving me home." To Dallas if necessary.

"Emiliano, you can't leave the hospital yet."

"Can. Will. In this stupid hospital gown if I have to." He pressed the call button for the nurse and demanded to have his IV removed.

The nurse refused, calling for a doctor when Emiliano started peeling back the tape himself.

"You're an idiot," Ace muttered. "She's *gone*." He up-ended a small duffel bag and tossed clean clothes at him.

"How long ago?"

The orthopedic surgeon on rounds walked in and Emiliano made it clear he wasn't staying. "I'll rest at home. Go to my follow-up."

The doctor scribbled out two prescriptions. "And you'll take these antibiotics or I'll see you back here in worse shape than you're in now."

"Yes, sir." It wasn't easy dressing with one hand and it was morale-lowering to need Ace's help buttoning his jeans and shirt, but at least they were moving in the right direction.

"How long has she been gone?" he demanded as Ace drove to the ranch.

"Barely an hour," Ace admitted, glumly. "She wanted more of a head start."

"I bet she did." Emiliano was calculating the time. If he was lucky, she hadn't gotten away from the ranch yet. "How was she getting back to Dallas?"

"She said she had it under control."

A cab or a ride-share service? Either was possible, he thought. Probably she asked a new friend. "Step on it," he said as he first called Claudia and then Jade to see if they'd heard from Marie. They hadn't.

His hopes sank again, remembering what she'd said about family in her letter. She could have tapped any number of contacts at Colton, Incorporated, the people she considered family. The upper corporate had vast resources and all of them thought the world of Marie, valued her as an employee and a friend.

They weren't her *family*. That was the role Emiliano wanted to claim. He wanted to build that with her, give her the foundation of love and stability he'd had. He was half-way out of the truck before Ace had come to a complete stop in front of the house. He hurried inside, ignoring the griping shoulder. She couldn't be gone yet. The alarm system chimed as he walked in and he stopped long enough to punch in his code.

Hearing Marie's voice pleading with someone, he moved as fast as possible toward the guest room. Was she under attack again? Why hadn't he brought a gun?

He checked his headlong rush at the doorway, taking in the scene. Marie was trying to pack up her things and Scrabble was sitting in one half of her open suitcase, nipping and tossing things back out without moving.

"Stop that," Marie said again. "You're a menace."

She reached for his dog, and rather than shove her aside, she cuddled Scrabble close. "I'll miss you too." She put the dog on the floor and Scrabble leaped up and back into the suitcase.

"Menace," Marie repeated, her voice full of tenderness.

"Sure, kiss the dog goodbye." Emiliano stepped into the room. "But not me."

Scrabble stood up, her body wriggling and a grin on her face, though she held her position in the suitcase.

Marie faced him, her eyes red and her eyelashes spiked with tears. "You shouldn't be here."

"Where else would I be after that ridiculous letter?"

"Ridiculous?" Temper flashed through her deep eyes, gone in an instant. "You're pale." She drew him to the chair under the window, made him sit down.

"Emiliano, I…" Her voice trailed off, her gaze shifting to the view through the window.

"I love you, Marie."

She stared at him, her eyes wide and wet.

He reached out and tilted her chin, examining the bruise on her cheek. "Trust me not to let anyone hurt you again."

She took his hand in both of hers, and though she smiled,

it didn't hold much confidence. "You've been a wonderful protector."

"I'm *in love* with you," he said. "I should have said it sooner, the minute I knew, but I was scared." He raised his chin toward the bed. "Scared of this, actually."

He waited, giving her room to say something. She didn't. He wasn't wrong about her, about them. On the bed, Scrabble gave a low huff and settled into the suitcase, resting her chin on her paws, watching them.

No, he wasn't wrong.

"All my life I've searched for the joy and faithfulness, the partnership and laughter my parents have." He cleared his throat. How had he let his ex have that much sway over his life? "I took a detour, let one bad apple get into my head. Until I met you.

"All your life you've wanted family," he continued. "It's right here. I want that for you, *with* you." He reached out and brushed her long bangs from her eyes. "You don't have to leave first, Marie. You can trust me to stay. Always."

A tear trickled down her cheek and he wiped it away with his thumb.

"Your family has been here for generations," she whispered, sinking to her knees beside the chair.

"A testament to the Ortega stability and stubbornness," he said. "Trust what we've started. Count on *me*, Marie."

A smile teased the corner of her lips. "I am afraid," she confessed. "I love you too, Emiliano." She shook her head and her hair fell like a curtain around her face. "I'm afraid of everything I don't know about being in a family."

"I know it." She was thinking about the wreckage in her past. He pulled her closer, longing to turn her focus to the present, the future. "Just as I know our family won't be complete without you, without us, bringing up the next generation. Marry me, Marie. Be my family, and we'll figure out the rest of it as we go."

"It's a dream I gave up on," she admitted with a quiet sigh. She lifted her eyes to his. "Until you."

The sunlight from the window caught the flecks of gold in her gorgeous eyes, illuminated the depth of love he'd almost given up on. "Is that a yes?"

She leaned forward and carefully touched her lips to his. "Yes."

"You'll need a ring."

"First, you need a hospital."

"The doctor said I only need rest. I'll get more of it here, with you." He aimed a look at the bed behind her.

Her soft laughter filled his heart as she helped him down the hall to his room with Scrabble dashing ahead as escort. When he was as comfortable as she could make him, she stretched out along his good side and Scrabble settled at the foot of the bed.

"We'll need a bigger place in Dallas, too," he said after a few minutes basking in the quiet wonder of being loved by Marie. "I know how much you want to get back to work."

"We have some time," she replied. "I called in and Fowler told me to take the rest of the year."

Time. It was a gift nearly as beautiful as the heart of the woman beside him.

She laid her palm over his chest, the warmth sinking deep into his soul. "We could find a place here in Shadow Creek. Telecommuting is a workable option for me."

He caught the skittish tremor in her voice and wanted to ease all her fears. He tipped up her chin, waited for her to meet his gaze. "You've given that some thought."

She trailed a finger along his jaw. "I might have wished on a star or two for what could be."

"What will be," he promised. "We'll celebrate tomorrow or maybe the day after." He kissed her softly. "This is the best healing a man could ask for."

"This will be the best Christmas ever," she whispered, snuggling close.

"I promise to make each one better than the last."

"You can try," she teased, her dimples showing. "Since you're my first Christmas miracle, it will be a challenge."

He stroked his fingers through her hair, equally stunned and content. "Challenge accepted, my love."

* * * * *

Dear Reader,

It's always a joy to write a book set in the world of the Coltons! This is a family that has seen their share of troubles, and yet at the end of it all, they stick with each other through thick and thin. While the characters in this book aren't Coltons by blood, they forge strong friendships with the members of the clan. And really, aren't friends the family we choose for ourselves?

I'm fortunate to have some truly great friends in my life, and I'm happy that we still keep in touch despite our lives taking us in different directions. Like Dario and Felicity, my friends are very important to me, and I treasure every one of them.

I hope you enjoy this story. Dario and Felicity face a lot of hurdles in a short period of time, and it's quite the roller-coaster ride! Grab your favorite holiday treat and settle in for an exciting time!

As always, thanks for reading!

Lara

THE MARINE'S
CHRISTMAS CASE

Lara Lacombe

For O. Can't wait to meet you!

Chapter 1

It was a nice party...for an engagement celebration.

Dario Ortega stood in the corner, nursing his beer as he watched the group. The ranch house was packed, the walls practically bulging as friends, family and well-wishers crowded in alongside the usual menagerie of dogs and cats that always seemed to find his parents. The two veterinarians had soft hearts and never had been able to say no to an animal in need. He and his brother, Emiliano, had practically grown up in a zoo, and as he watched one of the members of his family's current pack nose the guests in a hopeful manner, he couldn't help but smile. Some things never changed...

All the bodies made the house warm, but Dario didn't mind. He enjoyed being around his family; he traveled a lot thanks to his freelance tech work, so it was nice to stay in one place for a bit and spend some time with his parents and brother.

He'd never seen Emiliano so happy before. His brother was normally serious and reserved, but Dario didn't think he had stopped smiling in days. And it was all thanks to the woman by his side.

Marie Meyers was a beautiful lady, made even more pretty by the love shining in her eyes as she looked up at her fiancé, laughing at something he said. Emiliano had his arm around her, and it was clear from the way their bodies were angled toward each other that they were sharing a private moment despite standing in the middle of the crowd. Dario was happy for his brother and the love he'd found, but he had to admit he didn't understand Emiliano's desire to get married.

Dario didn't have anything against relationships, per se. He loved women—their smell, their laugh, the way they moved and talked. He enjoyed hearing their thoughts and figuring out what made them tick. And he didn't mind having an exclusive relationship with one at a time. In fact, he preferred it that way.

But there was something about the whole till-death-do-us-part-forever-and-ever-amen aspect of marriage that made him tense up. Maybe he was just cynical, but Dario liked going into a relationship knowing that he had an escape option if things went south. And while divorce was a possibility, it was often a messy, drawn-out process. Besides, what kind of a pessimist thought about divorce as they were getting married?

"There he is!" Emiliano's voice boomed over the din of conversation. "Get over here, best man!"

Dario smiled and pushed off the wall, threading through the crowd until he reached his brother's side. "You rang?" he said drily. He nodded at Marie, who smiled at him.

Emiliano clapped him on the back. "I did. Why are you skulking in the corner? This is a party! You need to mix and mingle."

"I'm sorry," Dario replied. "I didn't realize I was being so evasive." He truly hadn't meant to put a damper on the party, but perhaps his thoughts about marriage had affected his mood.

"You weren't," Marie said. "He just doesn't want to be the only one in the thick of things."

"She's right," Emiliano admitted, sounding a little sheepish. He glanced around, his eyes widening a bit as he took in the size of the gathering. "I didn't realize we actually knew this many people. And having them all in one place is a bit claustrophobic."

"Just wait until the wedding," Dario said. He grinned, taking a perverse pleasure in his brother's discomfort. "Mom has a list of guests as long as your arm."

Emiliano and Marie exchanged a loaded glance. "Uh, we were kind of hoping for a small, quiet affair," she said.

"Yeah," Emiliano put in. "We figured if we let her go nuts for the engagement party, she'd be more likely to back off on the guest-list demands."

Dario nodded and bit his lip to hide a smile. "I'll keep my fingers crossed for you."

His brother was right to look so worried. Natalia Ortega was a force of nature—as a petite woman who worked with huge horses all day, her job practically demanded it. Dario didn't envy Emiliano's predicament, and he chuckled to himself. *One more reason to stay single...*

As if summoned by their conversation, their mother walked over. She slipped her arm around Dario's waist and pulled him close, and he leaned down to kiss the top of her head. "I'm so glad you're home," she said. "Having both my boys home for Christmas is the best gift I could ask for."

Dario smiled. "I'm glad I was able to take a break. It's good to be here." Even though he lived in Houston, only a few hours away, he'd been working steadily over the past year, moving from job to job without pause. But his next project didn't start until January, giving him a few weeks to catch up with everyone and get to know Marie a little better before she officially joined the family.

His father walked over and joined them. "Is this an impromptu family meeting?"

"Something like that," Emiliano replied, angling his body to make room for Aurelio Ortega to step into the circle.

"Are you two enjoying yourselves?" Aurelio asked Emiliano and Marie.

"Very much," Marie said. "It's a wonderful party—thank you again for hosting it."

"Our pleasure," Natalia said, her smile stretching from ear to ear. She practically vibrated with joy, and Dario's heart warmed to see his mother so happy.

"We can't wait to officially welcome you into the family," Aurelio said. He glanced at Emiliano and Dario. "But for now, we need to mingle so our guests don't feel neglected."

Dario and his brother nodded. "I'm on it," Dario said, raising his glass in salute. He scanned the crowd as his parents slipped away, seeking out a friendly face. Maybe he could find an old family friend to chat with for a minute, to ease himself into being social.

Jade and Claudia Colton had found Marie, and the three women were talking and laughing by the Christmas tree. While he watched, his mother joined the group—she had long been the vet for Jade's horses, and Jade hugged her in greeting.

Dario's father caught his eye and nodded meaningfully at the crowd. Dario lifted his glass in acknowledgment. Message received.

He spied Mrs. Jenkins by the refreshment table. She'd been their neighbor for years, and she was always nice to talk to. Dario took a step in her direction but a flash of red caught his eye and made him turn.

She was standing by the window, sipping from a glass of white wine. She was limned by the glow of the Christmas lights lining the roof of the house, giving her an ethereal look. How had he missed seeing her before? With her long brown hair, full lips and delicately arched eyebrows, she was exactly the kind of beautiful woman he usually appreciated.

"Who's that?" he asked his brother, keeping his gaze locked on her lest she disappear.

"That's Felicity Grant. She just came back to Shadow Creek and is now working for Adeline Kincaid's PI agency."

"Excellent," he murmured. He started forward, but a hand on his shoulder stopped him.

"I don't think she's going to be interested, little brother." Emiliano nodded in her direction. "She looks like she wants to be left alone right now."

"We'll see," Dario said, shrugging off Emiliano's hand. "I'm sure I can put her at ease."

He heard his brother's soft chuckle. "This ought to be good," Emiliano muttered. But Dario ignored him, focusing instead on the beauty across the room.

He started toward her, taking his time so he didn't seem too eager. He wasn't exactly looking for a relationship right now, but he couldn't pass up an opportunity to get to know such a lovely woman better. And if she wanted to have a little fun while he was home? Well, that was just fine by him...

Her eyes landed on him as he approached. He offered her a suggestive smile designed to melt feminine resistance. In his experience, women usually blushed and giggled after such attention. But she didn't.

One eyebrow arched slightly, but her expression didn't otherwise change. His confidence faltered; perhaps Emiliano had been right, after all? But he'd come too far to stop now, and he was aware of his brother's eyes on his back. If he veered away at this point, he'd never hear the end of it.

So Dario took a deep breath and pressed forward. One conversation—they could both get through something as simple as that. Maybe he could even coax a smile out of her. The thought stiffened his spine and filled him with determination. He had yet to meet a woman who was immune to his charms.

And he loved a good challenge.

He's coming this way!

Felicity's stomach twisted as the handsome cowboy drew near. She'd spied him the minute she'd walked into the party, and not just because of his shiny boots and bolo tie. He was a difficult man to ignore. He was tall and broad-shouldered, and his dark hair had a mussed look that made her want to run her hands through the strands. She couldn't tell the color of his eyes from this distance, but it didn't matter. His gaze was intense, landing on her like a touch.

The smile he aimed at her was full of sensual promise, and she knew without a doubt he could deliver on his offer. Heat suffused her limbs at the thought of those full lips on her body, and she shivered as she imagined the rasp of his beard stubble scraping across her skin. For a brief, thrilling second, she allowed herself to indulge in a vivid fantasy involving an empty bathroom, the sexy cowboy and a locked door. It would be so easy to slip away and discover if he felt as hot as he looked.

She shook herself free of the enticing thought. The idea was appealing, but she wasn't interested in a fling. She'd come back to Shadow Creek to start a second career after leaving the Marines. Whoever he was, the man approaching her was a distraction she simply didn't need.

"Hello." His voice was deep and soft, the tone better suited to whispering sweet nothings rather than making polite conversation.

"Hi." She nodded once in acknowledgment, hoping he wouldn't take the gesture as an invitation.

He did.

"I don't believe we've met before." He stuck out his right hand. "I'm Dario Ortega. Emiliano is my brother."

Felicity considered not touching him, but she didn't want to appear rude. "Felicity Grant," she replied, slipping her hand into his.

Instead of shaking her hand, he smoothly turned it over and brought it to his lips. His kiss was featherlight, the barest whisper of a touch, and the warmth of his breath on her skin sent sparks of sensation arcing up her arm.

She gritted her teeth, determined to ignore her body's response. But if a casual touch had this much of an effect on her, how would she respond if he really kissed her?

Doesn't matter, she told herself sternly. *I'm not going to find out.*

"Nice to meet you, Felicity," he said, releasing her hand. His eyes were a warm hazel, a swirl of blue and green and gold that was mesmerizing. If she wasn't careful, Felicity could get lost in his gaze.

"I heard through the grapevine you've come back to Shadow Creek. Why haven't I met you before?"

She shrugged and his eyes traced the curve of her shoulder before landing back on her face. His blatant appreciation of her body was a little unsettling; it had been years since a man had so openly stared at her. When she'd first joined the Marines, she'd dealt with her fair share of catcalling and crude remarks. But once she'd proved to the men she was just as good as the rest of them, they'd stopped treating her like a woman and had embraced her as one of the guys. Their acceptance had made her feel proud, but she was no longer used to a man's romantic attention.

"I'm, uh, not sure why we would have known each other." She definitely would have remembered him—he was just the type her young heart would have pined over during high school.

"You didn't go to school here." It wasn't a question. "I would have seen you."

"I think I was a few years ahead of you."

He winked at her.

She lifted a brow. "Well, that explains it."

"I've always liked older women," he said. "Especially when they're as pretty as you."

It was an obvious attempt at flattery, but Felicity's stomach fluttered nonetheless. Ignoring her body's response, she rolled her eyes. "Does that line usually work for you?"

He grinned and twin dimples appeared on his cheeks, giving him a boyish appeal. "Yes."

His honesty was unexpected and she couldn't help but laugh. "Sorry to break your record."

"That's okay. I have other lines." He lifted a brow suggestively and Felicity shook her head.

"I'm immune." Better to stop this now, before he wore down her resistance and she forgot her resolve to stay focused on her new job.

"So you say." Dario studied her thoughtfully as he took a sip of his beer. "But I bet I could find one that works on you. I'm very talented."

That's what I'm afraid of.

He took a step closer and Felicity's breath caught. His cologne was subtle and smelled expensive. "Have dinner with me tomorrow."

She straightened her spine. "No."

Surprise flared in the depths of his eyes. "No?"

"You heard me."

"Are you sure? We should really get to know each other before I take you to my brother's wedding."

Felicity shook her head at his audacious assumption. "I don't remember agreeing to accompany you."

"Not yet." Dario tilted his head to the side. "But you will."

A loud voice broke into their conversation, saving her from needing to reply to his arrogant statement. "Felicity Grant? Is that you?"

She turned to find a middle-aged man staring at her, a look of surprise on his face. "Mr. Perkins. What a nice surprise."

Her high school history teacher smiled and took a step closer. Dario shifted to include the man, and the tension in Felicity's muscles eased as she got some of her personal space back.

"I thought that was you!" Mr. Perkins said. He ignored Dario, focusing intently on her face. "Are you back in town on holiday leave?"

Felicity felt Dario's interest sharpen at the question and she mentally sighed. She hadn't really wanted to talk about her past with him, but it seemed there was no help for it.

"No, sir," she replied. "I retired from the Marines a few months ago."

"The Marines?" Dario interjected. He sounded a little astonished, and Felicity could tell that was the last thing he'd expected to hear.

"That's right, son," Mr. Perkins said proudly. "Felicity here joined the Corps after she graduated high school. She was the only one in her class to enlist." He turned back to Felicity. "Every time I ran into your father around town, I asked about you. He told me about your promotion to corporal, and when you shipped out to Afghanistan with the Third Battalion." His eyes shone with respect. "I was in the Third Battalion, too, you know. K Company."

A lump formed in Felicity's throat, and she blinked hard to clear her eyes. "I didn't know that, sir. I was in L Company, myself."

Mr. Perkins nodded. "Desert Storm. We were there for months but never lost a man—can you believe it?"

Felicity smiled sadly. "I wish we could say the same."

Afghanistan had been unlike anything she'd experienced before, and she'd seen her fair share of intense fighting. While her unit hadn't suffered many casualties, she'd personally known each marine who'd been wounded. And when one of their own had died—in a freak drowning accident, of all things—they'd grieved for months.

A faraway look entered Mr. Perkins's eyes, and Felicity knew he was recalling his days in the desert. "It was a different war for us," he said softly. "We didn't have to deal with insurgents and terrorists hunting us down."

"War is never easy, sir," she said. As far as Felicity was concerned, anyone who put on the uniform and served their country was deserving of respect. Some people liked to argue about which branch of the service had it worst, or which assignment had been the toughest, but she considered that to be counterproductive. Friendly banter between units was one thing, but she would never demean the experiences of another service member simply because they didn't match her own.

"Ooh-rah," he said softly. He shook his head, visibly casting off his memories. "It's good to have you back. Will you be staying long?"

"I hope so, sir," she replied. "I just took a job as a private investigator."

"That's wonderful." He smiled, appearing genuinely happy to hear it. "You let me know if you need any help settling in. That's an order."

"Yes, sir," Felicity said. She was touched by his offer, especially since she hadn't seen him in a dozen years. But that was the magic of the Corps—young or old, active duty or retired, the title of "Marine" lasted a lifetime.

Mr. Perkins stuck out his hand, and Felicity was happy to shake it. "Semper Fi," he said.

"Semper Fi," she repeated.

He melted back into the crowd, leaving Felicity alone

with Dario once again. She turned to face him and could tell by the look on his face he was brimming with questions. Felicity braced herself to rebuff him. It was one thing to talk about her combat experiences with a fellow veteran, but she didn't want to share those memories with a man she'd only just met.

"The Marines, huh?" he said simply. "That's pretty hard-core." He looked her up and down as if evaluating her in a new light. Then he stuck out his hand. "Thank you for your service."

"You're welcome." She slipped her hand into his again, and this time he didn't flirt with her.

"Dario!"

They both glanced over to see Emiliano beckoning his brother with a wave. Dario nodded and waved in acknowledgment. Then he turned back to her, one hand dipping into his jacket and reappearing with a business card.

He juggled his drink as he hastily scrawled something on the back of the card before offering it to her. Felicity took it, frowning slightly. "What's this for?"

"That's so you can reach me once you've decided where you'd like to have dinner." He grinned impishly. "Call me anytime."

Before she could explain she had no intention of contacting him, he winked at her and strode away, heading for Emiliano and Marie. Felicity watched him go, a mixture of relief and disappointment swirling in her chest.

Dario Ortega was a charming man, and she had to admit that knowing he found her attractive was a boost to her self-esteem. If circumstances were different, maybe they could have gotten to know each other better.

But now was not the time. Felicity had worked hard in the Corps and had earned her share of accolades and awards. But she was a civilian again, trying to start a new career. That didn't leave much time for romance, especially not with a charmer like Dario, who probably had a different woman in every city. She needed to focus on her cases and show Adeline that hiring her had not been a mistake. She didn't want to let her friend down, but more than that, Felicity's pride demanded she do her very best.

She had no other choice.

Chapter 2

The next morning was cold and clear, with a sharp chill in the air that made Felicity's lungs burn a little. She clutched her travel mug of coffee in one hand, holding it close to her face so the thin column of steam that escaped through the lid could warm her nose. Thanks to the Christmas shopping crowds, she'd had to park several blocks away and had spent the last few minutes working her way back to the office. Only a few more steps before she was inside and could thaw out by the space heater near her desk.

She had just stepped onto the sidewalk when a loud bang broke the stillness of the morning. In the next instant, Felicity found herself on the ground, kneeling in a puddle of rapidly cooling coffee, groping for a weapon she no longer carried.

Her heart thundered in her ears and she gasped for breath, her eyes scanning the area as she instinctively searched for threats. After a few seconds her rational mind caught up with things and she realized Shadow Creek was not, in fact, under a mortar attack.

She stood, surveying the sidewalk with a frown. Her travel mug was ruined, the pieces scattered across the cement. The coffee had soaked into her pants, and the fabric clung to her knees in a chilly embrace that made her shiver. She glanced at her watch—there wasn't enough time to dash home to change them. *At least they're dark gray*, she thought wryly. Once everything dried, the stains wouldn't be too obvious. And there were worse things in life than going through the day smelling like coffee…

"Felicity?"

She turned to find Mr. Perkins approaching. He carried a bag in one hand, and it was clear he was getting an early start on shopping.

"Good morning," she said, trying to sound normal.

His gaze took in the coffee stain on the sidewalk, the remnants of her mug and the damp spots on her pants. His features softened. "It was a dropped crate."

"I'm sorry?"

He jerked his head toward the small market at the end of the block. "They were unloading some crates from a truck, and one of them fell off the tailgate. That's where the noise came from."

"Oh." She felt her face heat, a little embarrassed to learn she'd overreacted in such a dramatic fashion to such a simple event.

"Don't beat yourself up over it. It took me a few months before I stopped jumping at every little noise."

"I don't even know how it happened," she confessed. "One minute I was walking along, minding my own business. The next thing I know, I'm on the ground."

He nodded, as if this made perfect sense. "Gotta love those battlefield reflexes."

She shrugged, acutely aware of the mess she'd made. She knelt and began picking up the pieces of her mug, and Mr. Perkins joined her.

"For what it's worth, it gets better," he said kindly. "When I first got back, I freaked out every time a door so much as slammed shut. But I'm living proof that doesn't last forever."

"That's good to know," she said. While she realized on an intellectual level she would eventually adjust to the normal rhythms of civilian life again, it was hard not to feel like a failure for spooking so easily. She'd been evaluated for PTSD as part of her retirement health screen. Fortunately, she had shown no signs of the illness, which made her reaction all the more puzzling. But hearing Mr. Perkins talk about his experiences made her feel less alone, less self-conscious. She'd spent the last twelve years living a very different lifestyle from the people around her, and she felt like a bit of an outsider. It was nice to hear from a fellow marine that wouldn't always be the case.

They tossed the broken shards of pottery into a nearby trash can. "Thanks for your help, Mr. Perkins."

"Anytime." He smiled at her. "And I think under the circumstances, you should call me Henry. I'm not your teacher anymore."

It was a nice offer, but she couldn't bring herself to do it. "Yes, sir."

He laughed. "All right, Corporal. Fair enough. Have a good day."

"Thanks. You, too."

Felicity took a moment to smooth her hair back and run a hand down the front of her blouse. Feeling marginally more put together, she walked the rest of the way to the office and stepped inside the warm lobby.

"Felicity? Is that you?" Adeline's voice floated out of her office, and Felicity winced. She was late, and apparently her friend—*No, my boss*, she reminded herself—had been expecting her.

She headed down the hall, unwinding her scarf as she walked. "Sorry I wasn't here earlier," she said. "I had a bit of an accid—" The words died in her throat as she poked her head into Adeline's office and saw that she had a visitor.

But not just any visitor.

Dario Ortega sat across from Adeline's desk, sipping

a cup of coffee. He winked at her, plainly enjoying her reaction.

"Oh," she said, unable to hide her displeasure. "It's you."

It wasn't the most gracious remark, but Felicity still felt frazzled from her earlier mishap. The last thing she needed right now was a visit from a smooth-talking, good-looking distraction.

If her reaction bothered him, he didn't show it. He smiled broadly. "In the flesh. Nice to see you again, Felicity."

"You two know each other?" Adeline looked from Dario to Felicity, curiosity in her eyes.

"No," Felicity said, just as Dario replied, "Yes."

Adeline raised one eyebrow, a smile tugging at the corner of her mouth. "I see."

"We met last night, at Emiliano's engagement party," Felicity explained. "That's all." She didn't want Adeline to get the wrong idea, and if the look on Dario's face was anything to go by, he wasn't about to correct any misunderstandings as to the nature of their relationship.

"I didn't get a chance to ask you—how do you know my brother?"

"I, uh, don't. Not really." She had read some of Emiliano's reports on the Colton, Incorporated, hacking case, but she hadn't had a chance to meet him in person until last night. Dario frowned slightly, and Felicity felt her face heat.

Adeline came to her rescue. "She went in my stead. Jeremy's company holiday party was last night, and the boss couldn't very well skip the event. I asked Felicity to go and represent the agency. I thought it might be a good opportunity for her to meet some new people and get reacquainted with a few familiar faces." She looked at Felicity, her head tilted to the side. "I take it my plan was a success?"

"Looks that way." Felicity offered her a tight smile. "I'd better get started on my day." She nodded at Dario. "Nice to see you again." She heard the note of forced cheer in her voice, but couldn't muster the energy to care. She'd made it very clear last night that she had no interest in seeing Dario Ortega in any kind of social capacity. If he couldn't take a hint, that wasn't her fault.

"Always a pleasure, Ms. Grant." His voice was deep and sonorous, and Felicity clenched her jaw as goose bumps stippled her arms. Her body was responding as if he'd touched her rather than simply spoken a few words.

Enough of that, she told her traitorous flesh. She nodded once, then turned and marched down the hall to her office.

She tried to ignore the world on the other side of her desk, but no matter how hard she focused on booting up her computer and stowing her coat and purse, she heard every word coming out of Adeline's office.

"I won't keep you any longer," Dario said. "It was nice talking with you."

"Likewise," Adeline said, genuine warmth in her voice. "You know you're always welcome here."

"I appreciate that. You'll definitely be at Emiliano's wedding, right? Jeremy didn't schedule any work functions that conflict with the nuptials, I hope."

Adeline laughed. "No, I made sure our schedules are clear. We'll be there—we're both looking forward to it."

"Excellent." Dario sounded pleased. "See if you can talk Felicity into coming as well, will you?"

Felicity rolled her eyes and shook her head. Would the man ever stop?

"I'll see what I can do," Adeline replied. "That's nice of you to want to include her." There was a speculative note in her voice, and Felicity knew her friend was probing for information.

Dario didn't miss a beat. "Just don't want to see anyone left out. I know my family would agree."

Oh, he was slick. Felicity could almost admire his easy confidence and suave determination. She'd never met anyone with such an abundance of charm, and Dario knew exactly how to wield that particular weapon. She imagined he had women eating out of his hand everywhere he went.

All the more reason for her to bolster her resolve. She had no desire to be Dario Ortega's girl of the moment. And it was likely her very refusal to succumb to his flirtations that made him so determined to get through to her. It was the thrill of the chase that motivated him now, not any genuine interest in getting to know her.

Felicity pushed thoughts of Dario aside and turned to her computer. She needed to focus on her case, not worry about the actions of Shadow Creek's local playboy.

Adeline had assigned her the Colton, Incorporated, computer hacking case, and Felicity's main priority was tracking down Sulla, the infamous leader of the Cohort, which was the group that had claimed responsibility for the hack. It was a high-profile case; the FBI was leading the criminal investigation, but the Colton family had hired Adeline's agency to conduct their own investigation, in the hopes of bringing the matter to a swift end. It was a measure of Adeline's faith in Felicity that she'd turned over the reins of the investigation once she had joined her agency.

As if summoned by her thoughts, Adeline rapped on the open door of Felicity's office. "Got a minute?"

"Of course."

Adeline stepped inside and sat, then steepled her fingers in front of her chin. "What do you know about Dario Ortega?"

"I know he won't take no for an answer," Felicity muttered before she could think better of it. She shook her head. "Sorry. I know he's your friend."

Adeline tilted her head to the side. "Oh, I wouldn't necessarily say that. We're friendly, but he's not someone I consider a friend like you." She dropped her hands and leaned forward. "I take it he's been hitting on you?"

"And how." Felicity smiled ruefully. "He's very determined."

"That sounds like Dario," Adeline confirmed. "He's got a bit of a reputation for being footloose and fancy-free. But I must say, I've never heard talk that any of his relationships end badly. I think he's careful to make sure the women he dates know the score before they get involved."

"How kind of him," Felicity said drily.

Adeline shrugged. "I'm just saying, if you're looking to have a little fun, he's a good choice. I know it's probably been a while since you've had any romantic involvement."

Felicity's shoulders stiffened. "What makes you say that?" It was true, but did she wear the evidence of her dry spell like a shirt for everyone to see?

"I thought the Marines had rules about fraternization. Or are you telling me you ignored them?" Adeline's tone was equal parts teasing and hopeful, as if she had her fingers crossed that Felicity had flouted regulations in the interest of love.

Or lust, as it were.

Felicity shook her head. "Sorry to disappoint you, but I did not break the rules."

Adeline sighed. "I figured as much. You always were so proper."

"It's served me well so far."

"I know. But I worry about you. It might be good for you to let your hair down and have a little fun."

Felicity considered the idea for a split second, then shook her head. "I have no interest in being the next notch on Dario's bedpost."

Adeline leaned back. "Fair enough. But I think you're

looking at this the wrong way." She smiled wickedly. "He'd make a great notch on yours."

"Adeline!"

Her friend laughed. "Couldn't resist. Teasing you is too much fun. But that's not why I actually came in here."

"Oh?"

"Believe it or not, Dario is a top-notch computer expert. He's a genius with all things cyber related."

"Is that right?" Felicity couldn't keep a note of skepticism out of her voice. The handsome playboy actually had practical skills?

Adeline nodded. "Yeah. I know it's hard to believe, but he has an impeccable professional reputation. He's even more skilled than Emiliano in some respects."

"Wow." That *was* impressive. Emiliano was a respected agent on the FBI's National Cyber Investigative Joint Task Force. The men and women on that team were experts in every aspect of computers, so Adeline's words were high praise indeed.

"Dario came to visit me this morning because he's currently between cases, and he offered to assist in the Colton, Incorporated, hacking investigation while he's in town."

"What did you tell him?"

Adeline shrugged. "I thanked him for his offer and said we'd consider it. I didn't want to bring him on board until I'd talked to you."

"I appreciate that," Felicity said, touched at her friend's thoughtfulness. Adeline ran the PI agency, so as her boss, she had every right to accept help from whomever she chose. But it was nice of her to ask for Felicity's input first.

"This is your case, Felicity. I'm not going to tell you how to run it. But I do think it would be a mistake to turn down Dario's offer. His help might be just what you need to break this thing wide open. And for what it's worth, I think he'd be professional about it."

Felicity nodded slowly. "Can I take some time to think things over?"

"Of course." Adeline stood and smiled. "Like I said, this is your case and I trust your judgment. I know whatever you decide, you'll get the job done."

"Thanks, Addy," Felicity said. "I appreciate it."

Adeline made it to the door, but then stopped and turned back. "Oh, I almost forgot! You were saying something about an accident when you walked into my office this morning. Are you okay?" Her blue-gray eyes searched Felicity's face and her brows drew together in concern.

Felicity waved her off. "I'm fine." She didn't want to get into her earlier scare. Adeline was her friend, but Felicity still felt a little embarrassed over her reaction. She knew Mr. Perkins was right and that her jumpiness would fade with time, but until it did, she didn't want people to think she'd come back from the war broken. "I just dropped my coffee on the walk in."

"Bummer," Adeline said. "I put on a pot when I arrived this morning. It should still be pretty fresh."

"I'll grab some in a minute," Felicity said. "Thanks."

Adeline left and Felicity turned back to her computer, her mind whirring. The Colton hacking case was proving to be difficult, and she was under a lot of pressure to discover the identity of Sulla. Zane Colton, the head of security for Colton, Incorporated, had emailed her practically every day over the past two weeks asking for updates, and she'd even gotten messages from T. C. Colton, the executive vice president, and Fowler Colton, the president of the company. The corporate bigwigs were very interested in the case, and they were likely feeling a little paranoid since one of their own had recently been surrounded by scandal. Hugh Barrington, the family attorney, had schemed to take control of Colton, Inc., and he'd very nearly been successful. The cyberattack couldn't have come at a worse time for the company.

Felicity had worked as an intelligence specialist in the Corps, so she was used to compiling and sifting through data, looking for patterns or other nuggets of information that she could piece together to form a bigger picture. She knew her way around a computer, but she recognized her skills were nowhere near Emiliano's level.

Or Dario's, apparently.

If the talk about his talent was true, it would be nice to have someone of Dario's caliber join the investigation. Curious, Felicity did a quick internet search, looking for independent confirmation of Dario's computer prowess.

A few minutes later, she sat back, satisfied he was probably as good as he said. Could they really work together, though? Would he be willing to cool his flirtations and focus on the case?

Even if Dario agreed to stay on his best behavior, he would still be a distraction. Felicity would have to muster every scrap of self-discipline to ignore the temptation of his mouth and the knowing glint in his hazel eyes. Just the thought of being on guard all the time made her feel mentally and emotionally exhausted.

But did she have another choice?

A quiet chime sounded, and she glanced at her monitor to see the email icon blinking. She clicked on it, and a message from Zane Colton popped up: Any progress?

"If that isn't a sign from the universe, I don't know what is," she muttered to herself.

With a reluctant sigh, Felicity dug Dario's card out of her purse. She'd slipped it in the bag last night when she hadn't been able to find a trash can. She'd never intended to actually use it, but now she was glad she hadn't managed to throw it away.

She stared at the numbers he'd scrawled on the back,

imagining all too easily his triumphant smile when he answered the phone and realized she'd called him. Under any other circumstances, her pride would have kept her from asking for his help. But this was no ordinary case, and if she had to dance with the devil to make progress on it, then that was what she'd do.

She picked up the phone and began to dial, before she changed her mind.

Chapter 3

Dario leaned back in his chair, trying to look casual. He didn't want Felicity to see how pleased he was to be meeting her. Something told him if she thought he was gloating, she'd turn around and walk out of the restaurant before he even got the chance to say a word. So he forced himself to relax and managed to keep a grin off his face while he waited for her.

Inside, though, he practically fizzed with anticipation.

Her call had been unexpected. When he'd offered his services to Adeline this morning, he hadn't known she'd assigned the case to Felicity. As soon as he'd learned that, he'd figured there was no chance Felicity would want to work with him. She was so very determined to keep him at arm's length, and he found her reluctance intriguing. Usually, he had no problem getting a woman to go out with him. Why was Felicity playing so hard to get? The question had dominated his thoughts ever since he'd met her, and maybe now he would get an opportunity to learn the answer.

The door opened with a gust of cold air, and Felicity stepped inside, her hand clutching the lapels of her coat tight against the frigid wind. He waved to get her attention, and she nodded in acknowledgment.

Dario stood as she approached the table. She eyed him warily and began to shed her coat and scarf, draping them both over the back of her chair. Once she sat, he did the same.

"I'm glad you called," he said.

"Before we get started, I want to make one thing inescapably clear." Felicity placed her hands on the table and leaned forward, holding his gaze. Her green eyes glinted with challenge, as if she was daring him to argue with what she was about to say. "I called you because of your reputation as a cyber expert. You offered to help investigate the Colton hacker case, and I'm willing to give you a chance to do that. But this is not personal in any way, shape or form. Our interactions will be limited to the professional, nothing more. No flirting, no teasing, no accidental touches. Treat me like you would your brother's fiancée."

Where's the fun in that? Dario merely nodded, though, knowing that if he did otherwise, Felicity would leave without a backward glance.

In truth, he was glad to be consulting on her case. It gave him something to do while he was in Shadow Creek, and it would help keep his skills sharp. The fact that he was going to spend more time with Felicity was simply the icing on the cake. She talked tough now, but he was confident that eventually she'd relax her guard and let him get to know her better.

Apparently satisfied with his response, Felicity relaxed into her chair. "Okay. Great."

The waitress chose that moment to saunter up to the table. "What can I get you, hon?"

"Uh…" Felicity hastily glanced at the menu, scanning the options with a slight frown.

"I can come back," the woman offered.

"No, it's fine," Felicity said quickly. "I'd like a cup of the tomato soup and a grilled cheese sandwich. Water for the drink, please."

The waitress nodded, scribbling on her pad. "And you?" She turned to Dario with an expectant look.

"Cheeseburger and fries for me. Iced tea to drink."

"Coming right up." The woman collected their menus and left.

Dario studied Felicity a moment as she unwrapped her silverware and placed the napkin in her lap. "Have you eaten here before?"

She shook her head. "No. But I did like to come here back when it was a pizza parlor." She glanced around at the café's cozy tables and soft green walls. "It looks a bit different now."

"If it's any consolation, the food is good. Emiliano and I ate here last week after I got back into town."

Felicity nodded but didn't otherwise respond.

Dario searched for something to say to break the ice between them. "I imagine a lot of things changed in the years you've been gone," he offered.

She lifted one shoulder in a shrug that was strangely elegant. "I suppose."

The waitress returned with their drinks, and Felicity offered her a smile of thanks. After the woman left again, she leaned forward. "Can you tell me what you already know about the case? I don't want to waste time."

He nodded. "Emiliano filled me in on the basic facts. Colton, Incorporated, was hacked by a group calling itself the Cohort, and the personal information of the company's employees was released to the general public. Emiliano posed as a digital freedom fighter and tried to infiltrate the group, but things unraveled before he really gained entry into the Cohort."

Felicity nodded. "That's one way of putting it," she said, referring to the shocking betrayal by Finn Townsend, one of Emiliano's FBI colleagues, who had secretly been working for the Cohort. "I heard he was shot."

Dario nodded. "But don't feel too bad for him. He did get a fiancée out of the deal."

Felicity shook her head, but smiled faintly at his joke.

"Did the FBI get any useful intelligence out of Emiliano's former partner?"

"Not that I know of," Dario replied. "To be honest, I'm not sure the man knows that much to begin with. I get the impression he was only told what he needed to know to play his part. I don't think he was privy to any of the bigger-picture stuff."

"Figures," she muttered.

"Adeline told me you're tasked with tracking down Sulla, the Cohort's leader."

"That's right." Her lips pressed together in a thin line, and he got the distinct impression she didn't want to say more. After a second, she sighed. "I hate to say it, but I haven't made as much progress on unmasking Sulla as I'd hoped."

Dario recognized how much the admission had cost her, so he said nothing. It was obvious Felicity was a proud woman and took her job seriously. Her failure to make headway on the case had to be frustrating, and it probably pained her to admit it out loud, especially to him.

It was a sentiment he understood all too well. He was a perfectionist, and he set very high standards for himself, especially in the professional realm. It wasn't uncommon for him to spend days working on a project, often to the exclusion of other aspects of his life. He saw that same drive in Felicity and knew that while she had currently hit a wall in her investigation, it wouldn't be long before she found a way around it.

"Let's go back to the beginning," he suggested. "What do we actually know about Sulla?" Maybe it would help her to talk over the evidence one more time, and his fresh perspective certainly couldn't hurt.

"Not much," she said. She paused as the waitress deposited their food on the table and blew out a breath, her lips pursing slightly in a manner that was entirely too appealing. In another time and place, he'd have interpreted the expression as an invitation. But Felicity had made no secret of the fact she wanted to keep their relationship on an impersonal footing, and she didn't seem like the type of woman to act the tease. She likely had no idea how sexy he found her, and for a fleeting instant, he regretted volunteering to help with the case. It had seemed like a good idea at the time, but now that he was faced with resisting her unconscious charms for the next several weeks, he wasn't so sure.

Cold showers, he decided grimly, tearing his gaze away from her mouth. *That's my only hope.*

"So far, Sulla has claimed responsibility for the hack. But I don't know why Colton, Incorporated, was on Sulla's radar. Furthermore, I don't know if there are other strikes planned."

Dario nodded, redirecting his thoughts to the case. "I think it's safe to assume the initial hack might not be the only attack. The Cohort probably has more trouble planned for Colton, Inc."

"Yes, but why?" Felicity took a bite of her sandwich and chewed thoughtfully. "Of all the companies out there, why target Colton, Incorporated? The Cohort said it was against the collection of personal information, but there are lots of corporations nowadays that create extensive digital profiles of their customers. It seems odd to target one company for doing something so common."

Dario dipped a fry in ketchup. "Maybe the privacy story is just a smoke screen to conceal the group's true motives."

Felicity's eyes brightened with interest. "What are you thinking?"

Dario took a sip of his tea. "It's no secret the Colton family has a lot of enemies. Do you suppose the company was targeted as a way of doing more damage to the family and the Colton name?"

"That's an interesting possibility," Felicity said. She sounded a little surprised, and Dario hid a smile in his napkin, pleased that he'd shown her he could be useful to her investigation.

"That would mean Sulla probably has a personal connection to the family," she continued.

"Most likely," he agreed.

She thought for a moment. "That doesn't exactly narrow the field," she said wryly. "There's no shortage of people who hate the Coltons."

"We should probably talk to the Coltons themselves. They might be able to come up with a list of names to check out."

Felicity nodded. "That's going to be a big job. There are six Colton siblings alone living in Shadow Creek."

"Which means if we each pick three, it will take half the time to interview them."

"You'd do that?" She arched one eyebrow, plainly surprised.

Dario tilted his head to the side. "I did volunteer to help you," he pointed out.

"Sure, but I figured you'd just want to stick to the computer stuff. I didn't realize you intended to actually embrace all aspects of the investigative process."

Dario leaned back and clapped his hand over his heart. "You wound me," he said, affecting his best Southern drawl. "I'm not a dilettante."

Felicity laughed, a light, bright sound that made her seem almost girlish. "Forgive me," she said. "I certainly didn't mean to impugn your honor."

"The truth is, it'll be fun to talk to the Coltons. I usually do my work in front of a computer and don't really get to participate in other aspects of a case."

"It's not like you see on TV," Felicity cautioned. "This

job isn't always exciting. Most of the time, it can be down-right boring."

"That's okay," Dario said. "I'm just happy to help." Hopefully, Felicity would appreciate his efforts and relax around him.

She was silent a moment, then said, "Thank you."

Dario swallowed a bite of his burger and felt a surge of warmth at her words. It seemed she was softening toward him already.

"So which siblings do you want to interview?" he asked. "I know River was in the Marines, so maybe you should talk to him. He'd probably be happy to chat with a fellow vet."

"Sounds good. I'll talk to Jade and Claudia, as well. Can you interview Knox, Thorne and Leonor?"

Dario nodded. "No problem. Can you give me your phone number?" He kept his voice casual. "In case I need to reach you?"

Felicity hesitated only a second before reaching into her bag. She pulled out a business card and wrote her cell number on the back, then slid it across the table toward him. "The main office line is on there as well, in case you need Adeline."

"Great." He quickly memorized her number, then put the card into his wallet. "Now, what about my badge?"

"Your badge?" Felicity frowned, her confusion plain.

Dario couldn't contain his grin. "Don't you need to deputize me or something?"

She nodded thoughtfully. "Of course. How could I forget?" She stood abruptly and grabbed her purse, then walked away from the table.

Dario sat there in shock, unsure of what was happening. He'd only meant to tease her; had he somehow overstepped his bounds and offended her? Was she headed back to the office to explain to Adeline how she couldn't work with him?

He needn't have worried. Felicity returned a moment later and tossed him something. "Here you go."

He caught it reflexively, then examined the object. It was a shiny gold plastic star stamped with the word *sheriff.* She must have gotten it out of the coin-operated toy dispensers located by the entrance to the café. Dario stared at it for a second, hardly believing his eyes. The gesture was so unexpected he wasn't sure how to respond, but after a second his laughter took over. It seemed the straitlaced former marine had a sense of humor, after all...

"I trust that's sufficient?" There was a spark of mischief in her eyes he'd never seen before, and Dario felt an answering flare of heat in his belly. He liked seeing this side of Felicity.

He sniffed, pretending to consider it. "I think I can work with this."

"I'm glad to hear it." She studied him over the top of her water glass. "Do you think you can get in touch with your group of Colton siblings today?"

He nodded, appreciating her sense of urgency. This was a big case, and the sooner they made progress, the better. "I'll start calling after we're done here."

"Excellent." Felicity glanced around and gestured to the waitress for their check. Apparently, she didn't want to linger. He shoved the last bite of his cheeseburger into his mouth and lifted his hip to pull out his wallet. It seemed their lunch was over.

Time to get to work.

One hour later, Dario parked in the driveway of Thorne Colton's home and killed the ignition. The house was a pretty ranch-style rambler with lots of exposed wood and a large front porch. Rocking chairs and a porch swing swayed gently in the breeze, adding to the picture of domesticity.

He climbed out of the car, his boots crunching on the crushed gravel of the driveway. He heard the distant sound of horses neighing, the noise carrying easily in the cold winter air. He knew from the drive in that Thorne's house was tucked away from the barn and other ranch structures, but he spied a paddock about fifty yards away where a beautiful palomino horse grazed peacefully as a smaller bay horse frolicked around. *Mother and foal?* he wondered as he climbed the porch stairs.

Dario pressed the doorbell, and a loud squeal sounded from inside the house. *What the—?*

A series of loud thumps sounded, accompanied by the murmur of a deep voice. After a few seconds, the door opened to reveal a tall, dark-haired man and a small, bright-eyed baby sporting a onesie that read Mommy's Little Cowboy.

"You must be Dario Ortega."

"That's me. Nice to meet you." He extended his hand, and Thorne reached for him.

The baby, sensing his father's distraction, chose that moment to make a break for the freedom of the outside world. He lunged forward, arching his back and angling his body away from his father's chest. Thorne made a grab for the child, but the little one was slippery, and his eyes filled with horror as he lost his grip on the baby...

Without stopping to think, Dario stepped forward and scooped up the child before he wriggled free of his father's arms. "Hey there, little man," he said calmly.

The child blinked at him, apparently stunned at this sudden change of circumstances. He studied Dario warily, glancing to his father for reassurance. Not wanting to scare the little boy, Dario stepped inside the house and handed him over to Thorne.

"Thanks," Thorne said. He looked at the boy in his arms. "Way to knock a few years off my life, Joseph."

The baby cooed, grinning at this pronouncement. He wriggled his legs, and Thorne tightened his grip on his offspring. "Come on in," Thorne called over his shoulder as he carried the baby down the hall, headed for the warm glow of the room beyond.

Dario followed at a slightly slower pace, feeling a little self-conscious. The house was warm and cozy, and the hallway was lined with what appeared to be pictures of family: he recognized the sheriff Knox Colton in a few of them, along with Thorne and his wife. He stepped into the living room to find Thorne sitting on the floor, stacking blocks with his little boy.

"Have a seat," Thorne said. "Sorry it's a little chaotic here today. Maggie's gone to the grocery store, and Joseph just woke up from his nap, so he's got a ton of energy to burn."

"It's no problem." Dario lowered himself to the couch and watched the two of them play, trying to reconcile what he knew about Thorne with the man sitting in front of him. Thorne Colton had a reputation as a quiet, reserved man, and yet here he was, laughing and playing with his son as if he didn't have a care in the world.

"You're Natalia Ortega's son, right?" Thorne glanced at him curiously. "The equine vet?"

Dario nodded. "That's my mom," he confirmed.

"She's taken care of some of our animals before. Excellent vet. You have her eyes."

"Thanks," he said. It wasn't the kind of observation he'd expected Thorne Colton to make, but he was pleased to know the man was impressed with his mother's skills.

Thorne must have recognized his surprise. "Sorry. Before Joseph came along, I never would have commented on your resemblance. Lack of sleep has removed my normal filter." He shook his head, then reached out to muss the little boy's hair. "A lot has changed."

"I imagine so." And that was the biggest reason Dario didn't want to settle down and have kids. Life after children was never the same, and he liked things the way they were now. He had the freedom to do what he wanted, when he wanted, with no one to answer to or consider. It was nice to be able to pick up at a moment's notice, and a wife and kids just seemed like an anchor that would hold him down.

Thorne seemed to be enjoying fatherhood, but despite the cozy picture he and his son made, Dario wasn't convinced this was the life for him.

"Are you sure this is a good time to talk?" Joseph had scrunched up his face and was emitting a soft whine.

Thorne picked him up and set him down a few steps away, next to a pile of picture books. "I'd hate for you to waste a trip," Thorne said, grabbing one off the stack and holding it open. Joseph began to pat the thick cardboard pages with his chubby hand, jabbering happily as Thorne flipped through the book.

"Well, as I said on the phone, I'm helping Felicity Grant investigate the Colton, Incorporated, hacking case. We're trying to unmask the leader of the group, and there's a very good chance it's someone known to the Colton family. Probably someone who harbors ill will toward your family, maybe feels like they've been wronged in some way and is looking to exact revenge. Can you think of anyone who fits that description?"

Thorne snorted, and his breath ruffled his son's fine brown hair. Joseph shivered, and Dario couldn't help but smile. He really was a cute kid, even though he never seemed to stop moving for very long.

"You know who my mother is, don't you?" Thorne's tone was heavy with sarcasm, and Dario nodded, smiling ruefully.

"I'm familiar with her reputation," he said carefully. He didn't want to start off on the wrong foot by offending Thorne. Livia Colton was a bona fide psychopath, and it sounded like there was no love lost between them. But she was still Thorne's mother, and that wasn't a bond that was easily broken.

"It would take days to tell you about all the people she hurt. Not only the victims of her crimes, but her former business partners who have an ax to grind."

"I take it she cheated them?"

Joseph waved his hands, grabbing a rattle his father held. He shoved it into his mouth and began to chew enthusiastically. Thorne smiled absently at his son.

"Livia is a user. She preys on people, identifying their weak spots and taking advantage of them. She has no conscience, no remorse at all. And no sense of loyalty. She gets what she wants from someone and then cuts them loose, no matter the cost."

"It sounds like she has a lot of enemies."

"That's putting it mildly," Thorne said.

Joseph squealed as if in punctuation, and even Dario had to smile at the child's evident joy.

"Can you think of anyone in particular whose anger toward Livia might extend beyond her? Someone who might choose to target the Colton family since Livia is now in hiding?"

Thorne's expression turned thoughtful. "I might be able to give you some names," he said after a moment. "But to be honest, I didn't really stay up to date on all of Livia's dirty laundry." He shook his head. "I tried to keep her out of my life as much as possible."

A low rumble sounded through the room. Joseph's eyes widened. Thorne stood and picked up the baby. "My wife is home," he called, heading for the other room. "Come on back and we can keep talking."

Dario followed the man and boy into the kitchen to find the baby staring at the door that presumably led to the garage. After a moment, the door opened to admit a pretty blonde woman, her arms laden with bags.

Joseph let out a squeal and lurched forward, clearly seeking his mother's arms. Thorne walked over and handed her the baby before giving her a smacking kiss, collecting the bags from her in one smooth motion. "Welcome back," he said.

The little boy pressed his face to his mother's cheek, clearly thrilled to be with her again.

Something flipped inside Dario's chest at the sight of this little family, so in love with one another. They were obviously a team, and he had no doubt that whatever life brought them, they would all face it together. Perhaps there was something to be said for that...

"Oh! Hello. I didn't see you." Thorne's wife offered Dario a smile. If she was bothered to see a stranger in her kitchen, she didn't show it.

Thorne made the introductions. "Maggie, this is Dario Ortega. He's working on the Colton hacking case. Dario, this is my wife, Maggie."

She balanced Joseph on her hip and extended her hand, which Dario shook. "Nice to meet you," he said.

"Likewise."

Thorne placed the bags on the kitchen counter and began unpacking them. Dario watched as he pulled out box after box of what looked like sugar cookies. "Um, babe?" Thorne frowned in confusion. "What's all this?"

"Cookies," she said, her tone making it clear that this should be perfectly obvious.

"I can see that," Thorne said. "But why did you buy all these?"

"For the cookie decorating tomorrow," she explained. She rifled one-handed through another bag, withdrawing tubes of icing and containers of brightly colored sugar sprinkles.

"I thought you were going to bake them," Thorne said.

Dario inwardly cringed, immediately recognizing Thorne's mistake. *Oh boy...*

Maggie leveled a stare at her husband, and to his credit, Thorne blushed.

"Sweetheart," she began, her tone saccharine sweet. "Do I look like I have time to bake six dozen sugar cookies?"

Thorne immediately shook his head. "Of course not. This is perfect. I only asked because I was looking forward to the house smelling so good."

Maggie reached into another bag and plunked a candle on the counter. Dario smiled to himself as he read the label: Sugar Cookie Wonderland.

"Knock yourself out, honey."

Thorne laughed and leaned over to kiss her cheek. "I see you thought of everything. As always."

Maggie shook her head, smiling wryly. "Flatterer." She glanced at Dario. "So you're working on the Colton, Incorporated, case? Are you with the police?"

"No. I'm consulting with Adeline Kincaid—one of her investigators is trying to track down the leader of the hacking group, and since I have some computer forensics expertise I volunteered to assist while I'm in town."

"Have you found any leads yet?" Maggie extracted her necklace from Joseph's chubby grip and grabbed a bottle from the fridge.

Surprising himself, Dario reached out and took the bottle from Maggie's hand. He quickly stuck it in the microwave, then aimed a questioning look at Maggie. She told him the correct time, and he punched the buttons for her. "Thanks," she said.

"No problem."

The microwave dinged, and Dario retrieved the bottle. Maggie tested the formula, then began to feed the baby. Dario watched them for a moment, then returned his attention to Maggie's question. "It's a tough case," he said. "My brother, Emiliano, is an agent on the FBI's cyber-crime team. They're working on it as well, but so far, there haven't been any credible leads. That's why I'm here— I was hoping your husband might know of anyone who would want to hurt the family."

"How much time do you have?" Maggie said sarcastically.

"That's what I told him," Thorne said, folding the empty paper bags flat.

"I'm beginning to think this avenue isn't going to be as helpful as I'd hoped," Dario admitted. He'd thought the Colton siblings could help narrow down the search for Sulla, but if the family really had that many enemies, it would take forever to comb through all the potential suspects.

"Have you talked to anyone else?"

Dario shook his head. "Not yet. I'm supposed to interview Knox and Leonor, and my partner is going to talk to River, Jade and Claudia. I was hoping to get in touch with Knox this afternoon."

"Why don't you just come over tomorrow for the cookie decorating?" Maggie suggested. "Everyone will be here— it's a Colton holiday tradition. Bring your partner, too. What's his name?"

"Her name is Felicity. And are you sure about this? I don't want to intrude on a family event." He glanced at Thorne, but the other man nodded.

"Absolutely," Thorne said. "It'll save you from having to track everyone down one by one. And it'll give me more time to come up with a list of names for you, as well."

"That would be great," Dario said. "If you really don't mind us crashing the party."

"Not at all," Maggie assured him. "The more, the merrier."

"I'll talk to my brothers and sisters and let them know what kind of information you're looking for," Thorne said. "That way, they can be thinking about it before tomorrow's event."

"I really appreciate that," Dario said. "It's a huge help."

Joseph wriggled his legs, and Maggie shifted the baby in her arms, readjusting the angle of the bottle as she moved.

"I'll get out of your way now," Dario said. "Can we bring anything to tomorrow's gathering?"

"Just yourselves," Maggie said. "Thorne is going to grill some burgers and hot dogs, and we'll spend a few hours eating and decorating cookies."

"You're going to grill?" Dario couldn't keep the surprise out of his voice. "I thought we have a chance of snow tomorrow."

"We do," Maggie confirmed. "And to any sane person, that would be reason enough to cook inside."

Thorne scoffed. "I'm not going to let a few snowflakes keep me away from Bessie."

Dario shot Maggie a questioning look. "He named his grill," she said, her expression one of long-suffering patience.

"Of course I did," Thorne said. "It's only right. We spend so much time together."

Maggie grinned and rolled her eyes, and Dario chuckled. "Sounds fair to me," he said. "What time should we come tomorrow?"

"The gang will start getting here around noon," Maggie said. "Food should be ready between twelve thirty and one. Come by around then so you can eat before we start working on the cookies."

"Yes, ma'am." Recognizing an order when he heard it, Dario nodded. "Looking forward to it."

Chapter 4

"I can't believe we're doing this."

Dario glanced at Felicity before returning his focus to the road. "What's the matter?"

Felicity shifted in the passenger seat, struggling to find the words to explain her discomfort. "It seems wrong to intrude on their family event. Especially since we don't really know any of them on a personal level." She'd spoken to River and his wife, Edith, yesterday, and she'd liked them. River was also a veteran of the Marine Corps, and even though they had served in different units, they still had quite a bit in common. It had been nice to talk to a veteran her own age; she knew Mr. Perkins had offered to lend an ear if she needed it, but she had a hard time thinking of him as anything other than her high school teacher. River appeared to be adjusting to civilian life well, despite the loss of one eye. Perhaps once this investigation was over, she could talk to him about her worries and learn how he had dealt with his own…

"For what it's worth, I tried to refuse the invitation," Dario said. "But Thorne and Maggie insisted we come. If the rest of the family is anything like them, I think they'll be quite friendly and welcoming."

Felicity frowned. "I just hate to interrupt their celebrations with questions about the case. I'm sure the last thing they want to talk about is Livia Colton's enemies."

"It'll be fine," he said. "They don't seem like the type to stay gloomy for long."

Felicity envied his confidence. Hopefully, he was right. She'd feel terrible if they ruined the Coltons' holiday celebration.

Silence descended in the car. Felicity searched for something to say, wanting to make conversation. It would be easier to work on the case with Dario if she knew a bit more about him. But she had to be careful—she'd made it very clear she wasn't interested in any romantic involvement, and she didn't want to give him the wrong idea.

"How are your cookie decorating skills?"

He chuckled. "Rusty. I haven't decorated a cookie since I was a kid. I'm really good at eating them, though."

"Something tells me that won't be a problem," Felicity said.

"Probably not," he replied. "What about you? Did your family have any Christmas traditions?"

"We had a baking day," she said. "The second Saturday of December, my mom and I would spend the whole day baking cookies and breads. We'd box them all up and deliver them to the neighbors, and my dad would take some to his coworkers."

"That sounds like fun."

"It was." She hadn't thought about baking day in a while, and the memories made her smile. The tradition had fallen off after she'd joined the Marines. She hadn't always been able to get leave over the Christmas holidays, and when she had been home, she'd been more interested in sleeping and catching up with friends than baking. A pang of sadness speared her chest at the thought of the missed time with her mother. Maybe they could bake a few things together this year and recapture some of that holiday magic. It was exactly the kind of tradition she'd like to pass on to her own children someday.

Felicity made a mental note to call her parents later. "Your turn," she said, resuming the conversation. "Tell me about the Ortega family Christmas."

Dario glanced at her, a glint of surprise in his eyes as if he hadn't expected her to show interest in his life. "Well, we didn't have anything quite so formal. My parents often had to work over the holidays, since sick animals don't care about what day it is. When my brother and I were really small, one of my parents would make sure to stay home if the other had a call. But once Emiliano and I got a bit older, the whole family would go. I remember a few Christmases spent in a barn while my mom treated a sick horse or helped a mare foal. Once that was done, we'd return home and pick up the celebrations where we'd left off."

"Sounds like you guys made the best of things," Felicity said.

He nodded. "We did. All I can say is thank God for the microwave—it saved us from a cold dinner more times than I can count."

"I can imagine."

He pulled up in front of a nice-looking ranch house and angled the car onto a strip of the gravel drive. A handful of other cars were already parked, which meant the party was likely already under way.

Dario glanced at her, one eyebrow lifted in inquiry. "Ready?"

Felicity took a deep breath and nodded. Her heart was already pounding at the thought of being in a crowd, but she pushed back against her mounting anxiety. There were no insurgents hiding in this family gathering. Just like at the engagement party, these people were gathered to celebrate, and there was no traitor hell-bent on destruction in their midst.

Dario waited for her by the car, and he placed his hand on her lower back to escort her up the stairs onto the porch.

His touch was light, more a sign of good manners than anything else. Still, Felicity had to admit she liked having his hand on her. It gave her something to focus on, a distraction from her irrational fears. She leaned back a little as they waited for someone to answer the door, subtly increasing the contact between them. She glanced at Dario's face, expecting to see a flash of smug satisfaction in his eyes. But if Dario noticed what she was doing, he didn't show it.

She could hear the din of conversation and laughter even through the closed door, and she relaxed a tiny bit. *This is what normal life is like*, she reminded herself. It was something she had taken for granted once. Not anymore.

The door opened, and a pretty, curvy blonde woman smiled at them. "Dario! So glad you could make it!" She stepped forward and lightly kissed his cheek, then turned to Felicity. "And you must be Felicity. I'm Maggie Colton. Please come inside."

"Thank you for including us today," Felicity said, stepping across the threshold. The house was warm and smelled deliciously of cookies. Felicity was immediately transported back to the kitchen with her mother, the pair of them laughing and talking as they worked. "It smells amazing in here," she said. "Have you been baking all morning?"

Maggie's blue eyes sparkled. "Yes," she said with a nod. "Something like that." She winked at Dario, who smiled and ducked his head at what was clearly a private joke.

Interesting, Felicity thought. It seemed her initial assessment of Dario was correct; the man was a born charmer, and apparently even married women weren't immune to his charisma.

Oddly enough, this realization made her soften toward him. When she'd first met him, she'd assumed Dario's carefree, flirtatious attitude had been an act designed to manipulate people into giving him what he wanted. Now she saw that wasn't the case. He had the type of personality that drew people in, made them want to get closer. It was an effect she'd been fighting for the past few days, and for the first time, she began to wonder if her resistance was worth the effort.

"The gang's all here," Maggie said. "Thorne is just about to put the burgers and hot dogs on the grill."

"He's grilling in this weather?" Felicity said, incredulous. "Doesn't he know it's snowing?" The flurries had started on the drive in, and the week had been cold enough that the flakes were probably going to stick. It made for picture-perfect holiday weather, but it wasn't ideal for cooking outdoors.

Maggie rolled her eyes and smiled. "He sees the snow as a challenge rather than a sign to stay inside. I've given up trying to talk sense into him—I figure if he wants to freeze, then who am I to stop him?"

Felicity and Dario both laughed and Maggie led them down the entry hall into a large living room. All the Colton siblings were there; Felicity recognized River and his wife, Edith, and Knox, the sheriff of Shadow Creek. She spied Jade in the corner talking with a tall, striking redhead and a petite blonde woman. *Those must be her sisters*, she thought.

Maggie waved to get the group's attention. "Hey, everyone! Our guests have arrived!" She made the introductions and Felicity committed the names of the Colton siblings and their spouses to memory as she was guided around the room. She'd been right; the tall redhead was Leonor, and the other blonde woman was Claudia Colton. A moment later, Thorne popped his head into the room and waved.

"Good to see you again," he said to Dario, passing a baby off to Maggie. "And nice to meet you, Felicity."

Everyone was welcoming and Felicity soon found herself holding a mug of hot cider. Dario was pulled aside by Josh Howard, Leonor's husband, and Felicity drifted into the corner where she could watch the group. A young boy streaked through the room.

"Cody!" Both Knox and his wife, Allison, called out at the same time. "No running in the house," continued Knox.

The boy stopped, but Felicity could tell by the way his frame practically vibrated with energy that it wouldn't be long before he needed another reminder.

"Dad, it's snowing! Can I go outside and play?"

Knox and Allison exchanged a look, and Knox made to stand. "It's my turn," he said to his wife. "You stay warm."

"Both of you stay warm," Thorne instructed. He carried a plate of hamburger patties and hot dogs in one hand and a set of tools in the other. "I'll keep an eye on him."

Cody darted after his uncle. "Put your coat on," Allison called after him.

The baby Maggie was holding spied Dario, and his little face lit up. He stretched his arms out, clearly seeking Dario's hold.

Dario glanced down and grinned. "Hey there, Joseph." To Felicity's shock, he picked up the boy, settling him easily on his hip.

Maggie laughed. "Oh my. You made quite the impression yesterday," she said.

Dario laughed. "It's always good to have a friend."

"It's time for his bottle. Would you mind feeding him?" Maggie asked.

"I'd be happy to," Dario said easily.

Maggie stepped into the kitchen and returned a moment later with a bottle. "Let me know when you get tired of him," she said.

"No worries," Dario said. "Joseph and I will be just fine." He found a seat and settled the baby in his arms, then set about feeding him.

Felicity couldn't tear her gaze away from the sight. Dario hadn't struck her as the type of man to be interested in kids, but he looked like a natural sitting there with a squirming infant in his arms.

Something shifted inside her chest as she watched him interact with the baby. Dario patiently watched Joseph as he ate. The baby gulped audibly as he drank from the bottle and he hummed, clearly enjoying his meal. Dario smiled down at him, his expression one of genuine affection. Who was this man? He certainly didn't look like a carefree playboy now. Clearly, there was more to him than met the eye, and Felicity felt a pang of guilt at her assumption he was a one-dimensional flirt who was only interested in the next good time.

"Good to see you again." The quiet words interrupted her thoughts, and Felicity reluctantly looked away from Dario to find River Colton standing next to her.

She quickly took a sip of her cider, hoping to cover her interest in Dario. "It was so nice of your family to invite us," she said.

River glanced around the room at his siblings and their partners. The soft buzz of conversation filled the air, punctuated by the occasional laugh. It was a cozy, familial sound, the kind of noise Felicity wanted in her own home one day. "It's nice to have friends around, too," River said.

He turned back to study her, and Felicity tried not to fidget under his gaze. "You're doing really well," he said softly.

"I'm not so sure," she murmured.

"No, you are," he insisted. "It took me a long time to adjust to standing in a group of people. I got nervous being around my own family, it was that bad. You look great, though."

Felicity laughed softly. "Looks can be deceiving. I feel pretty wobbly inside."

"That will pass," he said confidently. "I know it doesn't feel that way now, but you will adjust." He lifted his arm as Edith walked over, and she snugged against his side. Felicity smiled, hoping it hid the weight of envy that settled on her shoulders as she saw the love shared by River and his wife. She wanted that someday—the closeness with someone, the sense of safety and belonging. Of feeling understood and accepted, flaws and all. She thought she'd had that once, but she'd been wrong and the memory of it still stung.

Edith gently poked River in the ribs. "Babe, would you mind getting me a cup of cider?"

"Not at all," he said, releasing her at once. He headed into the kitchen and Edith leaned closer to Felicity. "Are you okay?" Her brown eyes were full of compassion and understanding, as if she knew exactly what Felicity was feeling right now. And she probably did, since she'd had a front-row seat as River had adjusted to civilian life.

"I'm good, thanks."

Edith nodded. "Yeah, I've heard that line before." Felicity knew the other woman had seen through her social lie, but there was no accusation in Edith's tone. Just a matter-of-fact acknowledgment that Felicity appreciated. She got the sense that if she wanted to talk, Edith would listen.

"He's lucky to have you," she said.

Edith laughed and shook her head. "I'm lucky to have him," she corrected. "Or I guess you could say it's a good thing we found each other."

"I'm sure you helped him adjust to life after the war," Felicity said.

Edith tilted her head to the side, her expression turning thoughtful. "Yes. We've been good for each other." She glanced at Felicity's face and added, "You'll find that, too. The right man is out there."

"I'm not so sure," Felicity admitted. "I thought I'd found him once, but that wasn't the case."

"What happened?"

"We were high school sweethearts. We had big plans—marriage, kids, the whole nine yards. But then I joined the Marines, and he couldn't handle it. He had his reasons and didn't want to talk about it. So he dumped me the night before I shipped off to basic training." Felicity shook her head at the memory. Even twelve years later, the pain of his rejection still made her heart ache.

"I'm so sorry," Edith said. She gently touched Felicity's arm in sympathy.

Felicity shrugged. "It is what it is. Probably better things turned out the way they did. If our relationship wasn't strong enough to withstand my service, he wasn't the right guy, after all."

"That's true, but I'm sure that thought was cold comfort to you at the time."

"Yeah. It took me a while, but I've moved on."

"That's good," Edith said. "Are you seeing anyone now?"

"Ah, no," Felicity replied. She took a sip of cider, her eyes darting back to Dario. He still held Joseph, and now he was reading the boy a book. Her heart fluttered in her chest and she felt her resistance to him melt even more.

Did he know the effect he was having on her? Surely not. He couldn't be that calculating—he didn't seem like the kind of man to use a child as a prop to get into a woman's good graces. He looked far too genuinely interested in the boy for that.

"Something tells me you could be dating someone if you wanted," Edith said cryptically.

Felicity returned her focus to the other woman. "What do you mean?"

Edith's lips curved in a knowing smile. "You two

haven't stopped watching each other since you walked in here. Dario's doing well with Joesph, but he's been sneaking glances over at you when you've been distracted. And you've been doing the same to him. It's clear you're interested in him, and he returns it."

"Really?" Felicity felt equal parts dismay over being so transparent and giddy at the thought of Dario wanting her. When he'd approached her at Emiliano's engagement party, she'd figured he was just looking to flirt with a pretty face. But if his interest ran deeper than that, if he truly wanted to get to know her…the possibility made her feel warm inside.

"All I'm saying is that if you're feeling lonely, I don't think you need to stay that way. Unless that's what you truly want."

Felicity glanced at Dario again, her mind whirring as she considered Edith's point. Would it be so bad to go out with him once or twice? Adeline had said none of Dario's girlfriends had a bad word to say about him. Maybe he would be a good choice to reintroduce her to the dating scene, help her get her feet wet again. After years of being single, didn't she deserve to have a little fun?

At that moment, Thorne walked in the back door on a gust of cold wind, Cody hot on his heels. They both had snow in their hair and sported broad grins, and it was clear they'd had fun playing outside. "Food's up," Thorne called, carrying a plate of steaming hamburger patties and hot dogs into the kitchen. People began to drift into the other room, headed for the promise of warm food.

At the sound of his father's voice, little Joseph began to wriggle in earnest. Maggie retrieved her son with a smile, and Dario watched them go, then walked over to Edith and Felicity.

"Looks like you've been forgotten," Felicity said, her heart rate jumping at his nearness.

"That's okay," Dario said. "I think he was getting bored with me anyway."

"Kids can be rather fickle," Edith said. "But you made a great babysitter."

"Thanks." Dario grinned and glanced at Joseph again. The boy was now in Thorne's arms, his head against his father's chest. "He's an easy kid to get along with."

River joined them then and handed Edith a cup of cider. "Sorry it took me so long," he said. "I got caught up talking to Maggie in the kitchen."

"It's okay," Edith said. She turned to Felicity and Dario. "Are you guys hungry? We should get in there before it's gone."

River put his arm around Edith's shoulders, and the pair of them started for the kitchen.

Dario glanced at Felicity and tilted his head. "After you," he said gallantly. He gestured for her to precede him and fell in about a half step behind her. As they walked, his hand came to rest on the small of her back, and Felicity smiled.

He really needed to stop watching her.

Dario forced his gaze off Felicity and back onto the sugar cookies on the plate in front of him. Maggie had distributed the cookies after everyone had finished lunch, and Thorne had set up tubes of icing, bowls of sprinkles and dishes of small, pressed sugar pieces for use in decorating the treats. The entire Colton clan were gathered around the large farmhouse table, chatting over the soft din of Christmas carols drifting in from the stereo in the living room.

Fat snowflakes dropped lazily from the gray sky, completing the festive scene. It was exactly the kind of cozy, domestic setting that normally had him searching for the nearest exit, but today Dario found himself relaxing and enjoying the company.

It didn't hurt that Felicity sat across from him, her cheeks flushed from the warmth of the room and her hot apple cider. When they'd first arrived she had seemed a bit nervous. He'd meant to stay by her side until she felt more comfortable, but Joseph had claimed his attention and he'd had to leave her. Fortunately, River and his wife, Edith, had picked up the slack, and it hadn't taken long for Felicity to start smiling and chatting with the Coltons.

She sat between River and Edith now, and Dario was happy to see she appeared to be enjoying herself. She'd taken an instant liking to River Colton, a fact that had triggered a quick burst of irrational jealousy in his chest. Dario had squashed it immediately, knowing he was being ridiculous. It was only natural Felicity would feel comfortable around River, since they were both Marine Corps veterans who had been to war. They had the bond of shared experiences, something Dario would never be able to understand. The realization left him feeling a bit bereft in a way he couldn't fully explain. He had no desire to go to war, but there was a part of him that was sad to know he'd never be able to fully connect with Felicity on some levels. It was as if a piece of her was locked away, and he'd never be able to find the key.

Dario shook his head, dismissing the maudlin thoughts. It didn't matter anyway—Felicity had made it clear she had no interest in seeing him outside of a professional setting, so he had no reason to worry about how his lack of military experience would affect his ability to understand her.

But despite knowing they didn't have a future, Dario couldn't stop looking at Felicity.

Heaven help him, but he enjoyed watching her smile and the graceful movements of her hands as she worked to decorate her set of cookies. She was so beautiful, with a few tendrils of dark brown hair framing her face. She leaned forward, absorbed in her task, and he saw a flash of white as she gently bit her bottom lip in concentration. The sight hit him like a punch to the gut, and his stomach flip-flopped as he wondered if she'd apply that same focus to other, more pleasurable pursuits.

He slammed the door on the burgeoning fantasy and shoved back from the table a bit more forcefully than he'd intended. Everyone turned to look at him, and he felt his face heat. "Ah, I was just going to grab a glass of water. Can I bring anything back?"

There was a chorus of "No, thanks" and "Not right now." Dario nodded and walked into the kitchen, putting some much-needed space between him and Felicity.

He leaned against the counter and took a deep breath, then glanced around at the cupboards, trying to decide which one might hold glasses.

"Upper left," said Thorne as he walked into the room.

Dario followed his directions and retrieved a glass. "Thanks," he said, crossing to the sink to turn on the tap.

"No problem." Thorne leaned a hip against the counter and studied Dario as he took a sip of water. "Everything okay?"

Dario nodded. "Yep. Just got thirsty."

"Does she know?"

Dario glanced down, pretending not to understand. "Does who know what?"

Thorne merely tilted his head to the side and Dario sighed. "She knows I'm interested. She's not."

"I'm sorry, man. That's rough."

Dario shrugged. "It's not the first time I've been turned down." But for some reason, Felicity's rejection had stung. When other women had brushed off his attentions, Dario had moved on without a second thought. But Felicity's appeal went beyond the physical, and her refusal to give him a chance made him feel like he was missing out on something special.

"Is that why you volunteered to help with the case? Are you hoping to change her mind?"

"That's not the only reason," Dario said, sounding defensive even to his own ears.

Thorne held up a hand. "No judgment here. I might have something to help you get into her good graces." He stuck his hand in his pocket and withdrew a folded piece of paper. "I asked everyone to think of people who might have a grudge against us because someone in our family somehow did them wrong. Here's what we came up with." He passed the paper over and Dario unfolded it, surprised at the number of names on the list.

"I can't promise your guy is on there," Thorne said. "But for what it's worth, I hope this helps."

"This is fantastic," Dario said, scanning the paper before folding it and tucking it into his own pocket. His fingers tingled with the urge to touch a keyboard, and he couldn't wait to get back to his computer so he could start digging into the collection of potential suspects. If one of these people was Sulla, it wouldn't take him long to make the connection.

"I'm glad to hear that." Thorne clapped him on the shoulder as he walked past. "Now that you got what you came here for, are you going to leave right away, or can I convince you to stay and finish decorating your set of cookies? You know how hard Maggie worked baking everything."

Dario laughed and nodded. "I wouldn't want to upset the lady of the house."

"Smart man," Thorne commented. "With an attitude like that, I'd say you're ready for marriage."

"I don't know about that," Dario said. The thought of binding himself to one woman for the rest of his life usually triggered an automatic rejection in Dario's mind, but not this time. Having seen how happy Thorne was with his wife and child, and witnessing the other Coltons with their spouses, Dario had to admit the idea of marriage might not be as bad as he'd previously assumed. None of the Coltons appeared unsatisfied or unfulfilled. In fact, it was just the opposite. They all seemed quite happy. Just like his parents. Or Emiliano and Marie, for that matter.

He followed Thorne back into the dining room and sat across from Felicity once more. She glanced up and smiled at him, her eyebrows drawn together slightly in a silent question. Dario nodded, and her shoulders relaxed.

"That's a nice snowman you've got there," he said, indicating the cookie she was working on.

His comment drew the attention of the rest of the family, and a chorus of "oohs" and "aahs" broke out as everyone caught a glimpse of the finely detailed winter scene Felicity had created.

She blushed, but he could tell by the look in her eyes she was pleased people liked her work. "Thanks," she said quietly.

Cody craned his neck to see what all the fuss was about. "That's so cool!" He climbed out of his chair and walked over to stand next to Felicity for a better look. "You're really good at this. Can you draw an octopus and a shark on one for me?"

Felicity looked a bit taken aback by the boy's request and Knox chuckled softly. "That's a lot to fit on one cookie," he said to his son. He turned to Felicity and said, "He's really into all things oceanic right now."

Felicity nodded. "There's a lot of cool things in the ocean. How about I put an octopus on one cookie and a shark on the other?"

"Okay!"

"Here, buddy." River stood and gestured to his chair. "Take my seat so you can watch the master work without crowding her."

"Thanks, Uncle River." Cody climbed onto the chair

and leaned forward, elbows on the table, getting as close to Felicity as he could without actually crawling into her lap. She reached out to grab a fresh cookie, and Dario's chest tightened as he watched the two of them—woman and boy, one dark head and one light close together, the pair of them talking quietly to each other. Cody was rattling off facts about his favorite ocean creatures, and Felicity was asking him questions as she worked. It was clear she liked children, and for a brief, fantastical moment, Dario imagined what life would be like if he and Felicity had a baby together. What holiday traditions would they celebrate? Would their son be fascinated with the ocean like Cody, or would he be more interested in trains and cars? Either way, Dario knew Felicity would be a great mother. She seemed genuinely interested in what Cody had to say, and she tolerated his frequent interruptions with good grace and humor.

After a few seconds, Dario shook himself free of the spell he was under. It didn't matter that Felicity was good with kids, or that she had all the makings of a great mother. He didn't want to get tied down in a relationship, and children weren't in his master plan. He was all about enjoying life and the variety of beautiful women in the world. He needed to stop fixating on Felicity and start looking for someone else to have fun with. Someone who wouldn't make him question his choices and wonder about things that had no chance of happening.

No matter how intriguing they seemed…

Chapter 5

Felicity stared at her computer screen, reading the same sentence for the tenth time. It was hard to compose a response to Zane Colton's request for an update when her mind was occupied with thoughts of Dario.

He'd been strangely pensive on the drive back from the Coltons' yesterday. He'd seemed preoccupied, even, as if he'd been trying to work through a particularly knotty problem. After all her attempts at small talk had fizzled out, Felicity had stopped trying to make conversation and had embraced the silence. His lack of engagement hadn't bothered her—she understood the need for quiet while trying to think.

Had he been distracted by the case, or by something else? It was a question that still dogged her today and made her wonder just what was going on in his handsome head. The Colton siblings had given them a list of names yesterday, so now they had some leads to pursue. But was there something else bothering Dario?

She'd watched him yesterday, enjoying the sight of him with little Joseph. Dario had seemed to really like playing with the baby, but she hadn't missed the glint of surprise in his eyes every time Joseph turned to him or sought his attention. Was he currently rethinking his professed desire to remain footloose and fancy-free forever?

Doubt it, she thought with a snort. One afternoon with a cute infant probably wasn't enough to make Dario reconsider his enjoyment of serial monogamy. And why should it? Children were a huge responsibility, and while Felicity knew she'd like to have kids of her own someday, she wasn't ready to take that leap yet.

A rap on her office door broke through her musings, and Felicity looked up to find Edith Colton standing in the doorway.

Felicity rose from her chair. "Hi, Edith. What brings you in today?"

"I was in the area finishing up my holiday shopping, and I thought I'd stop in and say hello. Is this a bad time?"

"Not at all." Felicity waved her inside and gestured to the chair in front of her desk. "Please, sit down."

"Thanks." Edith plopped down and set her bags on the floor. "Every year I think I'm going to be more organized and get all the gifts bought early, and yet here I am on Christmas Eve, doing last-minute shopping."

Felicity laughed. "I can relate. I still need to find something for my parents." *And what about Dario?* The question popped into her head and Felicity froze. She had bought a little present for Adeline, but the two of them were more than just coworkers; they were friends. Still, she couldn't very well give Adeline something and not Dario. It seemed rude to ignore the fact that she and Dario had been spending so much time together lately, and she didn't want to exclude him from the office gift exchange later in the afternoon. She made a mental note to sneak out on her lunch break and search for a small token he might like. But what should she look for? She didn't have a lot of experience buying things for men, and Dario seemed like he already had everything.

"You okay?" Edith asked. "You have a funny look on your face."

Felicity swallowed. "I just realized Adeline and I are doing our gift exchange this afternoon before she leaves for the holiday. I didn't get anything for Dario, and I don't want him to feel left out."

"That's sweet of you," Edith said.

"Do you have any ideas? He always looks so polished and put together. I can't imagine there's anything he wants."

Edith considered the question for a moment. "I wouldn't try to get a personal gift, especially since you two don't know each other that well yet. There's a gourmet chocolate shop down the block. Why don't you get him some truffles? Everyone loves chocolate."

"That's a good idea," Felicity said. "I haven't seen him eat many sweets, though. He does drink a lot of coffee. He always seems to have a cup in his hand…"

"I was just in The French Press, that new coffee shop, and they have a lot of gifts on display," Edith said. "You'll probably find something there that will work."

"Perfect," Felicity said. "Thanks—you've saved me a lot of stress."

"No problem." Edith leaned forward, a spark of curiosity in her eyes. "Does this mean you're going to give him a shot?"

Felicity leaned back in her chair, wondering why everyone was suddenly so curious about her dating life. "I'm not sure yet. Why do you ask?"

"I think it would be a good distraction for you." Edith searched Felicity's face, her expression kind. "I hope you don't mind, but River told me some of the things you've been dealing with since you retired from the Corps. For what it's worth, he went through a lot of the same issues, too. It might be good for you to try something new, to take your mind off your worries."

"You might be right," Felicity murmured. She'd been thinking along those lines herself, and Edith's encouragement made her think it was probably the right thing to do.

At the very least, dating Dario would help her get out of her head and force her to interact with the world, rather than retreating to her lonely apartment every night.

Then another thought occurred to her, and Felicity's stomach twisted. "Say I do decide to go for it," she said. "How exactly do I approach him? I haven't been in a position to date anyone in years—I have no idea what to say!"

Edith shrugged. "In my experience, the direct approach is usually the most effective. And from what I know of you, I think it's probably your best option. You could invite him to a private holiday dinner or plan some other date. I don't think you'll have to worry about him saying no."

Felicity nodded, her mind whirring with possible activities. "Should I tell him right away that I just want to keep things casual?" Based on what he'd said to her before, she didn't think Dario was interested in anything serious or long-term. But would it kill the mood if she made it clear she felt the same way?

"It probably wouldn't hurt," Edith said. "But I wouldn't dwell on that. Kinda puts a damper on things, you know?" She winked mischievously, and Felicity had to laugh.

"Fair enough. Now I just have to work up my courage for the big ask."

Edith leaned forward. "That shouldn't be a problem. You're a marine. You have courage coming out your ears." She stood and gathered up her bags. "I've taken up enough of your time. I just want to say that I'm here for you if you ever want to talk. I know you and River have a connection, but if there's ever any girl stuff you don't want to say to him, I've got your back."

"Thank you." Felicity blinked against the sudden sting of tears. She stood and quickly rounded her desk, pulling Edith into a hug. "I really appreciate that. And I'm going to take you up on your offer."

"I hope so," Edith replied. "You've got to let me know

how it goes with Dario. I've got my fingers crossed for the two of you!"

Felicity smiled. "I think I'll have an update for you soon," she promised.

Edith left with a wave, and Felicity stayed in the middle of her office, considering her options. She glanced back at her computer, but she had no desire to finish composing her reply to Zane Colton at the moment. With her thoughts so centered on Dario, it was probably better for her to duck out and get his gift now. Once that was taken care of, she'd be able to focus on the case again.

Or so she hoped.

Dario tiptoed down the hall and retreated back into the relative safety of the temporary office Adeline had set up in the storage room just off the lobby. He'd accidentally overheard Felicity's conversation with Edith, and now his head was spinning. He needed quiet and privacy to think, and he didn't want Felicity to find him and think he'd been deliberately eavesdropping.

She liked him.

He'd suspected as much all along, but the confirmation made him smile. It was always gratifying to know a beautiful woman was interested in him, especially one as appealing as Felicity.

And he had to admit, he was pleased to know she also wanted to keep things casual. He'd done a lot of thinking after the Coltons' holiday gathering yesterday, and while he was no longer quite so against the idea of marriage and children, he knew those were milestones for a future time in his life.

From what he'd overheard, it sounded like Felicity was looking to ease back into the dating world. She must have had a bad experience, and for a brief second his heart ached for her. Her former boyfriend must have been a real jerk to turn her off of dating like that. Dario always took pains to make sure his relationships ended well, and he felt a spurt of disgust toward Felicity's unknown ex for not being as considerate.

Depending on how badly her former lover had hurt her, it might be quite a challenge to show Felicity that relationships didn't always mean emotional pain and regret. But Dario knew he was equal to the task. In fact, he relished the thought of being the man to show her how much fun dating could be.

He'd have to take things slow; that much was certain. Felicity was skittish, and he felt responsible for making sure they had a good time together. So as much as he wanted to walk into her office, gather her into his arms and kiss her soundly, he knew it was important to wait. To let her come to him.

And a little more than an hour later, she did.

"Have you got a minute?"

Dario glanced up and nodded. "Sure. Come on in."

Felicity stepped inside and sat down. She was still wearing her coat and scarf, and her cheeks were pink from the cold. "What's on your mind?" he asked.

"I was wondering if you'd made any progress on your half of the list of names the Coltons gave us." She began to unwind her scarf as she spoke, revealing the pale, slender column of her neck. Dario swallowed hard, his mind suddenly flooded with questions: Was the skin of her throat as soft as it looked? How would she respond if he kissed her just under the corner of her jaw?

She shrugged off her coat and his blood warmed. Even though there was nothing suggestive about her actions, Dario couldn't help but imagine her continuing to strip. He pictured her unbuttoning her jeans and peeling the fabric down those long legs. Lifting the hem of her sweater, exposing the skin of her belly, the curve of her ribs and the cups of her bra. And just what color was her bra? he wondered. A sensible white, or something more exciting, like red lace or black satin?

"Dario?" Her voice cut through his fantasy and he blinked, tuning back in to the conversation.

"Yes?"

She tilted her head to the side, her expression amused. "Are you okay? You seem a bit distracted."

There was a knowing glint in her eyes, and Dario realized his thoughts must have been more transparent than he'd realized. He felt his face heat and cleared his throat. "I'm fine. What was it you were saying?"

"I was asking if you'd made progress with your half of the names. I haven't been able to turn up much of anything. A couple of the people are dead, several have moved out of state and appear to have forgotten about the Coltons, and the rest don't seem to have the type of knowledge required to coordinate such a sophisticated cyberattack."

"They could always hire someone," he pointed out.

Felicity acknowledged his point with a nod. "True. I'm looking into what records I can, but so far I haven't found a smoking gun. Please tell me you've had more success."

"Maybe." Her expression brightened and he hastily amended, "I don't know for sure yet, but I've been hanging out on this forum that a lot of hackers frequent."

"Like an online coffee shop?"

"Something like that."

Felicity snorted. "I can't believe they'd be so brazen about discussing their actions. Sounds like a good way to get caught."

"Not exactly. The forum isn't on the regular web. It's part of the dark web, so most people don't even know it exists."

"The dark web?" Felicity sounded thoughtful. "Those sites are all heavily encrypted, right? And everyone uses throwaway names, so it's nearly impossible to connect a poster with a real person."

"Basically, yeah," Dario said, impressed at her knowledge. "That's why these guys aren't afraid to talk about what they've done. They feel protected by all the different layers of security set up, so they're a bit freer with their words."

"That makes sense. Do you think any of them are Principes?" she asked, referring to the term used for Cohort members.

"Almost certainly, but no one has admitted it yet."

"Have any of them bragged about participating in the Colton hack?" She sounded hopeful, and Dario wished he could say yes.

"No. At least, no one that I've found. I've been poking around a bit, asking the community if they know who was involved."

"Do you really think they'd tell you?" She wrinkled her nose. "These people are hyperparanoid about protecting their identities. I'd think they'd be suspicious of anyone asking questions like that."

"You'd be surprised," Dario replied. "Like you said, the users are very concerned with privacy. But mostly their own privacy. Most of them have no problem outing another user. It's a bit like the Wild West. And you're right—questions do tend to raise suspicions. But I'm a regular poster, and these people know me. I told them I'm interested in the details of the hack because I might have some work for whoever was responsible."

"Smart."

He smiled. "I'm glad you think so. Anyway, no one has responded to me on the message boards. But not too long ago, I received an email." He turned back to his computer monitor and, with a few quick keystrokes, pulled up the relevant message.

Felicity rose and moved to stand by his desk. She bent down to get a better look at the screen, and her breasts grazed the top of his shoulder. Dario caught his breath at the contact, wondering if she'd noticed. He risked a glance at her face, but she was so absorbed in reading his email she didn't seem to register the quick brush of her curves against him. Even though they weren't touching, he felt the warmth from her body and her scent filled his nose. She smelled faintly of coffee, and he fought the urge to lean over and bury his nose in her hair.

"Hmm." The sound she made was almost a purr, and he closed his eyes, letting it wash over him. It was exactly the kind of noise he enjoyed coaxing from women, and he wanted to hear it again under slightly different circumstances.

"What do you make of this?" Felicity straightened, putting distance between their bodies. Dario tried not to let his disappointment show. He glanced at the message, which was short and to the point: Look for ColtonQueen.

"To be honest, I think ColtonQueen is Livia Colton."

Felicity nodded slowly, her eyebrows drawn together. "Could be. Everyone knows she survived that accident. She's probably holed up somewhere, plotting revenge."

"If that's really the case, it makes sense she'd target Colton, Incorporated. What better way to get back at her family than to harm the company that bears their name?"

"Have you been able to find ColtonQueen user on your hacker forums?"

He shook his head. "Not yet. That's going to take a little more digging. Not everyone who is a member of the forum posts publicly."

"So it's possible ColtonQueen has seen your posts, and now she knows you're trying to find out more about her." Felicity looked down at him, her eyes bright with worry. "Have you just made yourself a target?"

"I don't think so." Dario stood and touched her arm in reassurance. "It's possible, but if Livia really is ColtonQueen, I'm betting she'll be flattered by my interest rather than angry. People like her have huge egos, and if she thinks I'm impressed by what she's done, she might contact me so she can brag about it."

"I hope you're right." Felicity still looked worried, and her concern set off a warm tingle in the center of his chest.

"Let's say it really is Livia Colton hiding behind a computer screen, or maybe someone working for her. What's the worst she could do to me?" He tried to sound casual, but he could tell by the look in Felicity's eyes she wasn't buying it.

"Lots," she said grimly. "You might want to do a quick search and get up to speed on her list of crimes. That woman is a true sociopath, and she won't hesitate to act if she feels threatened by you."

Dario studied her for a moment, surprised by the note of fear in her voice. Felicity didn't seem like the type of person to let her emotions rule her actions. "What are you saying? Do you think we should stop investigating this lead because of what Livia Colton might do? She might not even be aware of my inquiries in the first place."

"Of course I don't want you to stop," Felicity said, straightening her spine.

There she is, he thought with a mental smile. The Felicity he knew was back.

"I just want you to be aware of the potential dangers that you might face. Don't be careless, okay?"

Dario nodded, letting his smile show on his face. "I'll take every precaution," he said, stepping closer.

Felicity's eyes widened. "Good. That's, um, good to hear."

"It's sweet of you to worry about me." He reached up and tucked a stray strand of hair behind her ear.

Felicity swallowed hard, and Dario had the sudden urge to trace the line of her throat with the tip of his tongue. "You're doing me a huge favor by helping with the investigation," she stammered. "I'd hate to see you get hurt."

"Is that the only reason you care?" he murmured. His gaze zeroed in on her mouth, and he was rewarded by the sight of her tongue darting out to slick across her lips.

"Well, no," she admitted. "It's not the only reason."

That was all the invitation he needed. Dario dipped his head and captured her mouth with his own. Felicity gasped, and for a split second, he thought she was going to pull away.

But she didn't. She lifted her arms and threaded her hands through his hair, stepping closer to press her body against his. Her breasts flattened against his chest and he choked back a groan as his blood raced south.

He'd thought this would be a simple kiss, a getting-to-know-you gesture. A way for him to show her how good things could be between them. He'd meant to blow her mind and leave her wanting more.

But it was his world that got rocked. Felicity kissed him with a raw intensity that sent him reeling and left him aching for more. She burned hot and hungry, and he was only too happy to match her fervor.

Her hands left his hair, sliding down his back and then lower, anchoring their hips together. He slipped one hand between them, finding her breast. She moaned as he cupped her, her body rocking forward in wordless encouragement.

Dario's thoughts began to fragment as the intensity of his arousal grew. Flat surface. He needed to find something flat so they could get horizontal and then—

The jangle of bells and the slam of a door sliced through the moment, and Dario and Felicity both jumped at the unexpected racket.

"Adeline must be back from lunch," Felicity whispered. She began to hastily rearrange her clothes, and Dario didn't have the heart to tell her not to bother. Her lips were swollen and shiny and her skin flushed. She looked like a woman who had been thoroughly kissed, and no amount of smoothing and tucking was going to change that.

He ran his hands through his hair, feeling equal parts relieved and sorry that the kiss was over. The interruption had come just in time—a moment later, and they would have been on the floor, past the point of distraction. "Have dinner with me tonight."

Felicity glanced over, regret shining in her eyes. "I can't. My parents are flying out tonight for a Christmas cruise. I'm eating with them before I take them to the airport."

"What about tomorrow?" he pressed. He had to see her again, the sooner the better.

"I don't think anything will be open tomorrow. It's Christmas," she pointed out.

"Then come over for brunch at the Ortegas'."

Felicity shook her head. "Oh no. I can't possibly crash your family holiday gathering."

"I insist," he said gently. "You wouldn't be crashing. You'd be saving me from feeling like a fifth wheel." He grinned. "Besides, you can't be alone on Christmas."

"Do you really think it would be okay with your family?" she said doubtfully. "I don't want to impose."

"They'll be happy to have you join us."

She was quiet a moment, then nodded. "That sounds nice. Thank you." She turned and gathered up her coat, scarf and bag. "I'll, uh, I'll see you at the gift exchange later?"

"Sounds good."

Felicity nodded and stepped toward the door. "Hey," he

said. She paused and glanced back. Dario smiled at her. "I'm looking forward to seeing you again."

She smiled back, and his heart flipped over in his chest. "Me, too."

Chapter 6

Felicity rang the doorbell and ran her hand over her hair, then licked her lips as she waited for someone to answer the door. Her stomach churned with nervous excitement—she'd dreamed about Dario all night, and now she was going to see him again.

Yesterday's kiss had been...well, she was still searching for the words to describe it. *Amazing* didn't do it justice. Even now, just the thought of Dario's lips on hers sent zings of sensation through her limbs. She'd never experienced anything like it before, and the intensity of her reaction scared her a bit.

She hadn't expected Dario to kiss her yesterday. And she definitely hadn't expected her body to light up like a Christmas tree in response. But it was as if he'd unlocked the barrier she'd built to protect her heart, and twelve years of need and frustration had erupted inside her in a torrent that was impossible to ignore.

Truth be told, parts of yesterday's encounter were still a little fuzzy in her mind. As soon as Dario's mouth had met hers, her brain had short-circuited and lust had taken over, hijacking her body and taking control over her actions. She didn't know how long the kiss had lasted, or what, if anything, they'd said to each other. But she did know that if they hadn't been interrupted, that simple kiss would have turned into so much more.

It was a realization that both thrilled and scared her.

Her outsize response to Dario made it clear she was ready to connect with a man again. But they hadn't known each other for very long, and she was worried about moving too far, too fast. It had been a long time since she'd slept with anyone, and she worried about her ability to keep her heart protected.

The door swung open, and Dario himself stood on the threshold. He grinned widely, his hazel eyes glowing with warmth as he ran his gaze up and down her body. Felicity shivered, but it wasn't from the cold air.

"Merry Christmas." He reached out and laid his hand on her arm, tugging her forward and into the house.

"Merry Christmas," she replied. Dario leaned over and kissed her softly, a tame, polite version of what they'd shared in the office yesterday. But it didn't matter. Sensation arced through her, and just like that, she found herself wishing they were alone together so they could follow the kiss to its natural conclusion.

Dario reached for her bags and set them gently on the floor and then his hands were on her, unwinding her scarf, skimming across her shoulders and down her arms as he helped her out of her coat. His touch was light and probably looked impersonal to an outside observer, but Felicity felt as though he'd stripped her bare in preparation for a passionate encounter. Her nerve endings tingled, and she closed her eyes and took a deep breath, savoring the sensation and wishing it would never end.

Dario chuckled softly, and she opened her eyes to see him watching her. His knowing smile made it clear he knew exactly how his actions had affected her and he was enjoying her response.

Two can play at that game, she thought to herself. She stepped closer and laid her hand flat on his chest, then leaned in and nuzzled the curve of his jaw with the tip of her nose. Dario sucked in a breath, and she felt his heart start to pound against her palm. She hid her grin in the slope of his neck, pleased to know she had power over him, as well.

"Dario!" A woman's voice drifted in from the room beyond. "Did Felicity arrive?"

She drew back and smiled up at him, and he traced his fingertip across her lips. "Yes, Mom," he called loudly. "I'm just taking her coat." He leaned forward, his breath hot on her mouth. "We'll pick this up again later," he murmured. His voice was full of sensuous promise, and Felicity's stomach fluttered.

"Did your parents have a good flight?" he asked in a normal tone of voice. He grabbed her bags with one hand and placed his other hand on the small of her back as he led her toward the living room.

"They did, thanks," she responded.

"Do they go on a trip every Christmas?"

"Usually, yes. They started doing it after I joined the Marines. My mom said she couldn't bear to sit by the tree without me, so she talked my dad into starting a new tradition. They'd already made all the arrangements for this year's trip when they found out I would be here, and I told them to go and enjoy themselves one last time before we settled into our old routine again."

"That was nice of you," he remarked, leading her through the living room. A large tree sat in the far corner, the branches covered in twinkling white lights. Packages lay strewn on the red plaid tree skirt, and the homey sight triggered a sudden pang of loneliness. She was glad her parents were on their trip, but she missed them and the holiday traditions her family had built over the years. She hadn't even bothered to put a tree up this season, knowing no one would be around to celebrate with her.

Except, it seemed, Dario and his family.

He led her into the kitchen, where everyone was chatting and laughing. "Look who wandered in from the cold," he boomed, raising his voice to be heard over the din.

Everyone turned to look at her, and a chorus of voices rang out in welcome. A small corgi yipped in greeting, running over to sniff at Felicity's shoes and pants with great enthusiasm, while a larger dog continued to snooze in the corner.

"That's just Scrabble," Emiliano said, smiling. "She just needs to check you out, and then she'll leave you alone."

"Fine by me," Felicity said, bending down to scratch behind the dog's ears.

"I'm so glad you're here!" said Marie, stepping forward. She hugged Felicity. "I'm sorry I didn't get a chance to talk to you at the engagement party the other day."

"Don't worry about it," Felicity responded. "You guys were a little busy. I appreciate you including me now."

Dario's parents came over next, and his mother, Natalia, embraced her with a smile. "Welcome—it's always nice to meet one of Dario's friends." There was genuine warmth in her voice, and Felicity felt herself relax.

Emiliano handed her a cup of coffee. "Thanks for babysitting him for us," he said with a grin. "It's nice of you to let him play detective. We appreciate you keeping him out of trouble while he's in town."

"No problem," Felicity said. "Believe it or not, he's actually proved to be kind of useful." She winked at Dario, who pinned Emiliano with a mock scowl.

"Wow," Emiliano said. He punched Dario lightly in the arm. "I'll alert the media."

"Very funny," Dario said drily. He reached out and ruffled Emiliano's hair, and the two of them began to playfully wrestle in the middle of the kitchen. Scrabble danced around them, barking with excitement.

"Boys," said their father, Aurelio, his tone one of long-suffering patience. "How many times do I have to tell you? No roughhousing inside."

Their mother shook her head and aimed an apologetic glance at Marie and Felicity. "I'm sorry. I tried to civilize them. I really did."

"It's okay," Marie assured her. "There's only so much you can do when you're dealing with that much testosterone."

Felicity laughed. "Believe me, I've seen worse. The guys in the Corps were ten times as bad, and that was on a good day."

"I can imagine," Marie said. "Was it tough being surrounded by men all the time?" She wrinkled her nose. "Don't get me wrong—I like men. But there are times you just need to hang out with your girlfriends."

Felicity shrugged. "It was hard at first, but eventually I got used to it. Most of the time, they were professional." She didn't mention the occasions when the guys would turn off the self-censorship and really let loose. The things she'd heard and seen weren't the kind of topics people discussed in polite company. Still, there was a part of her that missed the camaraderie and that sense of belonging, even though as the lone woman in her squad she'd always been something of an outsider. The line separating her from her fellow marines had been bright at first, but as they had gone through training and then fought together, the men had viewed her as less of a curiosity and had grown to accept her as an equal. That, more than any medal or commendation, was the highest honor she could have received.

"And now you're working as a PI?" Aurelio asked.

"Yes. Trying to crack the Colton hacking case."

"I hope you're having better luck than I did," Emiliano said, smoothing the wrinkles out of his shirt. He and Dario had stopped their brotherly tussle and were now rejoining the conversation.

"Well, so far neither one of us has gotten shot, so I'd say we're ahead of you on that score," Dario teased.

"Boys, really." Natalia tsked softly.

"Ha ha," Emiliano said. He rolled his shoulder and winced a little, as if still pained by the injury.

The brothers continued their friendly banter as everyone settled around the table. Felicity enjoyed watching them tease each other, and their parents and Marie even poked fun at them a few times. It was so different from her experiences with her own family. She didn't have any siblings, and her holiday gatherings were a lot more subdued. They all loved each other, to be sure, but they didn't show it by joking back and forth like Dario's clan.

After a few minutes, Felicity began to join in the conversation. She was rewarded with a warm smile from Dario, and soon she felt like she'd been a part of the group for years.

Time seemed to fly by, and soon they were out of food. Marie stood and lifted her mimosa. "Time for presents!"

Everyone rose, and Dario took Felicity's arm. "Now the fun really begins," he whispered conspiratorially.

"I should go," she said, feeling out of place again.

"Not at all," he replied. They stopped before walking into the living room, letting everyone else go ahead of them. "I'd like you to stay, if you don't mind."

He sounded so hopeful she couldn't bear to disappoint him. "Okay. I did bring a few little things for your family, just as a token of appreciation for having me today."

Surprise flickered in his eyes. "That was sweet of you."

She shrugged. "I couldn't very well show up empty-handed. I even have something for you."

He grinned, his face lighting up with anticipation. "You have a present for me?"

"I meant to give it to you yesterday afternoon, but since

Adeline left early and we canceled the gift exchange, I brought it with me now."

He leaned closer, his breath warm on her neck. "I feel like you already gave me a present yesterday." His voice was low and intimate, for her ears only. She swayed toward him, unconsciously seeking his touch.

"I—I hadn't planned for that to happen," she said, feeling her cheeks heat at the reminder of the way she'd lost control. And in the middle of her office, no less!

"I know. That's what made it so great." He ran his hand lightly down her arm and a line of goose bumps sprang up in response.

"I'm glad you enjoyed it."

"Are you trying to pretend you didn't?" he teased.

She was saved from having to reply by the calls of his family. "Come on, slowpokes!" Marie called out. "We're sorting all the gifts!"

Felicity winked at Dario and walked into the living room to join them. He followed her and sat on the sofa while she retrieved her bag and withdrew the gifts she'd brought for Dario and his family. Once she was done, Dario gestured for her to sit next to him. She dropped onto the cushion, then sprang up again as her pocket began to vibrate.

She dug her phone out and offered an apologetic smile to his family. "Please excuse me for a moment. My parents are out of town, so I should take this in case something's gone wrong with their trip."

"Of course," Natalia said, waving her off.

Felicity retreated to the dining room and glanced at the phone, surprised to see Adeline's number flashing on the screen. "Hello?"

"Oh, thank God." Adeline sounded harried, and Felicity's stomach twisted.

"What's wrong?"

"Someone broke into the office," Adeline said. "The alarm company just called me. Can you meet the sheriff there? I'm really sorry to ask—you know I'd go if I was in town."

"Don't worry about it," Felicity assured her. "I'll take care of it."

"Thank you," Adeline said. She sounded relieved, as if Felicity had just taken the weight of the world off her shoulders. "I owe you big-time."

"It's not a problem. Just enjoy the holiday with your family."

"I'll try. Thank you again."

Felicity tucked her phone back into her pocket and returned to the living room. Dario turned to look at her as she walked in. "Everything all right?" he asked.

Felicity shook her head. "I'm afraid not. That was Adeline. There's been a break-in at the office, and she asked me to meet the police there." She began to circle the room, shaking hands with Dario's family as she said her goodbyes. "Thank you so much for including me today—I'm sorry to have to leave early."

Natalia and then Marie hugged her. "I hope everything is okay at your office," Marie said, frowning slightly. "I can't imagine why anyone would want to cause trouble like that on Christmas."

"I can," Emiliano said darkly. He tilted his head to the side. "I don't mean to question your abilities, but do you really think you should go by yourself?"

"She's not."

Felicity turned to find Dario standing in the doorway, holding her coat and scarf. He'd already donned his jacket, and he looked ready to head out. "I'm going with you."

She immediately rejected the idea, even as his offer made her heart lift. "No, Dario. I appreciate it, but you need to stay and celebrate with your family."

Dario opened his mouth to reply, but his mother beat him to it. "Nonsense," Natalia replied. "You shouldn't have to take care of this by yourself. Dario will help you."

"But your gifts—"

Aurelio smiled kindly. "This won't be the first time we've had to pause our holiday activities. We're used to it. You two go check things out, and we'll find something to do to occupy the time until you get back."

It was clear both Dario and his family were determined he should accompany her to the office. Recognizing defeat, Felicity nodded. "Thank you," she said simply.

Emiliano walked Felicity and Dario to the front door. "Be careful," he cautioned. "Please wait for the police to arrive before you go into the office. We don't need any heroes today." He aimed a meaningful look at Dario, who waved off his brother's concern.

"We'll be fine," he said. "There's no need to worry."

"I'll keep an eye on him," Felicity said with a smile.

Emiliano nodded. "Thanks. Good luck."

They stepped outside and a gust of cold wind stripped away the lingering warmth of the house. Felicity shivered, her nerves starting to jangle as she turned her thoughts to the office and what they might find there. A break-in sounded self-explanatory, but if her work in intelligence had taught her anything, it was that things were seldom as simple as they appeared.

She glanced over at Dario, grateful he'd insisted on joining her. She didn't think she'd have any trouble dealing with the sheriff and his men, but it was nice to know Dario was there if she needed him.

Still, she shouldn't get used to him being around. He'd made no secret of the fact he was only in town for his brother's wedding. And while Felicity wasn't opposed to spending time with Dario now, she had to make sure she didn't let him into her heart.

* * *

It didn't take long to arrive at the office—thanks to the holiday, there was no traffic. Dario parked in front of the entrance and shook his head at the sight of the door. Even from this distance, it was clear the lock had been badly mangled, and someone had tried to smash the glass panel that ran the length of the door. A million cracks ran through the glass, but by some miracle, it hadn't fallen out of the frame.

"Oh man," Felicity said softly. "What a mess." She unbuckled her seat belt, clearly intending to get out and conduct a closer inspection.

Dario placed his hand on her thigh and she stilled. "Not yet," he said. "I know you want to check things out, but let's be safe and wait for the police to arrive."

She nodded. "You're right. I just got caught up in the moment." She bit her bottom lip as she studied the scene. "Do you think whoever did this made it inside?"

"I hate to say it, but yes. It looks like the door is at a strange angle. I think it was wrenched open and now it can't close properly."

"Maybe we'll get lucky and whoever did this is still inside," Felicity said darkly.

"Don't get your hopes up," Dario warned.

A black-and-white cruiser drove up and parked a few spots away, its siren lights flashing. Dario squinted against the bright red and blue pulses that strobed the interior of the car. "Ready?" he asked Felicity.

She nodded, and the two of them climbed out of the car. No sooner had Dario shut his door than one of the responding deputies turned around and frowned. "Get back in your vehicle, please."

"We're here on behalf of Adeline Kincaid. She's the owner of this business," Felicity explained.

"Wonderful," said the man. "Now please get back in your car while we check out the place."

It was clear that any further conversation would only complicate matters, so Dario gestured for Felicity to return to her seat. She did, but as the minutes ticked by, it was clear her impatience was mounting.

"At least it's warmer in here than it is outside," he said, trying to improve her mood.

"Yeah." She was quiet a moment, then spoke again. "What do you think is taking them so long? The place isn't that big." There was a thread of worry in her voice and Dario had to admit, he was starting to get nervous, too.

Dario shrugged, trying to seem unconcerned. "I'm not sure. There's probably some kind of protocol the sheriff's department have to follow when they respond to a call like this."

"I suppose," she muttered. "I know it won't change anything, but I really want to get inside and determine if anything was stolen."

"Do you have a list of items?"

"No, but I'll be able to tell if the more expensive stuff is gone—the computers, the copier, the printers."

Dario glanced at the sidewalk in front of the office, and the road beyond. A light dusting of snow covered both surfaces, but unfortunately, there were so many tracks it was impossible to follow any trail the burglars might have made. "I think the copier is probably safe," he said, giving her shoulder a nudge. "That thing is as big as an old VW Bug. Not the kind of thing someone could simply waltz away with unseen."

"Fair enough," Felicity admitted with a small smile. "But I am worried about the laptops."

"That's a valid concern," he said. "If I had to guess, I'd say whoever did this was after the computers. Otherwise, why target a PI office? It's not like there's cash or other valuables stored inside."

"Do you think this is connected to the Colton case?"

Dario mulled over her question. "It's certainly a possibility," he said. "Hopefully we'll know more once we can go inside."

A moment later, the two deputies returned to the door and stepped outside. One gestured for Dario and Felicity to join them.

"Your names, please?"

Dario and Felicity responded. "We work for Adeline Kincaid. She called me earlier after being notified by the alarm company about the break-in. She's out of town for the holiday, so she asked me to meet you here and make sure the office is secure," Felicity said.

The deputy nodded. "Okay. There's no one inside, and the place looks undisturbed. But why don't you both come in and see if you notice anything missing?" The other deputy headed for the car, the radio on his belt squawking to life as he walked.

Dario and Felicity followed the man inside. He was shocked to find the officer was right—everything looked fine, without so much as a scrap of paper out of place.

"I don't understand," Felicity said as they walked from room to room. "Why would someone break in if they didn't intend to take anything?"

The deputy shrugged. "Who knows? Maybe whoever did this wasn't intending to rob the place—they just broke the glass and wrenched open the door as part of a stupid prank. Or maybe the culprits made it inside and realized they didn't have time to take anything and still get away."

Dario frowned, not buying it. It was the work of a moment to grab a laptop and run. If someone was motivated enough to force their way into the office, he didn't think they'd be deterred from taking what they wanted once inside.

Felicity didn't look convinced, either, but she didn't argue the point.

"Is there anything missing?" the man asked.

"As far as I can tell, no," she said slowly. "But it's possible Adeline will notice something when she gets back to work."

The deputy scribbled something on his notepad. "That's fine. Just give us a call if you find something later. We'll do what we can to find the people who did this, but without witnesses, it'll be tough. I don't suppose there are any security cameras set up in the office?" He didn't sound especially hopeful.

Felicity shook her head. "No. Just the security system. There might be some cameras on one of the nearby stores monitoring the street."

"Okay." The man made another note, then flipped the little book closed. "Like I said, feel free to call if anything comes up." He pulled out business cards and passed one each to Felicity and Dario. "We're here if you need us."

"Thank you," Dario said. Felicity echoed his gratitude. "We appreciate you coming out today."

"That's what we do," the deputy replied. "Merry Christmas." He walked out, leaving Dario and Felicity alone in the office.

She turned to face him, her features twisted in confusion. "Does this seem odd to you?"

"Yeah." Together, they walked through the rooms again, their pace slower. But just as before, everything looked normal. The laptops were safely docked in their stations on Adeline's, Felicity's and Dario's desks. The printers hadn't been moved, and even the contents of the desk drawers were undisturbed. It was as if someone had come inside, looked around and then left without touching anything.

They stopped in Felicity's office, and she began to thoroughly search her desk for any evidence of tampering. "What are we going to do about the door?"

Dario's chest warmed at her use of the word *we*. "I have some duct tape in my trunk," he said. "I'll tape a few strips onto the glass to stabilize it until we can get it replaced. If you're okay in here, I'll take care of that now."

Felicity nodded, and Dario stepped out into the cold to retrieve the tape. He found an old bicycle lock in the trunk as well and figured they could slip it through the outer door's handles to secure the entrance.

It only took a few minutes to apply the tape to the glass. Dario stepped back and studied the door with a critical eye. The hasty repair wouldn't last long, but hopefully it would buy them enough time to get it fixed properly.

That job done, Dario headed back to Felicity's office. Had she discovered anything missing?

"How's it going in here?" he called out, strolling into the room.

Felicity sat in her desk chair, examining what looked like a piece of fabric. Her posture was normal enough, but the look on her face made Dario tense. "Felicity? What's wrong?"

She glanced up, her face so pale he thought she might faint. "I found something," she said dully. Her hand jerked, and the fabric she held dangling on the tip of a pen fluttered.

"What is it?" He stepped closer, trying to get a better look.

"I think it might be a message." She extended her hand and he realized he was looking at a pink handkerchief. He took it from her, frowning.

"A message? What makes you say that?"

"She's known for her pink handkerchiefs," Felicity said, her tone stark.

"She?" Dario repeated. But he needn't have asked. The answer came to him as soon as the word had left his mouth.

Livia Colton.

Chapter 7

The next morning was cloudy and gray, the perfect complement to Felicity's mood. She stood in the small break room, staring impatiently at the world's slowest coffee maker as it sputtered and hissed.

"Come on," she muttered. She'd already had one cup this morning, slurping it down as she'd showered and dressed. But it wasn't enough. She'd barely slept the night before, and her body ached with fatigue.

When did I get so old? she wondered. Once upon a time, staying up all night would have triggered a few extra yawns the next day, nothing more. Now? She'd be lucky to keep her eyes open past lunch.

At long last, the coffee finished brewing. Felicity considered taking the whole pot back to her office, but decided the walk to refill her cup would help keep her awake.

Elixir in hand, she settled into her chair and booted up her computer. There was a message from Adeline, thanking her again for handling the situation yesterday and letting her know workmen would be stopping by today to replace the front doors. Felicity wasn't sure how her friend had managed to line up repairs so quickly given yesterday's holiday, but she felt better knowing the office would be made secure again.

She sighed as she clicked on her next message. The big man himself, Fowler Colton, had written for an update. She shook her head. "Don't you people talk to each other?" She was in regular contact with Zane; technically, it was Zane's job to keep the corporate bigwigs in the loop, but maybe Fowler thought he'd go straight to the horse's mouth this time.

Felicity leaned back in her chair, debating how much to tell the man. She and Dario had made good progress on the case, and thanks to his investigations on the dark web, they had a few more leads to pursue. She quickly typed up a response, then paused. Should she tell Fowler about the office break-in and their suspicions about Livia?

She opened her desk drawer and withdrew the plastic bag containing the pink handkerchief, studying it again in the vain hope of finding answers in the folds of the fabric. The *LC* monogrammed in one corner could have stood for a dozen names, but Felicity knew in her gut this was one of Livia Colton's handkerchiefs. The only question was, had she dropped it by accident, or had she deliberately left it behind to send a message?

A chill skittered through her and Felicity shoved the fabric back into her desk drawer. She'd called the sheriff's office yesterday after finding the pink square, but the deputies who had helped them earlier were busy.

We'll come by and pick it up tomorrow afternoon, he'd said. He had sounded unimpressed with her discovery, and Felicity suspected he didn't consider a handkerchief to be an important piece of evidence, despite Felicity's suspicions it was connected to Livia Colton.

Her thoughts were interrupted by a perfunctory rap on the door. "You're here early." Dario walked into her office, coffee in hand.

"Couldn't sleep," she admitted.

He nodded. "I had trouble, too."

Felicity eyed him up and down, taking in his pressed shirt and clean-shaven cheeks. He looked entirely too polished for a man who hadn't slept well, and Felicity felt even more rumpled in comparison.

"I just keep wondering why someone would go to the trouble of breaking in but then not steal anything," he continued. "And the handkerchief under your desk—do you think that was an accident?"

It was the same question she had pondered most of the night. "I don't know. But I'm beginning to wonder if the whole thing is some kind of message. Maybe Livia or one of her goons is trying to intimidate us, or scare Adeline into dropping the case."

"Like a warning?" Dario said. "Back off, or next time we'll do more than break your door?"

Felicity nodded. "Exactly."

"That makes sense." He was quiet a moment, then said, "How do you plan to respond?"

"If you're asking me if I'm going to stop digging, the answer is no," Felicity said. "But if you want to walk away, I won't think less of you. It's possible the next message will be more…personal, and that's a risk you didn't sign up for when you volunteered to help me."

Dario straightened and squared his shoulders, as if preparing to do battle. "Do you honestly believe I'd walk away and leave you to deal with this by yourself?"

"I'm not exactly alone," she pointed out. "Adeline can help me."

"No," he said flatly. "I'm sticking around. You can't get rid of me that easily." He winked, and a tendril of heat unfurled in her chest and spread through her limbs. Even though Felicity was confident she could take care of herself, it was nice to know Dario wasn't going anywhere.

"Hello?"

A new voice sounded from the lobby area, hesitant and a bit uncertain.

Felicity frowned and glanced at Dario. "Are you expecting anyone?" It was too early to be the deputies come to pick up the handkerchief, and she didn't have any appointments scheduled for today.

He shook his head. "Maybe it's a new client?"

They walked into the lobby, where they found Thorne Colton eyeing the door with a look of concern, his phone in hand. His face lightened with relief when he saw them.

"Oh good. I was just about to call Knox and tell him you guys were being robbed or something."

"Nothing so exciting," Felicity said.

"Someone smashed the glass and wrenched the door open yesterday," Dario explained.

"Oh man." Thorne shook his head. "Did they steal anything?"

"Not that we've noticed," Felicity said. "But Adeline will get back the day after tomorrow, and she might notice something's gone."

"That's a crappy thing to have to deal with on Christmas."

"Yeah." Dario nodded in agreement. "It wasn't the most festive way to spend the afternoon."

"Does Knox have any leads?"

"Not really." Felicity narrowed her eyes as an idea popped into her head. "But whoever did this left something behind. Would you mind taking a look at it?"

Thorne gave her a baffled look, but nodded. "Sure. If you think I can help."

Felicity quickly walked back to her office and grabbed the handkerchief, then retraced her steps. She held the bag out, trying to give it to Thorne. But he wouldn't touch it.

His eyes locked on to the pink handkerchief, and the color drained from his face. "Oh my God," he whispered hoarsely.

"Is this Livia's?" His reaction told her everything she needed to know, but she still had to ask the question.

He swallowed, his Adam's apple bobbing in his throat. He pressed his lips together and nodded. "It's hers." Thorne swore softly. "I thought she might be back. She's like a bad penny, always turning up where she's not wanted."

"What made you think she's come back to Shadow Creek?" Dario said. "The last I heard, she'd escaped. There's been rumors about her current location, but nothing concrete."

"That's actually why I came to talk to you both," Thorne said. "Is there someplace we can sit?"

"Of course." Felicity led them back to her office and they all settled into chairs.

"I don't have a lot of evidence," Thorne said. "But after seeing that—" he nodded at the handkerchief Felicity had placed on the desk "—I'm almost certain Livia is in town."

He leaned back and ran a hand over his hair. "You both know my sister Jade?" At their nods, he continued. "She's looking to expand her ranch, and before the holiday she put in an offer on some acres adjacent to her property. She called the Realtor this morning to check on the status of the paperwork, and the Realtor told her the land had already been sold—her offer never made it into the seller's hands."

Felicity frowned. "That's odd, but hardly reason to suspect Livia is back in Shadow Creek."

"No, you don't understand. The Realtor couldn't locate any evidence of Jade's offer. No paperwork, no emails, nothing. The woman remembers reading the messages from Jade before the holiday, but now it's as if everything has simply disappeared."

"Were any of her other files affected?" Felicity asked.

"No. That's what's so strange about it. Only Jade's communications and paperwork were gone."

"That sounds like a targeted hack," Dario said.

"That's kind of what I thought," Thorne said. "And since Livia hates Jade more than the rest of us, I started to wonder if Livia was targeting her, trying to make things difficult for her as a way of getting some revenge for turning over Livia's passwords to the FBI all those years ago. Jade's actions helped them crack the case wide open and allowed them to gather the evidence they needed to prosecute Livia."

"Is that possible, though?" Felicity asked. "To wipe out only a certain set of files without leaving any other trace of the hack?"

"Oh yeah." Dario sounded so casual about the possibility it made Felicity wonder just how often that kind of thing happened.

"Let's say the Realtor's computer was hacked," Felicity said. "Do you think the Cohort is responsible?"

Thorne nodded. "I do. I know you suspect Livia is the leader of the hackers, since they targeted Colton, Incorporated. I think since the cyberattack worked so well, she decided to use that strategy again. But this time, she went after Jade."

"Okay." Felicity nodded, willing to entertain his suspicions. "But that doesn't necessarily mean Livia is physically around. She could be anywhere that has an internet connection."

"That's what I thought, too," Thorne said. "Until you showed me her handkerchief."

"If it really is hers," Dario pointed out. "Maybe someone is trying to frame Livia."

"I suppose anything is possible," Thorne said. "But I think Livia is behind it all. The Colton, Inc., hack and Jade's missing files." He nodded at the handkerchief. "Have you told Knox you found that?"

"Yes," Felicity responded. "The deputies who came to investigate yesterday said they'd be back this afternoon to collect it."

Thorne frowned. "I'm going to call Knox, if you don't mind."

"Go ahead."

Thorne rose and pulled out his phone, then paced a few steps away to speak to his brother. Dario leaned forward, and Felicity did the same.

"What do you think?" he asked softly.

She shook her head. "I'm not sure. I'd like to talk to the Realtor and see if she'll give us access to her system. If she really was hacked, maybe we can find a digital signature or some trace of the person responsible."

"Good idea," Dario said. "I've been studying the method the Cohort used to hack into the Colton, Incorporated, system. If I can look at her computer, I can determine if her system has the same back doors and vulnerabilities to exploit. It won't be a smoking gun, but it might help advance the case."

"We might get lucky," Felicity said. "If the Cohort really is responsible for sabotaging Jade's bid, maybe they made a mistake that will help us catch them."

Thorne rejoined them with a sigh. "Knox is sending some deputies over now to pick up the handkerchief," he said. "He's also going to increase patrols in this area, and tell everyone to keep an eye out for anyone matching Livia's description." He aimed a direct look at Felicity. "I hope you won't be offended by what I'm about to say, but I think you shouldn't be in the office alone."

Felicity's first instinct was to roll her eyes, but she resisted the urge. There was no chauvinism in Thorne's tone or expression; he seemed genuinely worried about her safety.

To her surprise, Dario came to her defense. "She's hardly helpless," he said. "I'm sure the Marines taught her a few things."

"I'm sure they did," Thorne agreed. "But Livia is dangerous. Don't give her an opportunity to cause more trouble."

"We won't," Felicity said, touched by his concern. It was sweet of him to care, especially since they didn't know each other all that well. But from what she'd heard and seen lately, Thorne Colton was one of the good guys.

Thorne took a pen and the notepad from her desk and scribbled something, then handed the paper back to her. "This is Knox's personal cell number. If you get so much as a funny feeling, call him right away."

"I doubt he'd appreciate that," Felicity said jokingly, but Thorne's expression was serious.

"He won't mind. Trust me. He'd rather respond to a hundred false alarms than miss the one opportunity to catch Livia."

"Thanks."

Thorne nodded and let out a quiet sigh. "I'll let you both get to it, then."

Felicity and Dario both stood. "Please tell Jade we'll be in touch," she said.

"I will. And good luck. I have a feeling you're going to need it."

As Felicity watched the cowboy walk out of her office, she couldn't help but feel he was right.

Dario leaned back in his chair and stretched his arms above his head, trying to loosen his muscles. He and Felicity had been working steadily for the past couple of hours, and he was ready for a break.

He glanced over at Felicity. If she was growing tired, she didn't show it. Her back was ramrod straight as she concentrated on her laptop monitor, typing away with military precision.

She'd surprised him when she'd asked if he wanted to share her office. He'd immediately taken her up on the offer, and it hadn't taken long to drag his desk in from the supply room. He'd spent the first ten minutes or so distracted by her presence, sneaking covert glances and enjoying the subtle scent of her perfume that seemed to linger in the air. But fortunately, he'd soon lost himself in his work, and the sound of her breathing no longer sent his imagination running wild.

"Want some coffee?" It was about time for a midmorning refuel to top off his caffeine stores.

"Hmm?" she said absently.

"Coffee," he said, raising his voice a bit to break through her focus.

She blinked at him, and he saw her awareness return as she shifted her attention back to him and her surroundings. "Oh. Yes. That would be nice." She reached for her empty cup and stood, stretching a bit.

The movement pulled the fabric of her shirt taut across her curves, and Dario swallowed hard at the unexpected reminder of the beauty of her body. It had been two days since their mind-blowing kiss, and his palm tingled as he recalled the weight of her breasts in his hand. In the aftermath of the break-in, he'd pushed his attraction to Felicity aside so they could deal with the immediate issues, like talking to the deputies and securing the office. But now his libido came roaring back to life, and he suddenly wasn't interested in coffee anymore.

"Dario?" Felicity's voice broke into his thoughts, and from the look on her face, this wasn't the first time she'd said his name.

"Yeah?" He shook his head, trying to remember what they'd been talking about before the sight of her stretching had short-circuited his brain.

"Coffee?"

"Yes. Right. I could use a refill."

Felicity nodded and gestured for him to walk with her.

"Have you found any more posts about the Cohort on your hacker forum?"

"Campus Martius? Not really," he said. "There have been veiled references, but nothing obvious and nothing that appears to be helpful to the case."

"Figures," she muttered. She added coffee to his cup and then her own. "I hope the Realtor will let us access her computer so you can look for evidence of a hack."

"Did she give you any idea of when her boss would make a decision?"

Felicity shrugged. "She wasn't sure. I think if it were up to her, she'd agree immediately. But she has to clear things with her boss first, since they'd be giving us access to their system. I guess there are some privacy concerns, and in light of the recent troubles Colton, Incorporated, experienced, I think they're trying to be more diligent about protecting their clients' information."

"Can't really blame them for that," Dario said, taking a sip of his coffee.

"I know. I understand their reasoning, but it's a little hard to be patient when their system might hold the clue we need to find Livia Colton."

"Or it could be another dead end," he said. He didn't want to be overly negative, but he also didn't want Felicity to get her hopes up. There were limits on what they could do, and even if he found evidence Livia was behind the hack of the Realtor's system, there was no guarantee he'd be able to lead the authorities to her hiding place.

Felicity was quiet for a moment, studying him over the rim of her coffee cup. "That sounds a little defeatist. What happened to the brash, confident guy I met a few days ago?"

"I'm still confident," he said, sounding a little defensive even to his own ears. "I just think we need to manage our expectations a little. So far, nothing about this case has been easy." It was true, but there was more to it than that. It suddenly occurred to him that the reason he was trying to downplay his skills was because he didn't want to disappoint Felicity.

The realization made his stomach flip-flop. Normally, he didn't worry about failure—most of the time, the thought didn't even enter his mind while he was working. And on the odd occasion he ran up against a difficult problem that he couldn't solve? No big deal. He simply found a work-around or informed the client what they had asked for was impossible. He didn't lose any sleep over it or stress about letting anyone down. It was all a part of doing business, a risk that people understood before they hired him.

But things were different with Felicity. She definitely wasn't a normal client; in fact, he didn't think of her like that at all. He'd volunteered to help Adeline, yes, but not because he needed the work or because he was especially interested in the Colton case. It had just seemed like a good way to pass the time. But when he'd learned Felicity was in charge of the investigation, that had been an added bonus. He'd wanted to get to know her. And as he'd learned more about her, his feelings toward her had gone from the shallow hormonal surge of lust to a deeper, more complicated pool of emotion that had him second-guessing everything he thought he knew about what he wanted in his life. It was enough to drive a man crazy.

"That's true. But I have a feeling our luck is about to change."

He snorted quietly. "You don't strike me as the superstitious type."

Her cheeks flushed pink and she glanced down. "I'm not, really. But the guys I served with were. It kind of rubbed off on me."

"Oh yeah? How?" Dario found Felicity's stories about her time in the Marine Corps fascinating. It was a topic she didn't discuss all that often, so when she gave him an opening he jumped on it.

She leaned against the counter of the break room, getting comfortable. "Well, you have to understand all branches of the military have their own little superstitions. It's considered bad luck in the Navy to wash a coffee cup, for instance."

Dario glanced at his mug and winced. "Really?"

Felicity nodded, smiling. "Really. I once heard of a sailor being written up for scrubbing a superior officer's coffee cup clean during a fit of anger."

He laughed. "Please tell me you wash your mugs."

"Oh yeah. But I won't eat the candy out of an MRE. And I won't eat apricots, either."

"Wait—what?" Dario leaned forward, enchanted by this side of Felicity. "What have you got against candy and apricots?"

"A lot of the Meals, Ready to Eat have Charms candy as a dessert," she explained. "They're these fruit-flavored hard candies. And everyone knows that if you eat them, it will rain. Big-time. The green ones are the worst."

"I see," he said, nodding. "And the apricots?"

She tilted her head to the side, considering his question. "I'm not really sure how that one got started," she said. "I never bothered to ask. It was just part of the culture."

"And you still won't eat them even though you're no longer a marine?"

She gave him an affronted look and drew herself up. "I beg your pardon. I may no longer be on active duty, but I'm still a marine."

Dario held up his hand, palm out. "My bad. I apologize."

She settled back against the counter with a nod and a sly smile. "That's fine. You didn't know."

"It really is an identity, isn't it? Being a marine."

"Well," she said thoughtfully. "Yes. It's a brotherhood—

that's the best word I have for it, even though more and more women are joining the ranks."

"No wonder your high school teacher was so excited to see you at Emiliano's party."

"We have a common bond," she confirmed. "Doesn't matter if you never served together—when you find a fellow marine, you feel a connection to them."

Her words triggered a burst of irrational jealousy. *He* wanted to bond with Felicity and have her feel a connection to him. But did he even stand a chance?

"We should probably get back to work," he said abruptly. He straightened, wanting to retreat to the safety of the office where he could focus on work and not think about all the ways he and Felicia weren't right for each other.

If Felicia was surprised by his abrupt change of subject, she didn't show it. "Good idea." She pushed off the counter and together they walked down the hall. "I have a question for you," she said. "Can you show me how you'd trace the methods the hackers used to gain access to the Realtor's computer system? I'd like to learn more about forensic computing methods."

"No problem." He appreciated her question, and he felt himself relax as he turned his thoughts to teaching her the process he used during these types of investigations. "It's a lot easier than you'd think." He sat and pulled his laptop closer and gestured for Felicia to do the same. She pulled her chair next to him and leaned forward, clearly eager to learn.

"So I usually start by looking for any weak spots in their security software," he said, typing as he spoke. "Take this, for instance." He highlighted a line of code, but the computer didn't respond. "That's odd," he muttered. He clicked again, but nothing happened.

"Did it freeze up?" she asked.

"Maybe," he said, frowning. He reached for the keyboard, intending to reboot the machine. But before he could press the appropriate keys, the display on his screen changed.

"What's going on?" Felicity asked.

"I—I don't know." He watched in confusion as the text appeared to melt down the screen. "Maybe the computer has been infected with some kind of virus." He punched at the keyboard, but it was no use. He watched in horror as file after file opened and disintegrated in front of his eyes. All his most recent work on the Colton case, gone in seconds.

Felicity shoved out of her chair and grabbed her laptop, dragging it over to face them. "Oh my God, mine is doing the same thing." There was a note of fear in her voice, and Dario felt a swell of helplessness rise in his chest. She was looking to him to fix this, and there was nothing he could do.

It was over in a matter of minutes. The last files dissolved from their screens, leaving them both in a state of shock.

Dario exhaled. "Well, that was—"

An image suddenly appeared on the screens. It started out small, but quickly grew in size to fill each monitor.

"Is that—?" Felicity said.

"Yeah," Dario confirmed. "It is."

Livia Colton stared at them from their computer screens, a crooked crown on her head and a chilling smile on her face.

Chapter 8

Felicity stared at the picture of Livia Colton, revulsion and anger filling her as the image of the woman responsible for destroying her computer flashed tauntingly on the screen. Suddenly, Livia's face disappeared behind a wall of red letters.

Stop digging, or people will start dying.

The message sent a shiver down Felicity's spine and she reached out to slam her laptop shut. Dario cursed softly, then reached out to close his own computer.

Felicity turned to look at him, her heart pounding. "What do we do now?"

He shook his head. "I'm not sure." He sounded like he was in a daze.

That wasn't the answer she was hoping to hear. Given his expertise in computers, Felicity had been counting on Dario to know how to fix this new problem.

"Should we call the sheriff?"

"Probably," he said. He shook his head again as if breaking free of a trance. "I'll call Emiliano as well—the FBI can probably do more to help us than the local sheriff's department." He pulled his phone free and called his brother, and Felicity dialed Knox Colton.

It didn't take long to explain the situation to Knox, and he promised to come over right away. Satisfied she'd done what she could, Felicity hung up and waited for Dario to finish his call.

"Emiliano is going to meet us here," he said. "He's going to confiscate the laptops as evidence."

"Do you think there's any way of recovering the files?" It was a long shot, but maybe they would get lucky.

"Probably not," he confirmed. "But I'm sure the FBI team will try. As long as the digital storage system is intact, we should be okay."

"How do you think she was able to hack into our system?"

Dario frowned. "That's a good question. Adeline has the latest and greatest in firewall and antivirus software. I'm surprised Livia was able to find an opening in the security."

Felicity eyed her laptop, wondering if she'd accidentally done something to compromise the system. "Maybe she used a website as a Trojan horse, to sneak past the defenses."

"That's possible," he mused. He eyed the laptops, as if he could unlock their secrets by sheer force of will. "I think I can discover how she did it if I can spend some time dissecting the computers."

Livia's warning flashed in her mind again, and Felicity's anxiety spiked. Livia Colton wasn't known for making idle threats. If Dario pursued the investigation, he was risking his life.

"I don't know if that's such a good idea," she said. She knew Dario was itching to discover how Livia had managed to pull this off, but Felicity would rather he let the FBI take over. The agents were trained to defend themselves if necessary, and they could call for backup if Livia tried to threaten them. Dario didn't have that luxury.

He glanced at her, surprise evident on his face. "What do you mean? We can't back off now. We're getting close."

"What makes you say that?"

"Why else would she target our computers?"

His words made sense, but they did little to loosen the knot of worry in her stomach. "I don't like this."

"I don't, either," he said. "But I've never been forced off a job before, and I'm not going to start now."

"You've also never gone up against Livia Colton," Felicity pointed out.

Dario studied her thoughtfully for a moment, as if reassessing his impression of her. "Are you really that scared of Livia?"

Felicity shrugged. How could she explain her emotions? People always thought that because she was a marine and had been in combat, she was fearless. But the opposite was true. War had taught her that life was precious and could be gone in the blink of an eye. She'd seen too many people cut down in their prime, all because they'd made a careless mistake. She'd learned to be cautious and to avoid taking unnecessary risks in both her professional and personal life.

"I'm not afraid of her," she said slowly. "I knew when I took this job I might face dangerous people and situations. That doesn't bother me. What does frighten me is the thought of Livia targeting innocent people as a way to get to me." She stood and paced, needing to burn off energy. "My family didn't sign up for this. I'd never forgive myself if something happened to them."

Dario stood and reached for her, but she evaded his touch. "Hey," he said calmly. She let him catch her as she walked past again. "Hey," he said again, his voice gentle. "That's not going to happen. Livia isn't going to hurt them."

"How can you be so sure?" She wanted to believe him, but she couldn't ignore the voice of doubt in her mind.

"Well, for starters, they're out of town. I doubt even

Livia has the reach to get to them while they're on their cruise."

"That's true," she admitted. "But she could always set some kind of booby trap in their home." She'd seen the results of such sabotage before; it was a common tactic insurgents had used in Afghanistan, with deadly results.

"I'm sure we can talk Sheriff Colton into stepping up patrols in your parents' neighborhood."

"Maybe." Then a terrible thought occurred to her, and Felicity froze as her blood ran cold.

Dario felt her stiffen in his arms. "What's wrong?" He drew back to look at her, his eyebrows drawn together in concern.

Felicity pulled his head down until his ear was close to her mouth. "What if she hacked the microphones on the computers? Do you think she's listening to us now?"

Dario leaned back and his eyes went wide as he considered the possibility. *Maybe*, he mouthed.

Felicity's stomach sank. If her parents weren't on Livia's list of targets before, they certainly were now. Had her careless talk put them in danger?

Dario released her and walked over to the laptops. He opened them both up and Felicity tensed, expecting to see the image of Livia and her hateful message again. But the screens were blessedly blank.

Dario pressed some keys, but the machines didn't respond. He held one of the laptops up to his ear, listening intently. Then he lowered it.

"They're not on," he said. "She may have been listening in before her stunt took effect, but she can't hear us now."

Felicity exhaled in relief. She smiled weakly at Dario, but he was still studying the laptop in his hand. "That's odd," he muttered.

"What?" Had he found something wrong with the exterior of the computer?

"I think there's something in the USB port," he said absently. He set the laptop on the table and dug a Swiss Army knife from his pocket. He extracted a small set of tweezers and began to pry at the port, clearly trying to remove something. "Gotcha!" He held up a small, dark piece, his eyes bright with triumph.

Felicity drew closer, trying to focus on the device. "What is that?"

He passed it to her and she got a good look at the tiny chip he'd pulled from the USB port. "That," he said excitedly, "is how Livia Colton hacked our computers."

Felicity glanced at her own laptop but Dario was already checking it. He carefully withdrew an identical chip from the port on her computer and placed it on the table. "I'm willing to bet these chips contain the malware that deleted all our files."

The pieces clicked into place. "That's why she broke into the office," Felicity said. "She had to plant the chips so she could sabotage our computers."

Dario nodded. "Exactly. Far easier than trying to hack through Adeline's security features."

Felicity's heartbeat picked up. "Does that mean the network is still intact?"

"Probably. We'll need to check to be sure, but I imagine only our computers were affected." He noticed her growing smile and tilted his head to the side. "I take it from your reaction this is good news?"

"Oh yes," Felicity said. "I backed up my laptop yesterday to our cloud-based storage system. If Livia's malware didn't affect that, then most of my files are still intact!"

"Excellent," he replied. "I did the same as well."

"Sounds like Livia's attempt to derail our investigation wasn't as successful as she'd hoped." The realization filled Felicity with a smug satisfaction. Livia thought she was in charge, but she had miscalculated.

There was a shout from the lobby, and she and Dario moved down the hall to find Knox Colton headed toward them, Emiliano hot on his heels. They must have arrived at the same time, and they both appeared eager to know what had happened. Felicity led them back to her office, her nerves quieting as she and Dario explained everything. Livia might have the element of surprise on her side, but Felicity had a team of dedicated people helping her. Together, they would bring Livia down.

Dario reached for a French fry and dipped it into the puddle of ketchup on his plate. "Feeling better?"

Felicity nodded. "Much. This was a good idea."

Dario smiled and took another bite. It had taken several hours for Knox Colton and the FBI to finish asking questions about what they had seen during the hack, and Emiliano and his team had taken their laptops and the chips he'd found for additional testing. By that time, Dario's stomach had been audibly growling, and given Felicity's increasingly short responses, he'd figured she was hungry, as well. So he'd suggested dinner at the burger joint down the street from the office, and to his surprise, she'd accepted.

"We need to come up with a plan," she continued. "We can't afford to let this setback derail the investigation. And the sooner we stop Livia Colton, the better I'll feel."

"I agree," he said. "Tomorrow morning, I'll connect my personal laptop to Adeline's network and make sure the hack didn't compromise the firm's digital storage. If everything looks good, you can download all your files to a new computer and we can move on."

She nodded, chewing thoughtfully. "I've got my fingers crossed. And hopefully by tomorrow the Realtor's boss will have decided to let us check their systems, as well. The more evidence we can hand over to your brother's team, the faster they can catch Livia."

"I have to say, I'll be glad to put this case behind me." He shook his head. "I've never worked on a project that went sideways so quickly."

A shadow crossed Felicity's face, but her expression cleared quickly. "No kidding," she said. Her voice sounded a little forced, but before he could ask if everything was okay, the waiter returned with the check.

Felicity wiped her mouth and reached for her purse. "It's been a long day," she said, pulling a few bills from her wallet.

Dario felt a surge of disappointment at the impending end of their dinner. He'd hoped to use this as an opportunity to reconnect with Felicity, to bring back some of the magic he'd felt when they'd shared that kiss. But Livia Colton had gotten in the way, and now he wondered if he'd get another chance. Felicity seemed pretty confident they would be able to wrap up the investigation soon, and once that happened, he wouldn't have a legitimate excuse to spend so much time with her.

"When this is over," he began, fumbling for the words, "maybe we can go to a real restaurant and have a celebratory dinner."

Felicity smiled, and he caught a spark of attraction in her eyes. "I'd like that."

They fell into step as they walked back to their cars. His shoulder brushed against hers and he decided to take a chance. Dario slung his arm around her shoulders, and he was rewarded by Felicity snuggling closer. She was warm and soft, and the floral scent of her shampoo filled his nose.

They drew to a stop in front of her car, and she turned to face him. The streetlight cast her face in a soft glow and her eyes shone, dark and liquid, as she stared up at him.

"I really appreciate all your help," she said softly. "I don't know how I would have made it through today alone."

He reached up to trace his fingertip down the curve of her cheekbone. "I'm glad I was here with you." He hated the thought of Felicity facing Livia's threats alone—he knew she could take care of herself, but he had a chivalrous streak that demanded he protect her from danger.

She sighed softly, her breath ghosting across his lips. His heart flip-flopped and he couldn't stop staring at her mouth. Would their second kiss be as good as the first? Was that even possible?

He couldn't wait any longer to find out. He dropped his head and pressed his mouth to hers, raising his hands to cup her face as he kissed her.

Felicity responded instantly, coming alive in his arms. She threaded her hands through his hair and stretched, pressing herself against his chest. The thin fabric of his shirt was no barrier to the warmth of her body, and a flash of heat burned through his limbs.

He tasted salt and a lingering sweetness from her soda. Her tongue stroked his, and the blood drained from his head and began to pool in his groin.

His response did not go unnoticed. Felicity made a satisfied sound in her throat that only heightened his arousal.

Suddenly, she pulled away. Dario struggled to catch his breath. "What's wrong?"

"Nothing," she said, her voice husky. "I just remembered we're in public."

"We don't have to be," he said. He mentally winced. *Smooth, Ortega. Real smooth.*

"My apartment isn't far from here."

He did a mental fist pump and nodded. "Okay. I'll follow you there." Only the knowledge that he would soon be holding her in private allowed him to let go of her and take a step back. "My car's a few spots over." He jerked his head to the left. "Just give me a minute."

She nodded and turned to her own vehicle. He made

it a few steps away before her voice stopped him in his tracks. "Dario!"

Her fear was almost palpable, and his arousal died suddenly, quenched by a swell of concern. "What's wrong?"

"My car."

He was by her side in a matter of seconds, instinctively stepping between her and the car. She grabbed his arm, leaning against him as they stared at the driver's-side door.

A crown was scrawled on the window in garish pink lipstick, the shape immediately recognizable even in the shadows of the parking lot. But it was the list of names written on the door in white paint that made Dario's blood freeze.

"My parents," she whispered. "Adeline."

"Livia," he said hoarsely. "She's got to be close." The realization made the hair on the back of his neck stand on end, and Dario could practically *feel* eyes on him. He grabbed Felicity's arm and pulled her toward his car, glancing around as he guided her into the passenger seat. He didn't see anyone lurking nearby, but that didn't mean they were safe. Livia or one of her goons could be yards away, watching them through the scope of a sniper rifle.

Would he even hear the crack of the gun before he felt the bullet slam into his chest? He kept his head low as he darted around the hood and jumped into the driver's seat.

"What are we doing?" Felicity said incredulously. "We can't just leave. We have to call the sheriff's department. My car is evidence."

Dario grabbed his phone and tossed it into her lap as he cranked the engine. "Call them if you want. But we're not staying here." He slammed the car into gear and stepped on the gas. There was a screech of protest from the tires and the pungent stench of burned rubber filled the air as they shot forward. But Dario was too worried to care about his vehicle right now.

He had to protect Felicity.

Chapter 9

"What happens now?"

Felicity sat on the edge of the hotel bed and rubbed her arms, trying to warm herself. The graffiti on her car door and window had chilled her to the bone, and now she feared she might never feel warm again.

She closed her eyes and was immediately assaulted with the image of her parents' names scrawled in dripping white paint. The memory made her stomach cramp and she opened her eyes again, looking for a distraction.

Dario pulled the comforter off the second bed and draped it around her, then sat next to her. "We try to get some rest."

Felicity clutched the slightly scratchy fabric to keep it from sliding off her shoulders and laughed darkly. "Sure. That's going to happen."

"I could order room service?" he offered.

"I don't think I can handle eating anything right now," she said. She glanced around the hotel room, hoping to find a minibar she could raid for a stiff drink. But the room was disappointingly empty of alcohol.

"We could go down to the hotel bar," he suggested, as if he'd read her mind. "Maybe a drink will help take the edge off."

Felicity considered it for a second, but shook her head. She didn't want to be around people right now. She felt too brittle, as if the noise of the after-work crowd and the smooth jazz piped over the speakers might cause her to break.

"I don't think I'm up for that." She shivered and pulled the comforter tighter around her body.

Dario had driven them there while she'd spoken to Knox Colton. At first, she hadn't understood why he'd brought them to a hotel in nearby Austin, but he'd explained his worry about taking her home. "My name was on your door, too," he'd pointed out. "So I can't exactly take you back to my place." He was staying in one of the guest rooms at his parents' ranch, and Knox had assured Felicity he was sending officers to watch the Ortegas' home, along with her parents' house.

"Everyone on the list will get extra attention from my men," Knox had said. His declaration had made her feel a little better, but she was still a nervous wreck inside.

Dario's hand trailed down her back, a solid weight that pulled her out of her head. "It's going to be okay," he said. His voice was deep and calm, and Felicity wanted to wrap the sound around herself like a suit of armor. "Livia is just trying to frighten you."

"It's working," Felicity said.

"Try not to play into her hands," Dario said. "This is how she operates—she uses threats and intimidation to make people do what she wants. But she's not all-powerful. She won't be able to hurt the people you love. Especially now that Knox and his department are on high alert. And maybe we'll get lucky—it's possible she left behind some evidence that will help the deputies find her. They're checking over your car now, and hopefully they'll discover something useful."

Felicity shook her head. She wanted to believe Dario; she hoped with every fiber of her being he was right. But she couldn't turn off her worry like a spigot, not where her family and friends were concerned.

"I can't get the image of the car door out of my mind," she said. "Every time I close my eyes, I see it."

Dario draped his arm around her and pulled her close. She leaned against him, pressing her ear to his chest. His heart thumped reassuringly in a comforting rhythm, and she felt her muscles relax a bit.

"I'm sorry for what she did to your car," he said.

Felicity huffed in a poor excuse for a laugh. In truth, she hadn't even thought about the damage to her vehicle. "I'm glad you were there," she said quietly. If Dario hadn't been with her, she didn't know how she would have responded. She certainly wouldn't have had the presence of mind to go to a hotel instead of her apartment. Without Dario, she'd probably be sitting at home, an easy mark for Livia Colton.

She snuggled closer against him, seeking solace from his strength. The change in position left her half-draped across his lap, and Dario emitted a small, strangled sound.

"What's wrong?"

"Nothing," he said quickly. He shifted a bit, and she felt the bulge in his pants brush across her breasts as he sought to reposition himself.

His physical reaction struck a chord inside her, and Felicity was suddenly very aware of Dario's body. Warmth spread from every point of contact between them, suffusing her body until she felt like she must be glowing from within. She glanced at the skin of her arm, a little disappointed to find it looked normal. How was that possible, when she felt so alive inside?

"Dario," she said softly. She sat up slowly, deliberately grazing her breasts across the flat expanse of his chest as she moved. He sucked in a breath, and her nipples hardened, sending small zings of sensation to her core.

"Yes?" His voice was tight, and she could tell by the way he ground his jaw he was trying to rein in his arousal. In another time, she might have laughed at the idea of

Dario the playboy trying to resist a seduction attempt. But right now, she simply wanted Dario the man, the one she'd gotten to know over the past few days. The one she trusted.

The one who made her feel safe.

"Kiss me."

He squeezed his eyes shut and turned his head. "I don't think that's such a good idea right now," he said.

Felicity used her hand to gently turn his head until he faced her again. "I know what I'm asking you," she said.

His eyes popped open, the hazel depths bright with need. "Are you sure?"

"Yes." She nodded for extra measure. "I'm sure if you are."

The world spun suddenly, and she gasped as she found herself flat on her back. Dario rose over her, his deft fingers making quick work of the buttons on her shirt.

Cool air kissed her skin as he pulled the edges of her blouse apart. She shivered, but the chill didn't last long. Dario covered her with his hands, then lowered his head as he worked his way down her torso.

His breath was warm as it ghosted across her goose bumps, and she lifted her hips instinctively. Dario's large hands settled on her hips, and he pressed her down onto the mattress in silent instruction.

She was content to follow his lead, and her ready surrender surprised her a little. Felicity had always been take-charge in every aspect of her life, and the bedroom was no exception. But there was something about Dario that made her relax, made her want to cede a degree of control. For the first time in a long time, she felt safe with a man.

Her thoughts brushed against the memory of her last relationship. She and Ross had been high school sweethearts. Their fire had burned hot and bright, and every time Ross had looked at her she'd felt like the center of the universe. She'd thought they would last forever, but Ross hadn't been able to cope with her decision to join the Marines. His older brother had been a soldier in the army and had died in Iraq. When Felicity had told him about her enlistment, he'd been so afraid for her he'd actually cried. She'd tried to talk to him about it, but he hadn't listened. Unable to cope with her decision, he'd ended their relationship. He'd broken her heart, and while time had dulled the pain, she still had moments when she wondered what might have been if she hadn't put her country ahead of Ross's feelings.

"Hey." Dario's voice cut through her thoughts and brought her back to the present. "Where'd you go?"

She shook her head, feeling a little guilty at having drifted away from him. "Nowhere important. I'm sorry."

He ran his hand lightly down the side of her torso. "Don't apologize. There's a lot going on right now. We can put this on hold."

"No. I don't want to wait." She'd spent the last twelve years of her life putting her job before her personal desires. And while she didn't regret those choices, she was tired of being alone. Besides, she knew better than most that tomorrow was not guaranteed to anyone. With Livia Colton gunning for them both, Felicity wasn't going to take anything for granted.

She reached for Dario and pulled him down, capturing his mouth once more. His kiss was warm and sensual, and Felicity emptied her mind of all thoughts and distractions, focusing only on Dario and the way he made her feel in this moment. She opened her heart and her body to this man, reveling in the intensity of their connection. Some faint voice in her brain insisted she was feeling too much, too soon, but she dismissed the warning. Right now, she didn't want to think. She had surrendered to her baser instincts, and she craved the sensations that only Dario could provide.

He didn't disappoint.

* * *

He'd never experienced anything like this before.

Dario had slept with other women, sure. And he enjoyed sex. Who didn't? But this experience with Felicity was like nothing he'd ever imagined. For the first time, Dario knew what it was to fully open his heart to a woman.

It was a revelation. Never before had Dario felt simultaneously vulnerable and protected. He was used to keeping a small part of himself reserved, locked safely away behind an impenetrable wall. He enjoyed relationships, and because he kept that piece of his soul protected, he never had to worry about feeling the kind of heartache and loss that affected other people. It was self-preservation, pure and simple, and until now, he'd never questioned his strategy.

But Felicity changed all that.

He still wasn't sure how it had happened. What was it about this woman that had affected him so deeply? And how had he not felt his protective barriers weakening? How had he missed the signs?

She was in his arms, and for the first time in his life, he was truly naked with a woman. It frightened him, this potent intimacy. His first instinct was to retreat, but his pride wouldn't let him shy away from this new experience.

Every touch, every brush of skin against skin—it was familiar and yet strangely novel. He took his time discovering Felicity's body, learning what made her sigh, what made her writhe, what made her moan. It was an exploration he never wanted to end. But all too soon she pushed him down on the bed and rose over him, a sensuous smile on her face as she whispered something about payback in his ear.

His brain took a back seat as Felicity set about licking and teasing and caressing every inch of his body. She was enthusiastic about giving him pleasure, a fact that surprised him a little. His past lovers had tended to assume that his satisfaction was a foregone conclusion. But not Felicity. She did everything in her power to heighten his arousal, to make him feel like the center of her world. It was a heady rush to know this strong, confident woman was so dedicated to his enjoyment, and he felt both awed and humbled to be the focus of her attention.

Dario placed his hands on Felicity's shoulders and pulled her back up his body. Her flushed cheeks and mussed hair were nearly enough to send him over the edge, but he bit the inside of his cheek to stay in control.

His chest was so tight with need he couldn't speak. Instead, he gently guided her onto her back and positioned himself between her knees. But just as he was about to enter her, he realized what was missing.

"Oh God," he whispered hoarsely.

"No condom," she said, apparently reading his mind. "I'm on the pill." She sounded a little hesitant, though, as if uncertain that would be enough.

Relief flooded through him. "I'm clean," he blurted out, seeking to reassure her. "I got tested after my last relationship, which ended six months ago. But I'll run downstairs and get condoms if it will make you feel safer."

Her eyes shone with an emotion he couldn't name and she smiled at him. "It's okay. I trust you."

Those three words knocked the breath from his chest, and Dario could swear he felt his heart actually swell with emotion. He moved slowly, joining their bodies together with care, determined to savor every aspect of the experience as their relationship changed forever.

Felicity gasped and moved with him, her hands tightening on his shoulders. Encouraged by her response, Dario increased his pace until soon, they were both clinging to each other, panting with exertion and emotion.

He felt her clench around him, heard her call his name through the pounding of blood in his ears. Only when he was certain she was truly satisfied did he slip the reins of his self-control and allow his own pleasure to lead him to release.

The moment seemed to go on forever, stretched between them and suspended in time. He gave himself fully to Felicity, body and heart. But instead of leaving him empty, he felt more complete than ever.

He lay next to her on the bed and gathered her boneless warmth in his arms. She snuggled against him, emitting a sigh of feminine contentment that settled over him like a soft blanket. Filled with a bone-deep sense of peace, Dario drifted to sleep.

When he woke in the morning, Felicity was gone.

Chapter 10

Felicity stared at her computer screen, wondering why she'd even bothered to come to work. She wasn't focused on the case—no matter what she tried, she couldn't keep her thoughts organized enough to make any kind of progress.

She'd been distracted for the last three days, and it didn't take a rocket scientist to know why.

Sleeping with Dario had been a mistake, but she couldn't quite bring herself to regret it. The sex had been amazing, a mind-blowing experience like none she'd ever had before. But more than that, she'd felt deeply connected to Dario on an emotional level. She'd meant to keep things purely physical, to give in to hedonism, enjoy their chemistry and move on. But her heart hadn't been content to stay on the sidelines.

As soon as she'd opened her eyes the next day and seen his sleeping face, she'd known the truth. She was falling in love with Dario Ortega, and if she didn't extricate herself soon, she wouldn't be able to stop it.

He was the worst possible choice. After all, he was only in town until his brother's wedding. Then he would be leaving again, taking off for greener pastures and other beautiful women. Felicity knew that, and ignoring those facts was only going to end in heartache.

So she'd slipped out of his arms and left, hailing a cab

back to her apartment, where she showered alone, her tears mingling with the water.

She'd spent the past three days avoiding Dario, working from home or at a nearby café, ignoring his calls. It was the coward's way out, but the thought of explaining her reasons for leaving made her stomach cramp. He was so much more experienced at keeping things casual—if he heard she was having trouble keeping her heart under control, he'd probably run for the hills. The last thing he wanted was for a woman to try to tie him down.

Not that she would. Felicity still had her pride, after all.

"Can we talk?"

His voice cut through her thoughts and sent her heart pounding. Oh God, he was here! Standing in her office doorway holding two cups of coffee and wearing a friendly smile. Her first instinct was to run, but she couldn't very well shove him aside and race past. She took a deep breath and forced herself to calm down. She was an adult, and a professional, not to mention a marine. She could handle an awkward conversation.

"Of course." She gestured for him to come inside, and he approached her desk, setting one of the cups in front of her.

"Peace offering," he said quietly. Then he settled in the chair across from her desk.

When he didn't speak, Felicity decided to take charge. "Any new findings?"

He tilted his head to the side, and for a second, Felicity wondered if he was going to respond. "I checked over the network," he said, leaning back in his chair. "There's no evidence Livia's hack made it past our individual computers. Adeline's system integrity appears to be intact, so you don't have to worry that Livia is watching your every move."

Felicity nodded. "That's good." One less thing to worry about.

True to his word, Knox Colton had set up regular patrols of her parents' house. They had returned from their cruise late last night and had taken the news of Livia Colton's threats in stride. Felicity was still concerned for their safety, but she felt better knowing the police were keeping an eye on her folks.

"Why did you leave?"

She'd expected the question, but she hadn't thought he'd ask it so suddenly. "I— Ah, I had to get back to work," she fumbled.

Dario's hazel eyes pinned her. "That's crap," he said. "I've spent the past few days giving you some space, but after what we shared together you owe me an explanation. Why did you run out on me?"

Felicity's heart pounded in her chest and she ran her palms down her thighs to dry them. "What we did was a mistake," she said simply. "We never should have slept together. We should have kept things on a professional level and not brought sex into the equation."

"Is that all it was for you?" His eyes glittered with an emotion she couldn't name. "Just sex?"

"You're the one who likes to keep things simple," she fired back. "You tell me."

A muscle along the side of his jaw ticked and she knew her barb had struck a nerve. She considered apologizing, but decided against it. Better for him to walk away angry than to know how much she was coming to care for him.

"I hate to disappoint you," he said, his voice tight, "but that wasn't just another roll in the hay for me. And I don't think it was for you, either."

Felicity dropped her gaze but said nothing, not trusting herself to speak.

"I think you're scared," he continued. "And you know

what? I am, too. But unlike you, I'm not willing to walk away so quickly. I think we're good together, and I think we have a chance. I'm not going to pretend we don't simply to make you feel better about leaving me without even saying goodbye."

She felt her cheeks warm as shame rose in her chest. Dario was right—she should have at least left him a note. Sneaking out had been a low blow, and no matter how scared she was, Dario hadn't deserved that.

He stood abruptly and placed his hands on the edge of her desk, leaning forward slightly. "I'm not giving up on us yet, Felicity," he said quietly. "I don't know what's gotten you so spooked, but I'll be here when you decide you want to tell me."

Felicity watched him walk away, his back straight and head held high. Her heart ached to know she'd hurt him; that had never been her intention. She'd truly thought she was protecting herself and that he had seen their encounter as nothing more than a pleasant diversion. Part of her was thrilled to know her developing feelings weren't all one-sided and that Dario cared for her, too. But his words echoed in her mind, putting a damper on her emotional celebrations.

I'll be here when you decide you want to tell me.

"No," she whispered sadly. "You won't."

Dario parked in the gravel lot of Hill Country, Jade Colton's operation. He was there to talk to Jade about her bids on the neighboring property, in the hopes of getting more information that might shed light on the mysterious disappearance of her paperwork. He probably could have taken care of everything when he'd spoken to her over the phone, but given the tension between him and Felicity right now, he'd wanted to get out of the office, if only for a little while.

Damn stubborn woman! He'd seen the look in her eyes and known she had feelings for him. But why wouldn't she admit it? He'd practically bared his soul in her office, hoping that his confession would make her feel safe enough to express her feelings, too. But she'd remained silent, staring up at him with those big scared eyes that reminded him of a doe ready to bolt at the first sign of danger.

Well, he wasn't going to give her an excuse to run. Her disappearing act had stung, and he couldn't pretend it hadn't hurt to wake up and find her gone. But he wasn't going to hold it against her. He was feeling overwhelmed, too, and he knew they probably both needed time to process the changes in their relationship. Normally, he bailed at the first sign of trouble. But not this time. Felicity wasn't a fling—she was a woman he wanted in his life long-term, and he was going to do whatever it took to make her understand he truly cared for her.

He headed for the door of the main ranch house but a gust of wind carried the sound of a woman's voice. Redirecting, he followed the noise to find Jade in the pasture to the side of the ranch house, standing between two horses. She didn't see him; she was busy running her hands over her mount, checking the cinch of the saddle and the placement of the stirrups.

"Hello there," he said, careful to keep his voice calm and level so as not to spook the horses.

She glanced up. "Howdy," she replied.

The horses flicked their tails, their ears pricking forward at his appearance. Dario walked forward until he stood next to one of them, and the animal stuck its nose against his stomach, clearly searching for a treat.

"Sadie," Jade scolded affectionately. "You big flirt."

Dario ran his hand down the side of the mare's face, enjoying the feel of her velvet-soft coat. "Sorry, pretty girl," he said quietly. "I didn't think to bring any apples with me."

Sadie snorted, her breath warm and damp against his skin.

Jade turned her attention to the other animal, and Dario shifted to watch her work. "Did I come at a bad time?" he asked.

"Not at all," Jade replied. "I was hoping we could maybe take a quick ride while we talked. Are you up for that?"

"Ah, okay," he said, a bit taken aback by her suggestion. "But in the interest of full disclosure, you should know I haven't been on a horse in years."

Jade chuckled. "That's okay. I've got Sleepy saddled for you. She's a sweetheart, and she hasn't been above a trot in ages."

Dario eyed the brown mare with concern. She looked sturdy enough, but he wondered if she was too old to carry him. "Are you sure I won't hurt her?"

"I'm positive," Jade assured him. "Sleepy is fully capable of running—she just can't be bothered to do it."

"Sounds like a horse after my own heart," he quipped.

It didn't take long for Jade to finish her checks, and the two of them mounted and set off. It was a beautiful day for a ride, and as the sun warmed his back, Dario felt some of the tension leave his muscles.

The trail sloped gently as it meandered through a stretch of tall grass. They crossed a babbling brook and stopped to let the horses take a quick drink. Jade nodded to the land on the other side of the fence standing about fifty feet away. "That's the property I was hoping to purchase."

Dario nodded, taking in the green expanse, dotted with a few trees. "I'm sorry about your bids," he said.

Jade's shoulder jerked up in a shrug. "Not much to be done now," she said bitterly. "I just wish I knew what had happened."

"Do you have copies of the emails you sent to the Realtor?" Dario asked. "I can't make any promises, but if I can verify you sent the documents, and that the Realtor received them, you might be able to make a case that the land should have been yours."

"How can you do that?" she asked, frowning slightly. "The problems started because she had no record of receiving my bid paperwork. It disappeared."

"They were hacked," he said flatly. "I think by the same group responsible for hacking into the Colton, Incorporated, system. I've asked the real-estate company to let me access their network so I can look for evidence of the crime. If I can get your emails, I'll have a better chance of piecing together how they sabotaged your bid."

Jade nodded. "I'll send you what I have. I think there are copies of my emails in my sent folder."

"Perfect," Dario replied. "That should be enough to get me started."

They spurred the horses on, following the fence line for a few more miles. Dario was enjoying the ride, but he was also eager to get to work to solve the mystery of Jade's disappearing files. "Where are we headed?" he asked.

"There's a spot I want to check, just a bit farther," Jade replied. "Some of the hands have reported signs of what might be a squatter on the property, and I want to look around for myself."

A tingle of apprehension slid down Dario's spine. A squatter? That sounded a little ominous. His mind immediately conjured up the image of Livia Colton flashing on his computer screen, followed by the graffiti on Felicity's car. But he told himself to relax. Not everything was connected to the Colton, Inc., hacking case. A few teenagers had probably shared a bonfire, toasting marshmallows and sipping beer smuggled from their parents' refrigerators. Nothing to worry about. He and Emiliano had had their fair share of campouts as kids, and they hadn't always worried about whose property they were on when they'd pitched their tent.

A few minutes later, they came upon the evidence. Someone had taken the time to dig a small pit in the earth and to line the edges with rocks. A few charred logs sat atop a pile of ashes, and he caught the dull gleam of a dirty spoon, apparently forgotten after a meal.

Jade dismounted to poke around the site a bit. Dario glanced around and caught a glimpse of asphalt through the grass. "Is that a public road?"

"County service road," Jade replied absently. "Usually pretty deserted." She pulled a plastic bag from her pocket and deposited a few cigarette butts inside with a grimace. "Rude," she muttered, shaking her head.

"What do you think?" he asked as she mounted Sadie once more.

"Probably just teenagers," Jade said. "I'll have the guys dismantle the fire pit and post a few more no-trespassing signs. Hopefully that will take care of the problem." She reined Sadie around and Dario did the same with Sleepy. But as the horse turned, he saw a flash of pink in the grass a few yards away. He frowned, trying to find it again. But it was gone, obscured by the movement of the grass as it swayed in the breeze.

"You coming?" Jade called back.

"Yep." He nudged Sleepy, who obstinately refused to pick up the pace. Fortunately, Jade waited for them to catch up before setting off again.

"Everything all right?"

Dario debated telling her about what he'd seen, but decided against it. After all, there wasn't much to tell since he hadn't really gotten a good look. It was probably some kind of winter flower, or maybe a piece of trash left behind by the teens.

Definitely not one of Livia Colton's handkerchiefs.

The ride back passed quickly, and Jade turned down his offer to help unsaddle the horses. "I'll take care of it," she said, waving him off. "After I'm done I'll email you all the information I have on the bid. Let me know what you discover."

"Of course." He headed down the path, his thoughts still on the abandoned campsite and the flash of pink he'd glimpsed in the grass.

He heard the crunch of gravel before he saw the lot and drew up short as he spied a man by his car. "Can I help you?" he asked, striding forward.

The man jumped, apparently startled by the sound of Dario's voice. "Oh. No, I was just checking out your car. Is this the latest Mustang GT?"

Dario relaxed slightly. "Yes. I bought it a few months ago. Runs like a dream."

"I bet." The stranger ran his gaze along the car, nodding to himself. "Were the Shelby mods worth it?"

"Oh yeah." Dario grinned. "I've taken her out to the track a few times. Best money I've ever spent." He stuck out his hand. "Dario Ortega."

The man hesitated, then shook his hand. "Rodrigo Artero. I'm one of the ranch hands."

Dario nodded. "Artero," he repeated thoughtfully. "Where have I heard that name before?"

"My uncle was Fabrizio Artero. Jade's father."

"So that makes you her cousin."

Rodrigo frowned as if unhappy to be reminded of his relative. "Yes," he said shortly. "She is." He turned and began to walk away.

"Nice to meet you," Dario called after him. He climbed behind the wheel and shook his head, trying to make sense of the odd interaction. Jade hadn't mentioned hiring her cousin, but perhaps she didn't think it was news worth discussing with him. Still, there was something about the man's attitude that struck him as wrong, and Dario made a mental note to look into Rodrigo Artero's background.

He pulled onto the main road and, after a second's deliberation, took the first right that led onto the county service road he'd seen earlier. He'd just make one quick check of the site, reassure himself that he'd imagined the handkerchief and be on his way.

A few minutes later, he was bent at the waist, combing the grass in his own personal snipe hunt. "This is ridiculous," he muttered. "There's nothing here."

He heard a whisper of sound behind him, but before he could turn around, something cold pressed against his neck and a hard voice sounded in his ear.

"Don't move."

Chapter 11

"Where is he?"

Felicity glanced at her watch for the third time in ten minutes. Adeline had called a meeting in twenty minutes, wanting an update on the Colton, Incorporated, hacking case now that she was back in town.

She reached for her phone and dialed Dario's number, but it went to voice mail. Again. She knew he was probably still upset with her after their conversation that morning, but she'd left him several messages explaining the meeting. It wasn't like him to go silent like this.

Was he off sulking? Or was something else going on? Her thoughts drifted back to her car and the sight of Dario's name scrawled on that horrible list. There had been no sign of Livia Colton since that night, but Felicity didn't think the other woman had disappeared. She was probably biding her time, waiting for the right moment to strike.

Her worry mounting, Felicity called Jade. She knew Dario had gone out to talk to the rancher about her sabotaged bids, and perhaps he was still there.

"No," Jade replied. "He left about an hour ago."

Felicity thanked her and ended the call, unable to ignore the alarm bells in her head. Where was he? And why wasn't he responding?

She glanced at her computer. There was one way she could find out, but it was a violation of his privacy. Still, given the threats Livia had made against him, Felicity decided she would risk Dario's anger. She had to make sure he was safe.

Feeling a bit like a stalker, she pulled up the GPS program that allowed her to track the location of a cell phone and entered Dario's number. As long as his phone was on, the software could pull his location using cell tower triangulation... It didn't take long for the software to pull up a map, and she leaned forward, studying the blinking red dot on the screen that indicated the location of Dario's cell phone.

"That's odd," she muttered. It looked like he was in a field, just off a county service road. She enlarged the area, looking for nearby cross streets. There was an intersection a few miles back, but the location appeared fairly remote. It definitely wasn't the kind of spot Dario would regularly frequent, and a chill skittered down her spine as her imagination went wild.

Felicity pushed to her feet, committing the map to memory. It was probably just some glitch in the system, but she was going to have to check it out or else she'd drive herself crazy coming up with ever more fantastical theories about Livia Colton and her hired goons. She scribbled a note for Adeline, then grabbed her keys and her phone, and after a quick debate, she reached into her desk drawer for the small revolver she'd taken to carrying as Livia's threats had escalated.

"I can't believe I'm doing this," she said to herself as she climbed behind the wheel of her rental car. Talk about a wild-goose chase! But she had to see for herself. No matter how much she had tried to keep him at arm's length, Dario had gotten under her skin and she truly cared about him. Even though they had no future together, she had to make sure he was safe. She'd never forgive herself if something happened to him, something she could have prevented.

"Here I come."

* * *

Dario froze, his mind going blank as he realized he had a knife to his throat. His assailant took advantage of his shock and pulled his cell phone free of his pocket, tossing it away where it vanished in the tall grass. Then the knife was gone, and Dario spun around to see a petite, dark-haired woman glaring up at him.

"Livia." She was immediately recognizable, despite the dye job to disguise her signature blond hair. "I should have known."

She offered him a tight smile. "I believe you have me at a disadvantage," she said, her Southern-belle manners in full effect. "You are?"

"Dario Ortega. I'm the one who figured out you're behind the hacks on Colton, Incorporated. Do you still go by Livia, or should I call you Sulla?"

Recognition flared in her eyes and she laughed, a pretty, musical trill that seemed at odds coming from such a monster. "You say that like I should be impressed. I didn't exactly make it hard for you."

"Why'd you do it?"

She rolled her eyes. "Why do you think? To get revenge on my family! They betrayed me at every turn. It was only fair I punish them for it."

Dario shook his head, stunned by the raw hatred in her voice. He'd never imagined a mother could view her children with such scorn—it simply wasn't natural.

"How long have you been squatting on Jade's property?"

"Long enough," she said easily. "It's been the perfect place to hide in plain sight. No one thought I'd have the guts to come back here, after everything that happened."

"So what's your plan now?"

She jerked her chin at his car, parked about fifty yards away. "You and I are going to take a little ride."

"I don't think so," he replied. He had a good six inches and at least fifty pounds on the woman, and even though she had a knife, he liked his chances.

Livia lifted the hem of her shirt, revealing the butt of a gun that was tucked into her waistband. "Think again."

"Or what, you'll shoot me?" The sight of the gun unnerved him, but Dario knew if he cooperated with Livia, his odds of survival got considerably worse.

"Yes, that's exactly what I'll do. And then I'll go into town and pay a visit to that pretty little thing you've been spending time with. Do you think she'll see me coming?"

The bottom dropped out of Dario's stomach. He knew it wasn't an idle threat. His mind racing, he turned and began to slowly walk to his car. Livia fell into step a few paces behind him.

"How'd you do it?" he blurted. "That's the one thing I haven't been able to figure out. You're no master hacker. How did you manage to infiltrate the Colton, Inc., systems and the Realtor's computer?"

"I didn't," she said. "My associate did."

"Rodrigo Artero," he said, the pieces falling into place. No wonder the man had grown cold at the mention of Jade Colton. Had Livia poisoned him against his own cousin?

"That's right," she confirmed. "Good old Rodrigo. He's so gallant—excellent manners. His uncle was one of my former husbands, who died tragically." She tsked in false sympathy. "He's had it out for me ever since. When I told him my husband had been killed by that scheming bitch Livia Colton, he was only too happy to put his considerable technical skills to use to help me take my revenge on the family."

"He doesn't know who you are?" It was hard to believe. Livia's face had been plastered everywhere in the wake of her escape from prison. How had the man not recognized her?

"Rodrigo has only recently left Argentina," Livia said. "Jade hired him, thinking she was doing her cousin a favor. Little does she know he hates her and the rest of the family, and has been working to sabotage Colton, Incorporated, and Jade's business as well."

He must have helped hide her presence on the property as well, Dario realized. No wonder Jade hadn't known about the campsite until recently...

"And he never suspected your motives for the hacking?"

Livia shrugged. "He thinks I'm Jane Damian, a poor rancher's widow who lost everything, thanks to the Coltons." She sounded smug about her deception.

They were almost to the car and Dario slowed his pace, trying to stall. There had to be something he could do to stop Livia! But his fear for Felicity kept him from trying to act. He knew if he tussled with Livia and lost, she'd head directly to the office to kill Felicity. He wasn't naive—he figured as soon as Livia had disposed of him she'd focus on Felicity next, but if he could draw this out just a little bit longer, maybe Felicity would realize he was missing and could take steps to protect herself. It was a long shot, but he had to try.

He pictured Felicity's face, then planted his feet and turned.

And all hell broke loose.

Chapter 12

Felicity crouched in the grass, waiting for the right moment to strike. She saw the bulge of the gun in the woman's waistband and knew if she gave away her position too early, the woman—Livia, she thought; who else would it be?—wouldn't hesitate to shoot Dario in the back.

Sweat ran down her cheeks but she ignored it. Her time in the Corps had taught her to block out physical distraction. It had also left her in excellent condition, which was how she'd been able to park her car a mile back and hike into the area without being detected.

She'd told herself she was overreacting a million times. But as soon as she'd rounded the bend and seen the two distant figures—one tall, one small—her doubts had vanished. Felicity had yielded to her training then, employing all the tactics she'd learned to creep up on the pair, her weapon at the ready.

What she wouldn't give for her service rifle right now! If she'd been holding her M16A4, this wouldn't even be a contest. She eyed the small .38 Special in her hand with some misgiving. It was a solid enough gun, but it was a close-range weapon. She'd get only one chance to do this right.

Dario and Livia approached his car, which was parked about fifteen yards to the west of her. Just a few more steps, and Livia's back would be to Felicity's position. If Felicity played her cards right, she could break from cover and have her gun between Livia's shoulder blades before the other woman even knew she was there.

Come on, she coaxed silently. *Just a little farther...*

Dario stopped a few feet away from the car and turned to face Livia. At this angle, they were both in profile to her, so she couldn't move without risking exposure. She cursed silently. *Keep moving!* she shouted in her mind.

In the event, it didn't matter. Just as Livia reached for her gun to threaten Dario, a man ran out from behind Dario's car. He let out a horrible cry and swung at Livia. Felicity heard the *thump* as the pipe he was carrying connected with Livia's head. Livia crumpled to the ground, and the man stood over her, screaming in Spanish.

Dario put out a hand and the man turned on him, clearly intending to hurt Dario next. Rage and fear propelled Felicity to her feet. "Stop!"

Her voice split the air and both men froze. Dario wore an expression of almost comical disbelief as he watched her approach, while the stranger gave her a quick once-over and turned his attention back to Livia. He lifted his arms again, ready to beat her with the pipe.

"I said stop," Felicity repeated. She was close enough now that the man heard the *click* of the hammer as she cocked the gun. He froze and shot her a look of such anger it made her stomach quaver.

"Drop the pipe," she instructed.

He did, but she still didn't trust him. "Step away from the woman."

"She is not a woman," he said, sneering. "She is a monster."

"I won't argue with you on that," Felicity said. "But she's down. Move away."

He took a reluctant step, and Felicity nodded at a patch of grass a few feet to the left. "Sit there."

"Felicity—"

She spared Dario a quick glance, enough to assure herself he was unharmed. "Do you have any rope?"

His face went blank. "Uh, I have jumper cables in my trunk."

She'd used worse before to restrain a man. "Get them. Tie him up."

Dario quickly obeyed her orders, and only when the stranger was secure did she relax. "Call the sheriff."

"I can't," Dario said apologetically. "Livia threw my phone into the grass. I have no idea where it is now."

She pulled her own free and tossed it to him. "Here you go."

It only took a moment for Dario to make the call. He hung up with a nod. "Knox and some deputies are on their way."

"Good." Felicity relaxed a bit more at the knowledge the authorities would soon be there. "Why don't you tell me what happened while we wait?"

Dario launched into his story, but after a few minutes, he turned to the other man. "This is where you come in. What were you doing out here?"

"I followed you," he said simply. "I didn't trust you after meeting you in the parking lot, and when I saw you take a right instead of leaving the ranch, I knew you must be headed here. So I grabbed a horse and raced out here."

Dario frowned and glanced around. "I don't see your mount."

The man nodded at a copse of trees on the other side of the road. "I left him there. I didn't want to alert you to my presence. I snuck back over, intending to help Jane." His face darkened, and he glared at Livia's limp form. "But then I heard her talking and realized who she really is." He spit in Livia's direction. "Evil witch. She lied to me, making me think she had suffered at the hands of the Coltons as I had. I trusted her, helped her in her quest for revenge against that horrible family. But I was wrong."

A swell of pity rose in Felicity's chest. Livia had obviously tricked him into hacking Colton, Incorporated, a decision he clearly regretted. "I'm sorry she hurt you," she said. Given his involvement with Livia, he probably wasn't of lily-white character, but since he'd saved Dario's life she was willing to cut him a little slack in that moment.

"What about you?" Dario asked, stepping closer. "How did you find me?"

Felicity glanced down, feeling suddenly shy about telling him. "I used GPS to track you," she confessed. Dario laughed, but a flash of movement caught her eye. She watched in horror as Livia raised her arm and pointed the gun at Dario's unsuspecting back.

Before she could scream a warning, Livia fired. Dario fell against Felicity with a grunt. A second shot rang out, and Rodrigo grunted in pain. Acting on instinct, Felicity dropped to the ground and took aim, squeezing off round after round at her target.

Livia's body jerked, and blood bloomed on her shirt. She fell to the ground, a frozen smile on her face as her eyes stared up at the sky. Felicity ran over and grabbed the woman's gun, tossing it far away from her body. Then she turned back to Dario, her heart already breaking at what she knew she would find.

She spared a glance at Rodrigo, who was clutching his leg, cursing a blue streak in rapid Spanish. She knew she should help him, but her priority was Dario.

He was lying on the ground, a stunned expression on his face. "My God," he gasped, reaching up to clutch his shoulder. "That hurts!"

Felicity dropped to her knees, hardly daring to believe her eyes. "Dario?" she whispered, running her hands across his chest. "Don't try to talk. Just stay quiet. The ambulance will be here soon." Her view went blurry and she realized she was crying. She moved his hand to press her own over his wound, trying to stop the bleeding. "It'll be okay."

"I know it will," he said. His voice was heavy with pain, but he was surprisingly lucid for a man who'd just been shot. "She hit my shoulder. It hurts like you wouldn't believe, but it's not going to kill me."

It took a moment for his words to sink in. She blinked away her tears and realized he was right. His bleeding was slowing down, and the wound seemed to be centered in the fleshy part of his shoulder, just below his collarbone.

"Now I'll have a scar to match my brother's," he said, trying to smile.

Felicity stared down at him, unimpressed by his attempt at levity. "You could have been killed!"

He winced, and she realized she'd shrieked at him. But her emotions were all over the place, and she couldn't control the volume of her voice. "I thought you were dead," she said, choking back a sob. "I thought I was going to have to watch you die. And you think this is funny?"

"No, I—"

She shook her head and buried her face in her hands. "I killed her, Dario. I took her life because I thought she had taken yours."

"You did the right thing," he said.

The wail of approaching sirens saved her from having to make a reply. Not that she knew what to say. Even though she had been to war and seen combat, Felicity had never killed anyone before.

In a matter of seconds, Knox and his deputies swarmed the area. Paramedics clustered around Dario and Rodrigo, while Knox pulled Felicity away to talk. She told him everything she knew, but her gaze kept straying to Dario, still on the ground as the EMTs worked above him. Would he really be okay?

She wanted to go to him, but Knox and his men were insistent she stay and talk to them. So she could only watch as the paramedics rolled Dario into the back of the ambulance and took off, sirens blaring as they drove away with a piece of her heart.

Two weeks later...

Adeline threw open the door and reached for Felicity. "I'm so glad you could make it!" she exclaimed.

Felicity smiled as she returned her friend's embrace. "Thanks for inviting me. But I think I must be really early." She glanced back at the empty drive and frowned. "Where's everyone else?"

"Oh, they'll be along," Adeline said breezily. "Jeremy is upstairs getting Jamie dressed. Thorne and Knox both called to tell me they were running late due to kid challenges. Leonor and her husband are stuck in traffic, and Jade said she had a horse go into labor, so she might not make it at all. Claudia has apparently never been on time to anything in her life, and I asked River and Edith to stop at the store to pick up ice." Adeline smiled brightly.

"It was nice of you to throw a party for everyone," Felicity said.

Adeline shrugged. "It's my pleasure. We're all so happy to put this case behind us, it seemed like a good reason to celebrate."

Felicity smiled, but the reminder of just how the case had ended sent her into a spiral of doubt. "Are you sure this is a good idea? I know there was no love lost between Livia and her children, but I can't imagine they'll all be happy to see me after I killed their mother."

Adeline grabbed her by the shoulders and gave her a

little shake. "How many times do we have to go over this? You fired in self-defense. You did not murder her in cold blood. Although," she said thoughtfully, "if anyone deserved that fate, it was Livia Colton."

"I still feel bad," Felicity began, but Adeline cut her off.

"No. None of that. Not today. This is why I wanted you to come—so you could see the Coltons don't blame you for what you did." She guided Felicity into the expansive kitchen. "Now, grab a glass of lemonade and head outside. I need to finish putting some hors d'oeuvres together, and I don't want you moping around while I do. Get some fresh air and try to relax."

Recognizing a dismissal when she heard it, Felicity did as she was instructed. She walked through the sliding glass doors and onto the patio, then stepped onto the path that led to the garden. It was an unseasonably warm day, and even though there would be no flowers blooming, the walk would do her good.

Her mind drifted back to that afternoon, the image of Dario lying bloody in the dirt bringing tears to her eyes. He was recovering nicely, or so she'd heard. But that split second of terror when she thought she'd lost him forever had broken her heart.

I can't do this.

The memory of her words echoed in her ears, blocking out the birdsong in the yard. Dario had stared up at her from his hospital bed, his brows drawn together in puzzlement.

"What do you mean?" he'd asked.

"I can't keep seeing you. It's too hard for me."

Dario had tried to reach for her hand, but she'd moved away, knowing that if he touched her, her resolve would crumble.

"What about me? What about what I want?"

Felicity had forced herself to smile. "I'm giving you

what you want—the freedom to move on to the next pretty face. The way you always do."

Dario had flinched at her words. "I see," he'd said, his voice dull.

"It's better this way," she'd said. She couldn't let him know that she was falling for him. Even though it hurt, she'd rather end things now than have him dump her in a few months once he realized they had different goals.

Felicity wanted a husband and a family of her own someday. Dario had made it clear from the beginning he wasn't the marrying kind. But she didn't hold it against him—her heart had simply ignored that fact, and now she was paying the price.

Even though she knew they couldn't be together, she drew comfort from the fact he was still alive. The world was a richer place with him in it, and the memory of his laugh eased the ache in her chest.

And then suddenly, he was there before her.

She blinked, expecting him to vanish as quickly as he'd appeared. But he remained, solid and whole on the path in front of her.

"Dario?"

He smiled, and in that moment, Felicity decided that if this was a hallucination, she didn't want it to end. He extended his hand and she took it, allowing him to lead her into the small garden patio.

The scent hit her first. Roses. Their fragrance perfumed the air, bringing a breath of spring to this midwinter's day. She glanced around, amazed at the sheer number of bouquets on display. Red, white, pink flowers. Pale peach. Vibrant yellow. Every shade imaginable was present, the blooms surrounding her with their beauty.

"I don't understand," she whispered.

Dario gestured to a small table set in the middle of the

patio. As she approached, she saw he'd used rose petals to write a message.

Will you date me?

She turned to look at him, her happiness at his sudden appearance draining from her. "How can you ask me that?" she said, her voice quavering. "After what I said to you in the hospital."

"I've been doing a lot of thinking about you and me, and I figured out you're scared because of my playboy reputation. But that's not the life for me anymore. It's time for me to settle down. Adeline has offered me a job with the firm, right here in Shadow Creek. I'm going to start putting down roots, and I want you to be a part of that. Unless I've completely misjudged everything and you don't want that." A flicker of doubt crossed his face, and Felicity realized he truly didn't know how she felt about him.

She'd done such a good job of guarding her heart, she hadn't let the one man she cared about know how much he meant to her. And yet despite his uncertainty, he was still willing to take a chance on her.

On them.

"No," she said firmly. "I want that, too. I want you in my life, now and in the future. I need you to stay, if it will truly make you happy."

She saw relief wash over him and she felt an answering lightness in her heart. "You make me happy," he said softly. He reached for her, and she pressed herself against his chest with a contented sigh.

"This means we'll be working together, you know," he said in her ear. "And I seem to remember you saying something about how we shouldn't mix work and sex."

"That was a mistake," she said. "Forget I ever said it."

He chuckled, his chest vibrating against hers. "I'm so

glad to hear you recant your statement." He trailed one hand down her back and rested it on her bottom. "Because I have plans for us."

Felicity moved against him, reveling in the feel of his strong, broad chest against her curves. "Don't you need to rest and recover?"

"My doctor said exercise is good for me." He nipped gently at the top of her ear and she shivered.

"You're really going to stay?"

He drew back and looked down at her, his hazel eyes filled with warmth. "Do you really want me to?"

"Yes," she whispered, reaching up to cup his face. "I do."

He grinned. "Then it sounds like we have a deal."

She laughed. "Should we shake on it?"

Dario shook his head. "I have a better idea," he murmured. He lowered his mouth to hers, and Felicity lost herself in the promise of his kiss.

* * * * *

*If you enjoyed this suspenseful story,
don't miss the previous installments in the*
COLTONS OF SHADOW CREEK *miniseries:*

THE BILLIONAIRE'S COLTON THREAT
by Geri Krotow
MISSION: COLTON JUSTICE
by Jennifer Morey
CAPTURING A COLTON
by C.J. Miller
THE COLTON MARINE
by Lisa Childs
COLD CASE COLTON
by Addison Fox
PREGNANT BY THE COLTON COWBOY
by Lara Lacombe
COLTON UNDERCOVER
by Marie Ferrarella
COLTON'S SECRET SON
by Carla Cassidy

All available now from Harlequin Romantic Suspense.

And don't miss COLTON K-9 COP *by Addison Fox,
available now from Harlequin Intrigue!*

"Just what is it that you want me to do?"

Serena threw her hands up, angry and exasperated. "I
don't know," she cried, walking back around to the front
of the building. *"Something!"*

"I am doing something," Carson shot back. "I'm trying
to find the person who killed my brother," he reminded
Serena.

From what she could see, all he was doing was spinning
his wheels, poking around on her ranch. "Well, you're
not going to find that person here—and you're not going
to find Demi here, either," she told him for what felt like
the umpteenth time, knowing that no matter what he said,
her cousin was still the person he was looking for.

"If you don't mind, I'd like to check that out for myself," Carson said, dismissing her protest.

"Yes, I do mind," she retorted angrily. "I mind this constant invasion of our privacy that you've taken upon yourself to commit by repeatedly coming here and—"

As she was railing at him, out of the corner of his eye he saw Justice suddenly becoming alert. Rather than the canine fixing his attention on Serena and the loud dressing down she was giving Carson, the German shepherd seemed to be looking toward another one of the barns that contained more of the hands' living quarters.

At this time of day, the quarters should be empty. Even so, he intended to search them on the outside chance that this was where Demi was hiding.

Something had gotten the highly trained canine's attention. Was it Demi? Had she come here in her desperation only to have one of the hands see her and subsequently put in a call to the station? Was she hiding here somewhere?

"What is it, Justice? What do you—?"

He got no further with his question.

The bone-chilling crack of a gun—a rifle by the sound of it—being discharged suddenly shattered the atmosphere. Almost simultaneously, a bullet whizzed by them, so close that he could almost feel it disturb the air.

Find out who's shooting at Carson and Serena in
COLTON BABY RESCUE by Marie Ferrarella,
available January 2018 wherever
Harlequin® Romantic Suspense books and ebooks are sold.

www.Harlequin.com